A DIVINE WIND

Thriller in the Middle East

Taming a Tornado
Anticipating a Trillion Dollar Disruptive Technology
A Vision of Peace in the Middle East
An Allegory on the Biblical Book of Job

NORMAN M. JACOBS MD, MS

outskirts
press

A Divine Wind
Taming a Tornado Anticipating a Trillion Dollar Disruptive Technology A Vision of Peace in the Middle East
An Allegory on the Biblical Book of Job
All Rights Reserved.
Copyright © 2021 Norman M. Jacobs MD, MS
v2.0 r1.1

Outskirts Press, Inc.
http://www.outskirtspress.com

Paperback ISBN:978-1-9772-3632-6
Hardback ISBN: 978-1-9772-3621-0

Library of Congress Control Number: 2020922797

Outskirts Press and the "OP" logo are trademarks belonging to Outskirts Press, Inc.

PRINTED IN THE UNITED STATES OF AMERICA

DEDICATION

For Jake and Zeus,
and for Harley.
and for Peyote...

In their honor, a portion of the proceeds from the sale of each copy of "A Divine Wind," will be donated to local dog rescues as well as to national organizations giving aid to other neglected and abused animals sharing our planet with us. To further honor Jake and Zeus, their story is provided after the conclusion of "A Divine Wind."

A DIVINE WIND

The most learned among the Jewish orthodoxy studied Kabbalah, Jewish mysticism. One evening, they sat around a campfire, the pale light shining on weathered, aged, learned faces, each trying to recall their oldest memories. One remembered a time before there were cars, another before there were horses, another before there were animals in the forest or fish in the sea. Then they turned to a memory imbedded deeply in their collective unconscious. One remembered when there was gar nicht, when there was nothing, nothing but the dunes in the desert to hear, and nothing but the wind, a divine wind rumbling with a low vibrato across ancient desert sands, to tell the tale.

Adapted from May Antin and Rabbi Nahman of Bratslav

CONTENTS

CHAPTER 1

CAPTIVITY

DORON BEN AVRAHIM, an Israeli army lieutenant, was on his knees while a wickedly beautiful woman danced provocatively around him. Under different circumstances this might have been a prelude to something quite different. As she danced around him, an occasional drop of glistening sweat dripped off her brow falling unobserved upon Doron, moistening his blindfold until it ran down his face, to his lips. He promised himself he would remember this scent and the salty taste of her sweat, should he survive his current nightmare and should they ever, by chance, meet again. If she was ever nearby, Doron thought, whether in the darkest of nights or otherwise visually hidden or disguised, her scent, now embedded in his psyche, would give her away. Perhaps then, he would have his own chance to return, in kind, the tortured treatment now being bestowed upon him. As the lithe athletic woman danced around Doron, she held an 8-inch Russian Zuni serrated army knife in her hand, playfully brandishing, twirling, and sensually switching it between her left and right hands, running it across Doron's army fatigues, drawing a trickle of blood in a provocative dance before death. The woman's husband, Gamliel, smiled, laughing in derisive scorn of their Israeli captive.

Doron was motionless, appearing to silently accept his fate. A blindfold was intermittently put on him, which he was now wearing. Doron could see little, but perceived an intermittent green tint. The emerald sparkle of reflected light, he suspected emanated from Saron's green eyes, as she danced around him. Her unusual strikingly colored eyes, particularly for an Iranian, had significantly less melanin than the more common Iranian brown eyes. Her eye color genotype was inherited from Saron's Irish mother, combined with a mutation from her Iranian father. If, as has been said by poets and writers beginning with Shakespeare, "the eyes are a window to the soul," her eye color might have been more appropriately colored blue, to reflect her icy demeanor toward any woman and more particularly, any man approaching her. Her red hair was a gift solely from her mother, reflective of her strong-willed fiery temperament. Her richly golden-hued skin, now shimmering in the summer heat, appeared to be a perfect sensual blend of Iranian and European pigments. Her beauty was both admired and feared by the people who knew her the best. Her 8-year-old daughter, Nadina, sat in a corner playing with a worn-out Raggedy Ann doll. In her own oblivious world, she appeared unaware of her mother's actions. Two other Iranian terrorists, Aman Nefjani and Tesvan Recari, stood nearby sharing a cigarette.

Doron was being held captive within Iran, in a small nondescript house on the shores of the Caspian. He had lost thirty pounds during his imprisonment. His previously well-toned body now lay wasting beneath his army fatigues. Dirt and desert sand clung to his body, to his face, to his beard and previously auburn hair. His captors let him trim his beard to better see his face during the few times it wasn't covered with a blindfold. He had only showered once in the last month, not for his benefit but to minimize the smell exuding from unwashed clothing and caking perspiration.

The army lieutenant had been captured six months earlier on a secret Israeli mission in Iran, one week before his wedding. His fiance, Sarah, had just bought her wedding dress and was trying it on the day he was captured. The white of the gown accentuated her deeply tanned skin, sugary bronzed from working outdoors on a Kibbutz in the summer sun. The ruggedly handsome man with the auburn hair and quiet affect that had stolen her heart, would now be barely recognizable. They had met working together on a Kibbutz on the outskirts of Tel Aviv, dated for two years with her family, and only the small remnant of his family remaining, but all looking forward to their wedding.

After several failed negotiations for his release, the more militant faction in the Iranian autocracy argued with the moderates to let them kill him. It was only because of his fiance that Doron even cared if he lived or died. His parents were both dead—dying within minutes of each other, each working in the separate but adjacent North and South 9/11 Twin Towers when the attacks occurred. At the time of their death, Doron was only eight years old. That shock had ended his childhood, destroyed his innocence and left him with a lingering depression. This was only partially assuaged when he met Sarah who tempered his grief, replacing it with her tender affection. She hoped to one day see him laugh again—to see death and war recede from their collective memories and an insane world return to sanity and peace. Now that wish seemed a hopeless distant memory.

Doron's wistful blue eyes, rimmed with a thin border of gray, stared out through his cloth blindfold. Although imprisoned, his mind was still free to wander alone within the confines of his seemingly hopeless nightmare. His thoughts often turned to his fiance, now praying daily for his return, to distant memories of his dead parents, of a father who never thought his son measured up to his expectations and silent thoughts of a mother for whom he could do no wrong. By all appearances, Doron was completely alone with his captors, with his silent thoughts, on his knees, tied to a metal post in the middle of his prison home expecting at any moment to be killed, at times wishing it would be quick and his lonely nightmare over. Israeli intelligence, likewise, felt Doron's days were numbered.

Chapter 2
Lightning Strikes
the Wailing Wall

One month earlier. The Wailing Wall, Jerusalem. Sunset.

Rain pelted the dusty limestone blocks of the Wailing Wall like ancient tears. Without warning, lightning struck a Christian cross placed between the chiseled blocks, momentarily lighting the interior of the wall like the inside of a marble art deco antique column. The lightning bolt traveled through the wall, carving a circuitous path to the ground, igniting scraps of paper, bits of messages stuffed into the stone crevices of the wall like transcribed mortar, detailing the hopes and prayers, the collective unconscious of diverse unknown writers beseeching God to answer their prayers. Thunder boomed, reverberating off the desert dunes. Two people touching the wall near the lightning entrance point were knocked unconscious, but alive. One could still detect a lingering stinging odor of charred human flesh. Two ambulances arrived, sirens blaring.

Orthodox Jews knelt in prayer, kissing the wall with the tallit, their prayer shawls, then hugging the wall with their hands. Christians and Muslims together with their Jewish neighbors at the wall, prayed together as one mass of humanity. The multilingual prayers to God mixed into the air, sent heavenward, were difficult to separate from one another but all were sent with a fervent urgency.

Shimon and Ruven, 9 and 10 years of age, playing chess near the wall, stopped their game. Happening too suddenly to shield his eyes,

Ruven had a direct view of the lightning bolt. The startling ominous power of the event imbedded the scene indelibly in his memory. They both lay under their small table, as the storm continued. The rain and associated storm stopped several hours later, as abruptly as it had started. As word spread of the lightning strike, the religious and the curious gathered at the wall, a hundred turning into several thousand within hours.

Ten rabbis led prayers at the wall, putting on tefillin, placed on the head and hand, following the prescript to bind these words between eyes and hands. The rabbis recited words from Deuteronomy, that God was one and the commandment to love God with all one's heart and soul. Shimon and Ruven were not very religious, but they were Jews, and that day they prayed as fervently as the rabbis leading them, reciting their evening prayers with a contriteness and passion they had previously never displayed. There was a uniform belief among everyone at the Wailing Wall that the lightning strike had opened a spiritual pathway, a wormhole to the other side of the universe, and standing there, waiting no longer at that faraway doorway, was God.

"Dear Lord," Ruven prayed, "let peace come to Israel. Stop the endless wars. Let my Uncle Doron be alive." Ruven had a slight stutter, but surprisingly, not when he prayed. His Uncle Doron was born in New York to Israeli parents who had perished in the 9/11 disaster, both working in the Twin Towers that fateful day when the Towers violently crashed to the ground, creating a funeral pyre of smoke and debris. Doron could not understand why his parents were gone, but was old enough to feel an almost unbearable loss. He was flown to Israel and raised by an uncle and aunt. When he was eighteen, Doron joined the Israeli army, seeking to avenge the death of his parents. The Israeli papers said the Israeli army lieutenant had now been missing for six months. He disappeared, they related, during a secret mission in Iran. Ruven cried out to God, pleading, begging, "Rescue Doron, dear Lord, I beg of you; rescue Doron!" Tears streamed down Ruven's youthful face, mixing with the yellowed crumbled remnants of the prayers lying at the foot of the wall. He let his body lower as he knelt, hands outstretched against the wall, head bowed in prayer. At this moment, unbeknownst to Ruven, his Uncle Doron was also on his knees, blindfolded, captive in a nondescript house on the shores of the Caspian, an 8-inch serrated knife adjacent his skeletal ribs.

News crews came to film the gathering. "This is Rebecca Levy IBN Israeli Broadcasting News, reporting from the Wailing Wall. A few hours ago, lightning struck the Wall for the first time in recorded history. You have better odds in Las Vegas of winning a mega million lottery. The strike was caught on video by a sixty-seven-year-old apostolic minister visiting from Mississippi. Within hours of being placed on the internet, the video has already had two million views on YouTube." As 23-year-old Rebecca spoke, the amateur video played. A typical weekday group was initially at the wall observing and praying. Rebecca turned, pointing to the Wailing Wall, brushing her sun-lightened brown hair off her attractive olive-skinned face, as she continued her newscast. "The lightning struck the wall, instantly converting a metallic cross into a round blob in a wall crevice. Two people touching the wall near the cross fell to the ground unconscious. They have been taken to Tel Aviv General and we have word they are now conscious. In the background of the lightning strike, glistening with a golden hue in the setting sun, one can see the Dome of the Rock on the Temple Mount held sacred by Jews, Christians and Muslims. Often, after a storm, the sky clears and occasionally a rainbow appears. After this storm the sky has only darkened further, grays and blacks and deep auburn. There you can see a dust devil rising a hundred feet just above the Dome of the Rock, whirling with desert sand and debris."

As the evening wore on, the reporter glanced at the darkening sky--the moon now discernible, was just beginning an ascent above the horizon.

"At our studio we have our meteorologist, Steven Stern. So Steven, what do you make of this event?"

Steven was middle-aged, trained in meteorology at the Technion in Tel Aviv. His attractive charming demeanor helped attract viewers to his weather reports. He spoke English with a slight Hebrew accent. "Lightning does occasionally strike religious statues. Rio de Janeiro's Christ the Redeemer is often struck by lightning. The last time was Thursday, January 18, 2014 3:09 a.m. GMT when the right thumb was chipped by a lightning strike. But the Christ Redeemer statue is 125 feet tall and sits on top of Corcovado Mountain, 3000 feet high. The Wailing Wall sits in a desert valley without a previous recorded lightning strike in all of human history! Not an expected or common event. I have no explanation for it."

"What can you tell our viewers about lightning, since it strikes so rarely in Israel?"

"Here are some videos of lightning strikes around the world." The screen showed showers of lightning on land and over the ocean. Awesome streaks from cloud to ground, from cloud to cloud and cloud to ocean. As the display continued, Steven went on. "Lightning comes in many varieties, from the common forked type to shapeless flashes of light discharged between clouds, as displayed on the screen behind me. 1.2 billion lightning flashes occur around the world every year. A typical lightning flash lasts less than half a second, can be 25,000 feet long and may release enough energy to power a hundred-watt light bulb for three months. The temperature in the lightning channel can rise to 50,000 degrees Fahrenheit, four times hotter than the surface of the sun. This is what melted the metallic cross it struck in the Wailing Wall."

"Thank you, Steven," Rebecca stated, before continuing. "As you can see, the lightning not only struck the Wailing Wall but has awakened a spiritual cord in many people. The throng of people coming and praying at the wall has grown into the thousands, a remarkable response to the evening's events." The camera panned the Wall and the growing crowd. The reporter called to her cameraman, "Benjamin, we should..." As she turned to where he had been moments earlier, Benjamin and the rest of the camera crew were already gone, wending their own way to the Wailing Wall, transfixed in a lingering, deepening sense of awe and a palpable communal spirituality.

Fox News, CNN and ABC all telecast specials on the events of the preceding month. John Forsaith, the religion editor for CNN, gave his own commentary. "In the ensuing weeks the signature event in the Middle East has brought more converts to God than evangelical preaching had achieved in the past decade. From inside orthodox Jewish synagogues throughout Israel, rabbis say the signs of God had always been there." After interviewing one of the rabbis, he continued on.

"From evangelical pulpits in Mississippi, evocative soulful songs of worship echo amongst an enlarging throng of emotional parishioners filling overflow church pews." Images from a Southern Baptist church were displayed on the screen.

"It has been no different at the National Cathedral in Washington, DC, attended by the vice president of the United States, or at the Crystal Cathedral in California," Forsaith continued. "Religious gatherings worldwide are trying to shed meaning on the recent events in Jerusalem and their significance to the world."

"Now let us visit Saudi Arabia. From the air, we can see the golden dome of the Al Qhwari Mosque glistening in the morning sun. Even outside the Mosque one can hear the rhythmic mournful communal chant of a thousand Shiite Islamic faithful, heads bowed, dutifully praying within at a special convocation in Mecca. Following the prayers, numerous Islamic leaders are sharing their own interpretations to the Jerusalem events.

"A similar scene is also being repeated, now toward dusk at the Vatican in Rome where the Pope is praying with Catholics filling the courtyard outside the papacy, each person holding a candle, casting a surreal glow during the Papal prayer service, hoping for answers to events they cannot fully comprehend." A camera pans the crowds in Rome, lit by hundreds of candles.

A special event was held last week at the Kennedy Center by a joint committee of Christians and Jews. It started with poetry from the Bible with recitals from Job, from the Song of Songs, from Isaiah, read by American and British performers, by baritones booming the words of God, by philosophers and even ethical humanists, while ballet dancers evoked feelings of love and beauty. Here are some of the images and speeches from that event." Images from the Hubbell space telescope played on a huge screen. Forsaith continued. "Josiah Watson, a baritone recently retired from the Metropolitan Opera House at Lincoln Center, is now on stage in one of his rare appearances since retiring. Josiah was recently diagnosed with inoperable liver cancer, but has still chosen to perform. It is worth noting, Josiah's distant great great grandfather had been a slave on a cotton plantation in Mississippi. And I am sure somewhere in heaven he is looking down proudly at his descendant."

Josiah spoke in his inimitable deep baritone. "Who was there before there was a universe, before there was any man to even conceive of a universe? Who ignited the spark, the Big Bang, creating a universe for man to explore? Before Adam and before Eve? Whose breath sent forth the North Wind? Whose handiwork fashioned interstellar gas into the Pillars of Creation in the Eagle Nebula 7,000 light years from Earth, where new stars are yet being formed from the dust of creation? And who is humanity who cannot fathom a creator, the God of this creation? Humans who hypothesize a universe created from virtual particles smaller than a proton, smaller than an electron, lasting for a mere billionth of a second rather than believing in an author, a God of creation. Who would choose to marvel at the limited creations of humanity and yet not be in awe of God's creation of a universe thirteen billion light years in expanse?" A camera panned the audience who stood in rapt admiration then broke out in heartfelt applause.

Rabbi Herzfeld, 75 years old, gray beard, old saggy brown suit, deep piercing eyes then took the stage. He was the director of education at Yeshiva University in New York City. "The signs of intelligent design have been taken as proof of God by faithful Jews and Christians for over 2000 years. In spite of these signs of God's presence, of the reverent worship of God, Jewish history is fraught with incredible suffering, thus casting questions on the value of this faith in God, even the reality of God." With knuckles deformed by rheumatoid arthritis, the rabbi gripped the podium for support. He looked out at the audience as though giving a sermon to a Saturday morning congregation, wearing the same tallit he wore the previous Sabbath.

The rabbi continued. "Between the destruction of the Temple of Solomon in 586 B.C.E. and the destruction of the restored temple in 70 C.E. the Jews knew four conquerors—Babylon, Persia, Greece, and Rome. How could any nation survive such utter destruction, its people scattered to the wind? The persistence of the Jewish people is a mystery. And perhaps this too is a sign that God would not let this people, His people, vanish into oblivion. Embedded indelibly into the genome of each Jew is the remembered anguish from centuries of persecution."

An audiovisual attendant adjusted the rabbi's microphone and raised the volume as his voice quivered with emotion. "The Roman civilization, so powerful at the beginning of the Christian era, eventually faded into obscurity. The Jewish civilization, then on the verge of extinction, was banished into the Diaspora, enslaved, tortured in the crusades, gassed en-masse in the Holocaust. However, they would eventually make a miraculous recovery and return to this land, answering the cries first uttered at Masada and by countless other souls before their lives were extinguished. It lent credibility to the biblical prophecy in Isaiah; "For a small moment I have forsaken thee; but with great mercies shall I gather thee." Rather than dying off, Christianity and Islam grew out of its branches. The very survival of the Jewish people is an unmistakable signature from God!"

The rabbi again paused to look at his audience filling every seat at the Kennedy Center and spilling into the aisles. He continued. "That was the past. Where do we stand today? Jerusalem is imperfectly balanced at the center of three religions. Over 60 years after the birth of Israel, there are still questions regarding Israel's survival. A country the size of New Jersey lies surrounded by Arab neighbors. Beyond Iraq lies Iran, a theocracy on the verge of developing a nuclear weapon, a device it has promised to drop on Tel Aviv. The world is held at bay by Iranian oil and a desire for neutrality reminiscent of European appeasement of Hitler a half century ago. Skirmishes with Palestinian extremists escalate daily. Syria is in turmoil. Al Qaeda stalks the world, fomenting terrorism with a desire for a new world Islamic order. Isis, even more radical, more violent, threatens us all. Amidst these looming threats how are we to interpret the recent events at the Wailing Wall?

"To help answer this, we have invited a young witness to that event." With that, the rabbi introduced Ruven, one of the young chess players who had been at the wall. Ruven was bashful, concerned about his stutter. A few freckles dotted his tanned countenance. He wore jeans and a sky-blue shirt, matching his blue eyes. A small hand-sewn brightly colored yarmulke covered curly brown hair, lightened from the Middle Eastern sun. "Ruven," the rabbi said softly, "can you tell our audience what you saw that day of the lightning strike?"

Ruven did not turn to the audience, looking only at the rabbi. "I saw the face of God in the Wailing Wall," he stated matter-of-factly, without a stutter.

"You mean you saw the bright lightning strike," the rabbi said.

"I saw the lightning strike the wall, but in the wall I did not see lightning. I saw the face of God lighting the inside of the wall." He spoke with only a slight stutter, making him more comfortable on the stage.

"How can you say this?" the rabbi questioned.

"I could feel His presence, a warmth that filled me from head to foot, that filled me with this knowledge. Just like I know I see the large nose on your face." Again speaking with only a slight stutter. The rabbi smiled at Ruven's humor, as the audience let out a cheer and stood in united appreciative applause.

"Thank you, Ruven."

Over 50 candles surrounded the stage, creating a symbol of hope for a troubled precious land. A screen in the background showed images from the most recent events in the Middle East, as the rabbi continued. "On September twenty-third the sun appeared magnified as it set low over the Wailing Wall, a blood red manifestation of God." Rabbis were shown praying at the wall with their Jewish brethren, pressing tallit, their prayer shawls, to the wall. The elderly rabbi kissed his own tallit draping his shoulders.

Images on the screen showed evangelical Christians at the Wailing Wall saying their own prayers to Jesus Christ. In the ensuing weeks, vendors offered tee shirts and symbols of the Wall, silver and gold plated Jewish stars, crosses and Bibles. An artist at the wall drew charcoal portraits.

The rabbi continued. "After the lightning strike, the Israeli orthodox Rabbinate convened, interpreting the event as a revelation of God's presence and a warning; but a warning to whom and of what they did not say."

On the vast Kennedy Center stage, Rabbi Herzfeld looked up at his audience, speaking with a hushed solemnity. "There is a person we need to remember and honor this night. His Israeli name, "Doron," translates as gift in English. He has been a gift to the U.S. and to Israel. Tonight we need to remember and pray for him, as he remains captive, a prisoner in Iran. It is fitting that we at the Kennedy Center pray for him because he is also an American, born in New York City of Israeli parents that worked for an Israeli company with a branch in the U.S. His parents died in the twin tower destruction on 9/11. He lived in the U.S. for only eight years before moving to Israel. I knew Doron's parents very well and the boy, as well, from a very young age. As a child he started drawing and desired to become an artist. He drew pictures of far off worlds. Worlds with double stars he saw in his dreams." One of Doron's early paintings was shown on the screen, depicting an astronaut on a far off earth-like planet with butterflies flying from his hand." The rabbi continued. "Doron's father, Isaac, wanted him to be an engineer, saying to Doron his paintings did not depict reality. He believed the boy needed to live in the real world, not in his dreams. Within the dreams of our children may lie a child's innocent unrecognized strivings for a better future. The young man, to please his father, begrudgingly gave up his artistic passion and instead devoted his energy toward gymnastics. On the screen you can see a homemade movie of Doron ben Avrahim competing in gymnastics in the junior Olympics where he won many first-place awards. His parents told me, he broke his finger once in a floor tumbling routine and competed with his broken finger.

After his parents died, despondent and heartbroken, Doron quit all his studies, his art, even his gymnastics. He moved to Israel and when he turned fifteen enlisted in the Israeli army to fight terrorism on Middle Eastern soil to avenge his parents' murders and the murder of thousands of his fellow Americans, as a dual citizen of Israel and the U.S. So Doron gave up his art and gymnastics to become a soldier, a warrior, for Israel, for the U.S., and I believe for the sake of all humanity. Here is a picture of him in his Israeli Army uniform, a lieutenant in the Israeli army."

The screen showed a strapping young man of about 22, dirty blond hair, wistful blue eyes, rimmed with a bluish gray tint, clowning with a fellow soldier, toasting one another with a beer. Beneath the frolicking there was somehow a visible despondent affect etched in the young man's face and demeanor, perhaps from weathering too much grief for someone his age.

The rabbi continued. "He always requested the most dangerous details and over six months ago, on one of these missions he was captured. Let us pray for Doron's safe return and that God's return to Palestine heralds the peace we all seek." The lights in the Kennedy Center dimmed as the rabbi recited a prayer in English and Hebrew for Doron and Israel. The Kennedy Center was permeated with a hushed silence as the rabbi left the stage.

Several church groups, country singers and poets sang and recited worship songs and poetry to God, ending the evening in a prayer for peace in the Middle East.

Galbraith, the CNN religion editor, then continued his own report. "Every religious faction has their own interpretation of the signature event at the Wailing Wall in Jerusalem. The prevailing consensus outside Israel is that it was not ultimately Israelis, Palestinians or Christians that held title to this most sacred of all places but rather that it is the divine province of God. Last week Time magazine put an artist's depiction of the lightning strike on its cover with the title, "God takes Possession of the Wailing Wall." The screen displayed Time Magazine's cover.

Bill Mason, a reporter on Fox News, interviewed Richard Simmons, a well known scientist and atheist, showing him the latest cover of Time Magazine. "Have the recent events at the Wailing Wall changed your opinion about God? Mason asked.

"No," replied Simmons, returning Mason's glare. "Lightning strikes are a common occurrence. Lightning striking the Wailing Wall is just an unusual location of a common physical phenomenon. It..."

Mason interrupted, scornfully replying to his British guest. "Lightning may be common elsewhere but it has never previously struck the Wailing Wall. We're not talking about Kansas!"

"Is there any truth to the rumors circulating on Facebook and You-tube that you have converted to Judaism? You know it's ok if you have," Mason quipped.

Simmons laughed. "The pictures of me converting at the Wailing Wall are fabricated as is the video of my baptism in Rome!"

Churches that a week previously had trouble filling their pews now had standing room only. Synagogues had newfound members and new converts from other faiths.

Jay Landau, on his new comedy special, quipped that as soon as the corporate execs found him, God would be invited as a guest on his show but they would still interrupt Him for commercial breaks.

"Why did God wait so long to show up after Adam and Eve and the Ten Commandments?" Landau asked his audience. "If you knew your creation would rob and pillage and I'm not just talking about Congress, but knowing that in the future your creation was responsible for the lousy programming on ABC and NBC being broadcast throughout the universe you created, wouldn't you hide for a few thousand years, if you could?"

CBS sponsored "The Creation Debates," with the national audience voting on the results, an audience that proved larger than American Idol and proved to the execs at CBS that whatever the ultimate truth proved to be, there definitely was money in God. God was both the newest and oldest rock star. Rabbis, ministers, scientists and atheists participated in the emotionally charged debates with each side claiming victory. An empty chair was left in case God showed up to end the debate. The audience voted 70 to 30% in favor of the reality of God, citing the recent events at the Wailing Wall as the most convincing evidence.

Intermixed with the humor, hidden in the questioned mystery, dormant yet brooding, there was a solemn foreboding among the orthodoxy of all religions, a tremulous awe that the ancient God, the fire-breathing, vindictive God of the so called "Old Testament," the Hebrew Testament, was awakening as though from a deep slumber.

At the Wailing Wall, it was rumored by many, a low rumble could still be heard by a throng of both the religious and the curious, for several evenings after the singular event, reverberating off the desert dunes like lingering aftershocks from the recent storm. A blood moon rose in the evening sky, reddish rays sparkling through crevices in the Wailing Wall, pinpoints of light, like the reticle of a gun sight, perceived as an ominous portent of a future yet to unfold.

CHAPTER 3
HURRICANE ON THE SHORES OF THE CASPIAN

ARUL TURKMENISTAN ON THE CASPIAN SEA.

AMAN JEMALE, A 70-year-old sturgeon fisherman, stood on the banks of the Caspian staring at the sea. The deep azure of the Caspian continued to the horizon meeting and perfectly blended with the sky as though there was no sky, just an endless ocean of blue continuing heavenward at the horizon. It was no wonder that the ancient Romans thought the salty water was a sea that emptied into the ocean. They were not completely wrong. Five to six million years ago the Caspian was part of the Tethys Ocean. Due to continental drift, the Caspian became landlocked, becoming the largest enclosed inland body of water on Earth, classed as the world's largest lake or a full-fledged sea covering an area of 143,200 square miles, 3.5 times the size of all five Great Lakes put together. Its northern border with Russia freezes in the winter and waves at its shoreline can tower 30 feet high. Its size and variable ambient temperatures can create storm systems, much like the more common hurricanes and cyclones over the southern oceans.

The Caspian Sea is bordered by five countries: Russia, Azerbaijan, Turkmenistan, Kazakhstan and most significantly, Iran to the South. Aman stared at the sea, as he did every morning, deciphering the day's weather before venturing out. A hazy layer of fog nestled on the water surface this morning, like a rug rolling out toward the horizon. As he breathed in the cool salty air, Aman felt the morning chill. There was something foreboding about the lingering darkness this morning, as though the sun was hiding. No Caspian seals were out, no gulls, no terns.

Not far from Aman, bordering the Caspian, was the Iranian port city of Chaloos, only partially visible from Aman's location, too distant, too shrouded in fog. Inland from the nearby seaside of Cabul, lay Iran's Northern Caspian Hyrcanian mixed forest, surviving by moisture rising from the Caspian and the Alborz Mountain range of Iran. Within this forest there had once roamed indigenous Caspian tigers until they became extinct in the early 1970s.

A lone inhabitant on the sandy beach, Aman lit a hand-rolled cigarette. Six-foot waves lapped at the shore, roughening the water current. After a few minutes staring at the sea, Aman bent down, burying his half -finished Turkish cigarette in the sand. He could feel a storm brewing in his weathered bones. He would not venture out on the Caspian this day.

"We will kill you and then I will find the woman you want as your wife and tell her how you died like a coward. Then I will kill her!" Gamliel Gazzeri, six foot two, unshaven, grisly bearded, stood menacingly over his captive Israeli soldier. Despite his outward appearance, Gazzeri was a well-respected tenured mathematics professor at the Baghdad University of Science and Technology. His twenty-first century knowledge of mathematical theory was contrasted by a deeply held twelfth century radical Muslim theocratic world view. He saw no conflict, no anachronism living in both these worlds.

Gazzeri was an Iranian militant, a holy warrior, freedom fighter, Jihadist, raised from birth to hate Israel the Little Satan, to despise America, the Great Satan. He was totally committed, addicted to his cause. His world view was the perfect embodiment of the feudal religious Iranian autocracy, which instilled their beliefs in him from childhood, glorifying suicide and holy war. Doron was on his knees next to Gazzeri, still blindfolded. Gazzeri glared at his prisoner, grabbing his sun-bleached dirty blond hair, pulling his head back. The veins in Gazzeri's neck bulged as his words exploded in pent up rage. "I want to be the last person you see before I kill you!"

"Let me kill him!" shouted Gazzeri's wife, Saron. The two quarreled over the honor of killing the Israeli soldier. Most of her face was usually hidden, shrouded beneath a charcoal black niquab. For certain prayers and weddings, she would wear a green niquab to complement her emerald green eyes. The eyeholes of the niquab were separated by a thin vertical stripe of fabric, helping the niquab frame her eyes. A glance, a stare with those piercing green orbs, framed by long reddish black lashes was akin to a male spider being captivated by his black widow mate. Viewing only Saron's eyes left everything to the imagination. In Saron's case, less was more, more than most men could handle. Outwardly, she gave off an aura of a striking, wickedly exotic Islamic beauty. Numerous magazines wanted to use her as a model. She refused them all. Those who knew her, said her raw captivating exterior was more than balanced by her icy interior. As a soldier, she needed mobility and usually wore jeans and sneakers or army fatigues and boots, rather than a cumbersome chador, the full body cloak worn by many Iranian women. Nothing about Saron was ordinary, including her fiery temper and her strident terrorist ideology. At one point, she and Gazzeri had offered their only child Nadina at the age of two as a suicide bomber for an airplane hijacking and explosion. The plot was foiled, saving both the airplane passengers at London's Heathrow airport and Nadina's life.

Saron brandished her Russian Zooni army knife, brushing it along the skin of Doron's ribs. He caught momentary glimpses of Saron as she danced, barely visible, only a hint of her ghostlike visage seen through his blindfold.

Suddenly Saron stopped, noticing the Jewish star around Doron's neck. "You won't need this anymore!" Saron ripped it off, placing it in her pocket. Maybe she could sell it for the gold.

"Let me kill him now!" Saron wailed, turning to her husband.

In the corner of the room, 8-year-old Nadina continued playing innocently with her rag doll. Unlike her mother, Nadina had brown eyes and jet black hair. She appeared oblivious to the violence around her, hiding, many believed, in an autistic child's world, compensating, in her own innocent child's way, for the violence around her. She never smiled. She never laughed. Her childhood was embedded, lost within her parent's terrorist rhetoric and nihilistic world view.

Gazzeri did not respond to his wife's plea to let her kill Doron, but instead pointed the business end of his Russian made AK-47 at the Israeli lieutenant's head. This would be his killing, his honor. It was not the place of a woman.

Doron's bruised ribs appeared through his torn soldier's uniform. His prison home was in a small nondescript wood frame house in the town of Chaloos, on the northeast coast of Iran, on the Caspian Sea. A few gentle raindrops on the dusty windowpanes gave no hint of what was to come.

Hunters of African big game, as well as safari tour guides and the African indigenous people, will all tell you, the most dangerous African animal is not necessarily the largest, or even the strongest, but the cornered animal with no apparent means of escape. At the point of apparent greatest weakness to the animal, is also the point of greatest danger to the captor. And so it can be in war. During the outset of the Israeli Six Day War, October 6th, 1973, two Israeli army brigades were severely outnumbered and seemingly outmaneuvered by the Syrian army on the Golan Heights that fateful day. Although cornered and outnumbered, the Israeli brigades held until support arrived. By the third day, the defending Israelis went on the offensive, waging an aggressive prevailing counterattack, turning a seemingly impossible position into a victory studied to this day by military strategists.

Doron was likewise a cornered animal, with no means of escape, with seemingly no means to even call for support. To the casual observer of the scene, the situation was beyond hopeless. To the more astute observer, one might have noticed several pertinent details of unknown meaning at the time and certainly not recognized by his captors. Doron was not sweating like his captors. He was not showing any signs of fear, or anger and was not speaking, at least not outwardly. He appeared if anything, distracted, like Nadina, quietly residing in his own world. Doron heard the threatening words of his captors, but remained oblivious. Methodically, silently, speaking only inwardly to himself, he repeated the Shemah three times: "Hear O' Israel, the Lord is your God, the Lord is one." "Hear O' Israel, the Lord is your God, the Lord is one." "Hear O' Israel, the Lord is your God, the Lord is one."

The unspoken words, rolled over his cerebral cortex, causing changes in oxygen content, picked up by an implanted Microelectronic Biologic System (MEBS) coating the dura covering his cerebral cortex. The device, like a functional MRI, detected the cumulative but unique electromagnetic pattern created by 85 billion cortical neurons, imprinting a signal in the device, recognized as changes in cortical oxygen potentials through his silently spoken words. The inwardly repeated Shemah was a code sending off an emergency GPS radio signal from his cortical device to the bowels of an Israeli intelligence base in Hebron, Israel, silently instituting Operation Maimonides. Maimonides, in Hebrew known as Ramban, is considered one of the greatest and brightest Jewish scholars and philosophers of the medieval period.

I ignored my surroundings, the mocking anger of my captors, the shimmering presence of the dancer. Instead I was with my mother, watching her standing over her oven, baking in our small kitchen two blocks from the World Trade Center. The scent of terrorist sweat and body heat were now replaced by the warm nurturing aroma of baking bread. I was arguing with my father at age 10, on a fishing trip at a lake in upstate New York, fall leaves surrounding us as we missed yet another opportunity to connect as father and son. Then I returned to when I was age 13, my bar mitzvah just a month previous, now running towards the exploding 9/11 twin towers, my face and body covered in white dust like snow, till stopped by fire fighters, tears streaming down my face, my arms flailing in helpless hopeless crushing grief and anger, my world destroyed. Then I was with my fiance, Sarah, feeling her soft arms embracing me, while still oblivious to my captors as they mocked me. This went on for hours. I was physically captive, but my thoughts, my feelings, my memories wandered free. And then I recited the Shemah three more times as I had practiced in my hours of training.

Two days after the Shemah signal, the gentle rain mutated into a downpour and four days later the downpour became a hurricane blowing in from the Caspian. The storm outside quickened then raged, winds howling as though some vengeful God was sounding the Shofar of reprisal. Not apparent in the thunderous storm were two Israeli jets and numerous small drones racing from the scene. The drones were covered with a layer of stealth cloaking material, making them undetectable by radar.

The evening sky directly above the prison house was now filled with a circular classic supercell thunderstorm. A striated shelf cloud lay above the house and continued heavenward two miles. Sandy yellow clouds were interspersed with various hews of gray and dull black, ominous and

foreboding against the reddish hue of the setting sun. Lightning was followed by thunder with an ever-heightening crescendo with shortening intervals between them as the storm grew closer. From within the eye of the storm, a tornado developed, resembling an expanding nuclear mushroom cloud, as it gradually snaked its way until centered over the small wood framed prison home. The occupants were still oblivious to their fate. The rainfall, now thunderous, pounded the tin roof and windowpanes with a growing incessant clamor.

Repetitive streaks of lightning flashed within and above the vortex of the storm cloud, spreading across the sky, as though the very heavens were shaking. Lightning persisted, strobe like, across the entire expanse of darkening sky in crescendo scintillations, ominous and foreboding. As the storm gained in intensity, the howling wind ripped signs off nearby businesses. The tornado circled Doron's prison home, engulfing the wood-framed prison house as though made of paper mache. The house shook, helpless in the face of an angered God.

Nadina, lying alone, in a corner of the prison house was overwhelmed with fright. She felt she would die if she stayed in the home that was shaking with the storm's approach but unaware of the approaching tornado, now within several hundred feet of the wood framed house. She took her raggedy Ann doll, ran through the kitchen of the home and out a back door. The she ran to the front of the house and down the road leading away from the house. She did not turn to see what was shaking the house until she had run a hundred feet from the home. Partially turning, Nadina looked over her shoulder filled with trepidation and fear. She looked back at house she had just left, still clutching her raggedy Ann doll.

It was only then, for the first time, she saw the full height of the tornado, this monstrous creature extending from the ground to the clouds above. It was now within 50 feet of the house, the house holding her mother and father! It spiraled up with its high winds churning black and gray debris around it, dust and dirt rising from the ground into the maelstrom, as the tornado slowly snaked towards the prison home, the lone house stoically awaiting its destruction. Nadina, transfixed, couldn't help staring at the scene, the tornado whirling hysterically, an eerie high pitched sound emanating from it, only adding to her fright, filling Nadina with abject fear. Frozen in place, continuing to stare at the scene, Nadina dropped her raggedy Ann doll momentarily unable to move, or feel or think. Then she turned to continue running, ran a few steps, then realized she had dropped her doll. She ran back a few steps to pick it up, then continued to run from the house and the spiral monster approaching the house.

A few hundred feet away there was a large 50 year old leafless majestic oak tree with several low lying branches and steps that had been buit to allow children to climb into the low lying branches. She climbed the steps and reached the lowest limb of the tree, seeking refuge in its extending arms, thinking she could hide in its branches, away from the nightmare back at the house. Still holding her raggedy Ann doll she climbed into its lower branches. Then a flash of lightning near by made her decide to climg higher in the tree's branches, to further flee this new fright. Several additional lightning flashes and the accompanying thunder only drove her higher into the tree's branches until she was 30 feet up and from there climbed out along a long branch, hoping to escape the horror of the spiral monster and the lightning demon seeming to be chasing her. There she stayed, her eyes closed, her clasp of her raggedy Ann doll tightening, her mind riddled with fear, her body convulsing in shaking abject fear. Nadina's heart pounded within her chest. She lay elongated along an upper branch of the mighy oak, her sobs inaudible, lost in the shrieking whirlwind. Then a lightning strike hit a branch in the tree, causing Nadina to scream and lose her balance. She was now hanging, dangling 30 feet in the air, from her oak branch, holding on for dear life by one little child's hand, her other hand stubbornly still holding on to her raggedy Ann doll.

Within the prison house, the four Iranian militia crowded together, looking out the single window at the blackening sky, a small rodent flew by their window, caught in the storm vortex. The house creaked, swaying, shutters snapping. The pressure differential inside the house imploded the single window, the divine wind entering, uninvited, spiraling inside, causing the atmospheric pressure within the house to rise until it exceeded the ambient pressure outside. Gazzeri turned his AK-47 at Doron to be certain to kill him, even if he, himself, would die in the maelstrom. At that moment, without warning, the house lifted off its foundation, carrying the four Iranians with it. Gazzeri's shot misfired, coursing through the subcutaneous skin of Doron's left shoulder. But now Doron was also at the mercy of the violent storm.

The Israeli lieutenant was still tied to a drain piping until it too was torn loose and the soldier with it, thrust into the powerful maelstrom. One of his Iranian captors, Aman Nefjani, was the first killed, tossed several hundred feet to his death, impaled on the pointed metal fencing outside the foreign embassy of Kazakhstan. Gamliel Gazzeri was crushed under a wheel of a careening Venezuelan Citgo fuel truck, exploding in its own massive fireworks display. A third Iranian, Tesvan Ricari was shot by an Israeli sniper spotting his target through the reticle of his Manning Mark IV sniper scope, while riding on an Israeli Apache helicopter. The copter then further descended into the vortex, the engine straining in the violent wind. A gun sight signal on the copter console locked onto microelectronic sensors on the Israeli soldier, who was hurtling by. A Spike missile was fired from the helicopter, retrofitted with an encircling net, targeting sensors on Doron, engulfing him in a net which was then hoisted into the copter.

The Spike missile, like many technologies, arose out of a previous failure. Israel's Operation Edge was a response to 182 Hamas rockets and mortars fired into Israel in July of 2014. News reports, at the time, intimated that the U.S. was concerned about "heavy-handed" Israeli battlefield tactics. In response, the supply of U.S. made Hellfire missiles was halted to Israel. In response, Israel adapted the Spike antitank missile technology to the Apache, while still retaining Hellfire capability. The Israeli Spike proved superior to the Hellfire, providing nontrivial non-line-of sight firing capability. From there, further refinements using microelectronic sensor and radar technologies enabled it to provide unique rescue capabilities previously unheard of.

The Apache's engine rumbled and the rotors issued a pulsating vibrato, as the copter strained momentarily in the heavy storm winds. Doron spotted Nadina perched on the top of a tree, hanging precariously by her left hand from a limb, her right hand still clutching her rag doll, screaming between her tears.

"Save the girl!" Doron demanded, his voice rising emphatically.

The pilot turned to Doron. "We don't have time. Iranian ground to air rockets will soon be firing."

"Just do it!" Doron repeated. "We can't just let her die." The hair on the back of his neck bristled.

The Apache turned toward Nadina, fired a net-mounted Strike missile at her silhouette captured on a digital screen, radar targeted, the net catching her just as she fell from the limb, the missile path self-correcting in midflight. Nearby on the ground lay her semiconscious mother, Saron, just able to see Nadina hoisted aboard the chopper before passing out.

CHAPTER 4
WEDDING OF DORON AND SARAH

UPON RETURNING TO Israel, Doron recuperated for a month at an army hospital in Tel Aviv. "Let's not wait any longer to be married," he told Sarah, his fiance, looking at her for approval. Sarah, knowing how close to death Doron had come and uncertain of his future, did not hesitate. As hard as his captivity had been on him, Doron could sense that Sarah had also suffered both outwardly and inwardly from his captivity, in ways she was too kind to share. Although still beautiful, with chestnut hair and bronzed skin, she was thin, clearly from constant worry and fear of the worst, during the six months of his captivity.

"Can we get married at the cliffs overlooking the Caves of Rosh HaNikra?"

Doron knew it was a favorite destination of hers, at the northern border of Israel with Lebanon. "Of course," he told her, walking up to her and enfolding her in his arms. After a long embrace, they kissed passionately, longingly and gratefully.

Sarah unbuttoned Doron's shirt as he helped his fiance take it off. She then lifted his tee shirt, stopping, crying out, as she noted the numerous blood-tinged scars along his ribs. "Sightseeing souvenirs from my captivity in Iran," he told her, laughing to keep his fiance from crying. Sarah put her arms around him, not wanting to let him go. He kissed the tears seeping out the corners of her eyes. Their lovemaking that night was laced with a mixture of desire, longing and fear. They fell to sleep late in the night, wrapped closely in one another's arms.

Two weeks later, only six weeks after being freed from captivity, Doron and Sarah were married near sunset on a cliff overlooking the Caves of Rosh HaNikra. The majestic site was created over a span of thousands of years by the power of the Sea of Galilee eroding the chalk cliffs of the adjacent mountainside, creating a network of caves. Alexander the Great had hewn the first cave in 323 BC after besieging nearby Tyre.

A few facial bruises and bruised arms and ribs lingered, outward evidence of the recent storm and Doron's captivity. The inward damage shared by both appeared much deeper and little discussed.

Only a few guests were in attendance, Sarah's parents, several of her aunts, uncles, nephews and nieces, Doron's nephew Shimon, two of Doron's army buddies, his Uncle Steven and his wife Rebecca, and the 8-year-old Iranian child, Nadina, he had saved during the storm that freed him from captivity. Nadina had been watched by his Uncle Steven while he was hospitalized for several weeks after his escape. The rabbi performing their wedding ceremony, Shimon ben Yitschak, was an orthodox rabbi, 50 years old, who had known Doron, Sarah and their families since Doron had come to Israel. He recited prayers in Hebrew and for the sake of Nadina who knew a little English and no Hebrew also recited several prayers in English.

Sarah wore a simple, but elegant white wedding dress, looking happier than she had been in several years, older than her 23 years, stunning, her radiant features visible through a thin veil. Her betrothed, stood next to Sarah in his military uniform, ruggedly handsome, but thin and pale from his captivity.

Sarah spoke, gently reciting a heartfelt prayer, as the waves from the Sea of Galilee crashed into the caves of Rosh HaNikra, a deep rumble echoing through the caves as a backdrop to her words. Then Sarah turned from the rabbi to look almost pleadingly into Doron's eyes, as she spoke. "Dear Lord, almighty God, that created the moon, the earth and the stars and your people, Israel, thank you for the divine wind you summoned to bring Doron back to me."

Then Doron, looking into Sarah's eyes, spoke to his bride-to-be. "For over six months, I was a captive prisoner, almost every day expecting to die. It was only the thought of you, Sarah, my desire to look upon you once again, to not let you down, longing to hold you in my arms at least one more time, that gave me the strength to survive."

As Sarah looked at Doron, tears again welled up, barely visible through the thin veil, glistening like the sun sparkling off the nearby waves on the Sea of Galilee.

The rabbi then spoke. "The Caves of Rosh HaNikra display the power of God to join the sea and the land. Like the love story of Rosh HaNikra between the sea and the adjacent white mountain cliffs, I have witnessed the love of Doron and Sarah form and grow over many years. In this time of constant conflict, love is all the more precious." He told of their past and of Doron's parents who had died in 9/11 and then he recited seven Jewish prayers following an ancient orthodox tradition. The couple then slowly and gently placed a ring on each other's fourth digit. Following Jewish tradition, Doron broke a glass, symbolic that joy must always be tempered, whether because of future circumstance or the remembrance of the destruction of the Temple in Jerusalem.

Doron lifted Sarah's veil, revealing the beaming countenance of his stunning new wife, even that small gesture caused him to wince in a mixture of pain and pleasure.

Sarah and Doron kissed passionately, desperately, knowing their time together was precious, their profiles sharply etched in the foreground against the setting sun, as the waves from the Sea of Galilee shimmered, a million points of light crashing against the white chalk cliffs. Tears of pent up emotion streamed down both their faces as they held one another, and then the rabbi and soon all the guests save Nadina wept with them.

Rabbi Shimon ben Yitschak put his hands upon the heads of the newlyweds, saying, " Let us pray that God watches over the Israeli people in these most difficult and trying times and especially that God watches over two of His most precious children, now young adult newlyweds standing before us today, Sarah and Doron."

Deep within one of the caves of Rosh HaNikra was a secret catacomb where a Hasidic congregation was at the same time chanting evening prayers, barely audible, commingling with the low rumble of waves coursing through the cliffside caves. The rabbi and his students were later shown pictures of the couple during their wedding ceremony. The chief rabbi, 79-year-old Joshua Dresner, was as yellowed and hallowed as the Torah scrolls he read daily. He was most admired for being supremely perceptive and thoughtful from years of perusal of the Torah and lengthy debates on hidden meanings in individual Bible sentences. His weathered wrinkled brow and soft compassionate eyes were framed by straggly white hair, long pais curling at his temples and a white beard and mustache. His head was crowned with a worn, but multicolored hand-sewn yarmulke. He still led lengthy heated discussions with his rabbinical colleagues and their students. He was called simply Rabi, short for teacher, but not any Rabi, he was affectionately known as "The Rabi." Mirroring their practice of microscopically studying each word of Torah for every symbol, every nuance, every conceivable interpretation, so too did the Rabi and his students study every shade, every shadow, every point of light on the pictures of Doron and Sarah. Their shared consensus, their Kabbalah, their Jewish mystical and spiritual visionary insight was both grave and simple. To quote the Rabi, "The glistening points of light in these photos taken that wedding evening were tears sent from God."

Chapter 5
Meeting of the National Security Council

Pentagon: Arlington Virginia, Meeting of the
National Security Council.
November 10, 20--

SECRETARY OF STATE Arnold Schwarzmann glared at General
Carlson, a two-star general. Like his look-a-like and namesake, Arnold
Schwarzneggar, Schwarzmann was Austrian, had been a weightlifter
and had done some acting. He was, however, not a governor; he was the
53-year-old United States Secretary of State. Upon first meeting him,
he exuded an impressive persona. Six foot four, muscular build, biceps
bulging out from a long-sleeve gray fitted tee shirt with black bold
lettered NAVY on the front. The roles he had played as a charismatic
powerful force of nature had gradually become the same persona that
typified his working life. "How did the Israelis recently get one of their
imprisoned soldiers back from Iran and we couldn't even get Snowdon
out of Russia?" Arnold chomped on a stogie as he spoke, then squashed
it into an ashtray with obvious disgust.

General Carlson replied, a damp sweat moistening his brow. "We
think it was a coincidence that they had a helicopter heading into Iran
at the time the storm struck and luckily picked him up during the
confusion and havoc that ensued." The general looked awkwardly at
Arnold's crushed stogie in the ashtray, a drop of sweat falling from his
brow onto the desk in front of him.

"What the hell was an Israeli helicopter doing in the area?" newly elected United States President, 48-year-old Elijah Gomez asked. He was born in the U.S. of illegal immigrants, the first U.S. president of Mexican descent, one of the so called "dreamers." His actual birthplace was hotly debated during his campaign, but a U.S. birth certificate was accepted by the courts, giving him the legal right to run for president in spite of his DACA status at the time of his campaign. Surprisingly, he ran as a Republican, not wanting expansion of a welfare state, but promoting job creation and even desiring reasonable southern border security. His Latin charm and good looks, salty temples and genuine compassion for America created a bridge between Democrats and Republicans that elected him. 100% of "Dreamers," undocumented/illegal immigrants, now with voting rights, representing over ten million voters, crossed party lines and voted for him. The Democrats who had tried so hard to get voting rights for undocumented immigrants, thinking they would all be future Democrats were as blindsided as Egypt during the 1967 Arab Israeli Six-Day War. Although the 6-Day War was an immediate defeat for Egypt, Jordan and Syria, within Iran the Arab defeat only festered the open wound Israel's mere presence in the Middle East engendered, strengthening their own determination to destroy Israel. This manifested in their repetitive vocal tirades against Israel and their poorly veiled plan for a nuclear arsenal.

General Carlson continued, "We suspect the Israeli helicopter was in the area doing reconnaissance for a possible attack," the general answered, looking askew at the president, head slightly bowed.

Gomez turned to Raymond Schwarzmann, the Secretary of Defense. "I thought the Israelis agreed not to do a pre-emptive strike, unless they were first attacked?" The president turned from Schwarzmann who was silent, glancing around the room for an answer. There was none.

"What is the status of Iran's nuclear capability?" Vice President Vivian Tyson asked, breaking the disturbing silence. Tyson was both one of the first female vice presidents and one of the first black vice presidents. There was no doubt about her black ancestry. Both her parents were black. She was jet black, a brilliant student at MIT and Harvard Law. Her captivating physical presence often put opponents at ease, before being vanquished in debate by stinging arguments and rebuttals. She began her career as a Democrat but became a Republican when she came to the realization that blacks and other minorities were better served by a hand up rather than a handout. Her book, *Leaving the Victim Plantation-A Black Woman's Perspective*, was on the New York Times best seller list for 18 months. When reminded that she was a Democrat herself once, she echoed a simple reply she had heard as a child from one of her favorite people, Charles Krauthammer, "I was young once."

General Carlson replied, "Iran is at least five years away from enough fissionable uranium to create a bomb and another five years from the technology to deliver it."

"How accurate, how reliable is that information?" President Gomez asked.

General Carlson again responded. "The information comes from our CIA spies working in their nuclear facilities and from hacking their military computers. There is one unknown."

"And what is that?" President Gomez chimed.

"We don't know how much technology Iran is buying from North Korea. The North Koreans have nuclear weapons technology and an economy that has been in recession for decades. Offered enough money they would not hesitate to sell this technology to anyone, including Iran. Nuclear technology is their only significant export that can be monetized. They are amoral. Iran is amoral. We have successfully driven our enemies into an ignoble friendship. Two troublemakers see one another as admirable friends with a shared hatred of the West, America in particular, and all things American, encompassing the American form of democracy, ethics and culture."

"When was the last time a tornado struck Iran?" Senator O'Malley asked, changing the subject. He was the head of the Armed Services Committee.

There was a pregnant silence until Lieutenant Tiernan, a Pentagon meteorologist rose to answer. "We don't have a record of a tornado ever striking Iran. We think this incident is a part of weather volatility, climate change, due to global warming."

"Global warming--my ass!" Schwarzmann shouted, banging the table as his ashtray and stogie clanged onto the floor. "Is there any agency that has an idea what the hell is going on in the Middle East?" His jugular bulged from his neck as he spoke, a clenched left fist at his side.

"DARPA or the NSSL may have more information," Vice President Tyson said. DARPA was the department of Defense Advanced Research Projects Agency. It was created in 1958 in response to the Soviet Sputnik launch in 1957. Their charter was to prevent technology surprises but rather to create such surprises for our enemies. "One hundred geniuses connected by a travel agent," was the general quotation. NSSL was the National Severe Storms Laboratory in Norman, Oklahoma.

"Maybe we need a few of you to go to Oklahoma to get a background education before going to Israel to see firsthand what the hell is going on," the president suggested.

The president turned to Tommy Chu, the head of the National Security Association (NSA). "Next week have DARPA and NSSL give us their view on this tornado and hurricane, in one of our national security briefings." President Gomez glowered at his national security advisor, his forehead wrinkling, his eyebrows rising above piercing Latin eyes.

The president then turned to his audience. "Does anyone here think Israel would do a preemptive nuclear strike on Iran?" There was an ominous disturbing silence. "Tommy, as the head of the National Security Agency, you have certainly reviewed this issue. What the hell is your opinion?"

Tommy Chu stood up. "Although Israel does not publicly admit to nuclear weapons, they have had an operational nuclear weapon since

1967. Mass production began after the Six-Day War. They now have about 400 nuclear weapons, some in the megaton range. They also have neutron bombs, tactical nuclear weapons and even suitcase nukes. Israel is one of only a few nations with nuclear triad capability, able to deliver nuclear weapons by land, sea and air. Some of these systems would be invulnerable to a first strike by another country, so Israel has both first and second strike capabilities."

"And would they do a first strike?" Vice President Tyson repeated the president's question.

Chu continued. "When your country is as small as Israel, any nuclear strike on its soil would be catastrophic. We are aware of their Samson Option. This is Israel's ultimate deterrence strategy. Namely, massive retaliation with nuclear weapons, as a last resort against any country whose military has invaded, or otherwise destroyed much of Israel. As such it is not so much a deterrence policy but a policy to inflict overwhelming damage to any country inflicting such damage on Israel. Knowing this policy exists, is a deterrence, but if ever enacted, it would no longer have anything to do with deterrence. Iran has openly stated their desire to destroy Israel. As long as Iran does not have nuclear capability, they do not have the capability of inflicting overwhelming damage to Israel. But they will have nuclear weapons capability within ten years, with or without a nuclear treaty. We believe Israel would not do a preemptive nuclear strike against another country that did not have nuclear capability. However, if and when Iran has nuclear capability, all bets are off. If Israeli intelligence convincingly told the leaders of Israel of an imminent nuclear strike by Iran, what choice would they have?"

"What is the likelihood Iran will adhere to any nuclear treaty?" the president then asked.

Looking him squarely in the face, matter of factly General Carlson stated, "There is no likelihood they will adhere to any treaty provisions. We reviewed this with Trump before he had the U.S. resign from the

Obama nuclear treaty. You, we, all of us know we are dealing with religious fanatics." He peered around the room, scowling, looking for any objections to his comments. "Iran functions as an autocratic religious theocracy. They feel their actions as a purveyor of worldwide terrorism is justified by God, embodied in their fundamental Islamic beliefs, indoctrinated into their citizens at birth. They deny any desire for nuclear weapons while their centrifuges work tirelessly 24 hours a day, churning out fissionable uranium needed for nuclear weapons. They have enough oil to not need any nuclear power plants." The general asked the audiovisual personnel to show a movie of an Iran military display and the indoctrination of a five-year-old child brandishing a suicide device and bayonet while chanting "death to the big Satan," the U.S., followed by the chorus; "death to the little Satan" namely Israel.

The president stood up. "So why was all that time spent negotiating the first nuclear treaty with Iran, when they all knew it would be violated? The only thing it seems to have guaranteed was the successful Iranian development of nuclear weapons!"

Vice President Tyson stood up. She took off her ebony glasses before speaking. "The administration world view at the time, 'leading from behind,' meant the U.S. wasn't going to attack Iran. They followed the Neville Chamberlain approach of appeasement. This didn't work out very well for Europe against Hitler and it isn't worked out very well against another tyrant, the current autocracy of Iran. Benjamin Netanyahu's warning about Iran spoken to the American Israel Public Affairs Committee in 2012 should be heeded. His words at the time, "It's 1938 and Iran is Germany. Iran is racing to arm itself with atomic bombs. Believe him and stop him…This is what we must do. Everything pales before this." Netanyahu's words of warning were ignored and a nuclear arms treaty was negotiated with Iran. Apparently they hoped such a treaty would at least temporarily appease Israel, our military, our European allies, the Republican congress and our American electorate.

They outwardly maintained that through their successful negotiations, our country was made safer and that this negotiated treaty had ensured that safety. Everyone bought it but a number of Republicans and of course, Benjamin Netanyahu, then the Prime Minister of Israel."

President Gomez replied. "So was just a cover-up, delaying dealing with Iran for a few years? Kicking the proverbial can down the road, leaving the mess for someone else to clean up when the treaty failed and Iran ultimately became a nuclear power. Typical Washington politics." No one responded. "What is the odds ratio that we or Israel will be at war with Iran in the next few years, versus a peaceful solution?" Gomez asked.

General Carlson said, "We have run the numbers on our Cray supercomputers based on various scenarios. The war games experts at the Pentagon say the odds are a toss-up, 50-50 for war with Iran in the next five years but very high for war with Iran in the next ten years."

President Gomez stood, up looking over the entire group, his furrowed brow not hiding his growing fears. "What type of coalition can we put together to deal with Iran?"

Secretary of State Schwarzmann stood up but staged a dramatic pause within the eerily silent room. Everyone's attention was now drawn to the secretary. Only then did he speak with the strong Austrian accent issuing from his compelling commanding presence. "The UN is as usual powerless. The French, Germans, Russians, North Koreans and Chinese are all helping Iran develop a so called "peaceful" nuclear capability. They have a 130-year-supply of oil. They do not need this nuclear capability. They desire to destroy the United States as well as Israel. There is only the U.S. and Israel committed to this fight. For Israel it is a matter of survival. The Israelis say they are dealing with a madman, a Hitler prototype but now with a developing inevitable nuclear arsenal. Iran has highly regarded physicists well versed in 21st century nuclear physics, embedded within a religious fanatical theocracy governing with ethics at the level of the 12th century. The Supreme Leaders of Iran are wedded to a centuries old religious prophecy they believe was received by Islamic visionaries directly from God. This prophecy holds that when the Shia messiah known as the Twelfth Imam returns, a global Islamic kingdom will encompass the world. What can hasten his return? The return of 12th Imam will be hastened by mass chaos. What better way is there to achieve this, the Iranian theocracy reasons, in their warped end-of-days eschatology, than to set off a nuclear device? Iran is a closed society, embedded in the morality of the Middle Ages. It is like arming schizophrenics with weapons, not hammers and knives, not even just guns, but a nuclear weapon. Then, for good measure, throw in ballistic missile technology to deliver the nuclear weapon. It is a nightmare scenario. No wonder Israel feels they may have to revert to a preemptive strike, as they did in the Six-Day War. For the U.S., dealing with Iran is warranted beyond only defending and supporting Israel. Since 9-11 there is a recognition that our soil is clearly not safe from terrorists. Either we fight terrorists on their soil in the Middle East or we will deal with them on our own soil. Sleeper terrorist cells in the U.S. could leave a nuclear bomb in a suitcase anywhere. There is no firm coalition willing to jointly deal with Iran. It is us and Israel. Israel often feels they have been deserted. Left out in the cold to fend for themselves. For the Russians and Chinese, control of Middle East oil drives their actions and a desire to decrease U.S. influence and reputation."

"What are the possible military scenarios?" President Gomez asked. He had been elected as the president with a platform of change, a similar platform to President Obama, and now the change he was contemplating was a war with Iran, a final war, the final end of times biblically-predicted conflict between good and evil, Armageddon begun in the Middle East.

General Carlson asked all persons without top secret security clearances to leave. Several senators, secretaries and lower level policy officers had to leave. Then the room was lowered to where a screen covered 2/3 of the room similar to an Imax theatre.

General George Macy, four star general and the most respected strategist at the Pentagon spoke softly, reviewing several scenarios. The room lighting was dimmed, the audience silent, reverential. "If we attack Iran, the Middle East will explode. The Taliban, the al-Qa'ida network, will gain in influence and recruits. If Israel starts a war, the Russians may help Iran, if they think they can get away with it without our intervention. No other country will join the fight unless they are personally attacked. We have invited Shimon ben Yahudah, the head of Israeli Intelligence, to respond." A door was opened. Yahudah entered the room, was quickly introduced and then asked to give the Israeli perspective. Yahudah was not only the head of Israeli Intelligence but also a rabbi, contradictory pursuits anywhere but perhaps not in Israel.

Yahudah spoke with a British accent, having been educated as a historian at Oxford. He read from a prepared statement. "In the Knesset, the Israeli parliament, and in security meetings there is one word that says it all, 'Masada.' Let me review what happened there. In 73 c.e. the Jews of Rome revolted in a fortress at Masada on the shores of the Dead Sea. The Romans erected a battering ram and retired for the day, confident of their victory. At dawn they entered the fortress and found 960 dead bodies. Only two women and five children survived. All chose suicide over Roman slavery. Some historians say Masada never occurred. The evidence, our evidence, says it did, but revisionists do not accept historical facts. The older they are, the easier to revise. For me, the facts support the details I have described. What did survive the mass suicides, was the soul of the living and dead that vowed to never let Masada occur again. Within this spirit lies the soul of Israel that in the end survived Masada, survived wandering in the desert for generations, survived persecutions in Persia, Egypt and Rome, the tortures throughout the Middle Ages, the Diaspora, the Holocaust and multiple recent wars. In spite of all these wars, there is still no sign of peace. There are now recurrent Iranian threats of nuclear annihilation of Israel. Threats from a country that glorifies jihad, holy war, teaches hatred to its children and glorifies suicide as the ultimate noble sacrifice for an ultimate reward delivered in heaven. Of one thing I can assure you. We will not let Masada repeat itself. We will remember Masada!" Yahudah glared at his audience and marched out.

President Gomez stood up and turned to the generals, senators, officers and his staff. "So what the hell is going on there? Is Israel controlling the weather? Is that possible?"

All eyes turned to Lieutenant Tiernan, the meteorologist. The room lights were lowered. "Here is a satellite view of the recent tornado in Iran." An Imax 360-degree view of the storm was displayed on the ceiling screen. "It started from a hurricane that fed a supercell storm that mutated into the tornado that demolished seven nuclear sites and lifted the building holding a captive Israeli lieutenant. This storm had the equivalent energy of a small hydrogen bomb. The U.S. military does not have the capability of controlling, let alone creating a hurricane or tornado. DARPA and the U.S. military have had small groups looking into weather control for over ten years. They have had limited success. DARPA has a motto, "Anything not proven impossible, is possible." Weather control in their opinion is possible, likely, even inevitable, just not yet. There have been theoretical discussions of different types of civilizations that can control the weather. This was first described by the Russian astrophysicist, Nikolai Kardashev. A Type I civilization can control the energy of a planet and can control the weather. A Type II civilization can control the energy of their sun, 10 billion times more powerful than a type I civilization. A Type III civilization can control the power of their galaxy, 10 billion times more powerful than Type II." As he spoke, a large screen displayed the energy available to each civilization.

Gomez stood up. "So does Israel have the capability of an advanced Type I civilization?"

Lieutenant Tiernan looked directly at his commander in chief. "There have been rumors that Israel has been working on such a capability but the orthodox rabbis have also been in deep prayer, calling upon God to come to the aid of Israel in their deepest hour of need. They have been joined in prayer by many Christians in the U.S. and around the world that feel God has chosen to help, they say, His chosen people, Israel, in their time of ultimate need. We have also catalogued and are following fifteen small Israeli companies working on weather control and modification. Israel would be a desert if they could not control their environment and so weather control is strategic to their survival. Controlling rain is however very different from creating or directing a hurricane or tornado. We are..."

Gomez stood up again staring at Tiernan who stopped in mid-sentence... "Are the Israeli scientists controlling the weather or are the Israeli rabbis awakening God? Is that the question at hand?" Gomez turned to the audience of generals, scientists and senators waiting for an answer. There was none...

CHAPTER 6
NIGHTMARE
IN THE OVAL OFFICE

SEVEN IRANIAN JETS took off from airfields in Lebanon and Syria. They headed toward Israel where they were quickly picked up by Israeli radar. Within two hours they made it into Israeli airspace and the seven Iranian aircraft were met by five Israeli jets. Attempts at radio contact with the Iranian jets by Israeli air control, failed. Orders were given to engage the Iranian jets. All seven of the Iranian jets were shot down by a combination of the Israeli jets and ground-to-air missiles, with no Israeli jets lost during the 15-minute air scrimmage. Another seeming air victory for Israel, but all the Iranian jets were simply a camouflage for a lone Iranian jet leaving Iraq camouflaged as a small Iraqi air transport jet carrying its cargo into Israel air space. Instead of delivering its cargo on the ground, the pilot smiled as he pressed a button, opening two bomb doors on the underside of the plane, releasing its cargo a thousand feet over Tel Aviv where it detonated.

The resultant mushroom cloud, heat and expanding pressure front tore apart the lone Iranian jet left, sending the pilot to the supposed heavenly reward he was promised. One Israeli jet was likewise destroyed, leaving four jets intact, all straining to stay aloft as the pressure wave of the 10-megaton nuclear blast enveloped and expanded past them. Tel Aviv was destroyed, buildings blown away by the centrifugal pressure wave from the expanding energy front. The resultant radiation exposure would likely kill all living within a radius of over ten miles from ground zero, compounded by the resultant heat and expanding radiating plume of fire and an expanding pressure wave.

In Iran there was immediate jubilation. The untold death and destruction wrought, the global chaos that would ensue would, the autocratic Iranian regime believed, only hasten the Mahdi's arrival. President Ishmael Gomez, the recently elected president of the United States, was awoken at 3:00 a.m. and informed of the nuclear strike. As he quickly dressed, he wondered if maybe winning the election six months earlier from the Democratic incumbent was no longer the best thing that ever happened to him.

President Gomez stepped outside on his bedroom balcony, hoping the cool night air would clear his mind and help him assess his next course of action. Standing outside, clothed in striped pajamas, he noted a small jet flying through the restricted airspace over the White House. Was it another camouflaged Iranian jet with a nuclear cargo? the president wondered, with growing angst. He was filled with trepidation for both Israel and now the U.S. capital and more immediately, filled with growing concern for his own wife and family.

Gomez hastily ran back inside. There was no time to call the Pentagon, or even his secretary of defense. Would Israel even exist anymore? Should the U.S. declare war against Iran? There were two buttons on his desk. One red one, signaling war and an immediate missile launch against Iran. The other, a blue one, signaled diplomacy to gain European support for a multilateral attack.

President Gomez turned two keys, releasing the safety device preventing accidental thermonuclear war. The leader of the free world and president of the most powerful country on earth, stared into space. As the president of the United States pondered his limited but world-altering options, his 10-pound Bichon Frise little white puppy, Jake, jumped onto the desk and inadvertently, but decisively, stepped on the button for war...President Gomez screamed, but it was too late. His little fluffy white-haired Bichon, Jake, had inadvertently started Armageddon searching for a dog treat on the president's desk!

Suddenly, the White House shook, causing Gomez to look up,

observing a mushroom cloud appearing through the gossamer White House curtains covering the entrance to his bedroom balcony. President Gomez turned to the janitor cleaning on the other side of the room. "I never really wanted to be President," he quipped, then reverting to Spanish he ranted on incoherently in an increasingly abject soliloquy. He looked exasperated, forlorn, hopelessly dejected, sweating profusely. The janitor stopped his cleaning, giving his unbridled attention to the president, who rambled on. "My mother thought it would be good for a Mexican American to run for President. Right now, I'd trade jobs with you!" The president looked up at the janitor, tears in his eyes, seated in the Oval Office with the seal of the presidency behind him. "Would you like my job?"

On the verge of a nervous breakdown, he tried to maintain his composure. As the newly sworn in president of the United States attempted to convince the janitor to trade jobs, the president's wife, Jacinda, nudged him.

"Dear Ishmael, are you having another one of your Armageddon nightmares? You're ranting in your sleep. You're shaking like a leaf! What is it this time?" Jacinda frowned at her husband, sweat soaking their bed sheets.

President Gomez breathed a sigh of relief, realizing the Armageddon he had just witnessed was another one of his recurring nightmares. Whether it would ever become the reality he most feared was yet to be determined.

CHAPTER 7
DORON BECOMES A CYBORG

THREE YEARS PREVIOUSLY.

"ARE YOU READY to try your neocortex implant on another patient?" Martin Grossman, the research head of the Israeli Defense Department was speaking. With him, in his office at the Technion, was a 35-year-old Israeli neurosurgeon, Moshe Arendt, a graduate of Massachusetts General Hospital in Boston. MGH had tried to recruit him, but money and prestige weren't enough to sway him to stay. Israel had offered him a chance to turn his basic research on stroke into trials on living, but severely impaired, stroke patients. Some patients couldn't speak. Others had paralysis of an arm or leg. Such major impairments were often caused by the death of neurons in focal areas of the cerebral cortex, the surface layer, composed of focal gyri on the surface of the brain. It was difficult or impossible to implant devices on deep brain structures, so Grossman's research dealt only with injury to the surface layer, namely the cerebral cortex. The FDA didn't have any jurisdiction in Israel. The limitations of FDA oversight was, therefore, not present in Israel. This placed some patients at greater risk, but also expedited advances in research. His research work in Israel had progressed over the last five years from basic research in the lab to trials on seriously impaired stroke patients.

"What is the patient's medical state?" Arendt asked.

"He has no neurologic ailment, except maybe situational depression, which he has come by honestly. No stroke, no tumor, no neurosurgery."

"Then why do you want him to have risky neocortical implant surgery?"

"We want to be able to communicate with our soldiers nonverbally. To locate and communicate with them by their thoughts, not by spoken words. If one of our soldiers is held captive, we still want to be able to communicate with them. We want to be able to locate them. We want them to be able to disclose their level of danger, so we know the urgency of attempting rescue. If they are imprisoned, without any communications tool… If they are tied up, chained and cannot even speak, we want them to be able to communicate with us by their thoughts. We want to know where they are, whether it is possible to free them. Whether the risk of their impending death warrants the high risk of attempting rescue. Like Operation Thunderbolt, when our commandos of the Israeli Defense Forces succeded in a very high risk successful counter-terrorist hostage rescue at Entebbe Airport in Uganda in 1976. To free our soldiers or civilian prisoners and bring their captors to justice."

"To kill them."

"If they have killed our imprisoned soldiers, likewise to kill them."

"To seek revenge."

"To avenge the deaths of our soldiers, we would go to the ends of the earth, as we have done in search of living Nazi participants in the Holocaust. To kill the killers without mercy, without trial, to let them live every day in fear of revenge. As we avenged the killing of our Israeli athletes killed in Munich during the summer Olympics of 1972. Yes, if you want to put it in those terms, ' to seek revenge.' I would, however, choose use a different term."

"What is that?"

"Justice." Grossman looked squarely up at Arendt. Arendt was wearing his white doctor's jacket, still labeled with the MGH printing and below it, the Technion logo and Tel a Viv General Hospital below his name, Moshe Arendt, MD, PhD. Grossman and Arendt looked at one another for several moments.

"Tell me about the person you have chosen," Arendt asked, turning from Grossman's stare, to peer through a window. Children were playing in a little courtyard outside the Defense Department office.

"The person we have chosen is Doron ben Avrahim, an Israeli/American citizen, now an Israeli army lieutenant. He is not married, has no children, no parents..."

"No parents?" Arendt interrupted, surprised.

"None that are alive. They were killed in New York, in the 9/11 terrorist attack. They were both in separate Twin Tower buildings."

"How old is he?"

"Thirty. He has no immediate family. All our other choices have living parents, many have spouses and children. Only one has none of these, so he became our primary choice. He has also volunteered for our most dangerous missions, so his risk of capture is high and his willingness to take a surgical risk with you, I believe is also high."

"If Doron agrees to meet with you and is willing to undergo the procedure, can I send him to you?"

"In the U.S. no hospital safety committee would allow it."

"This isn't the U.S. and we fight for our survival every day. This technology can help save many lives."

"If it succeeds."

"There have been no serious complications in your last ten patients. We have the utmost faith in you."

"Flattery will get you nowhere."

"Can we send him to you?"

Ten days later, an army lieutenant sat in Moshe Arendt's office at Tel a Viv General Hospital. Arendt spoke to Doron. They shook hands. Doron looked in very good shape, about 200 pounds, 6 foot one, rugged and tanned from working outside, blue eyes, dirty blond hair, a small stubble of a beard. Arendt tried to size up Doron's suitability for the experimental neurosurgical procedure, as he spoke to him. "Research on various forms of a neocortex implant have been in development for over ten years. Over 20 years ago, functional MRI studies were shown capable of identifying specific cortical areas activated by sensory and motor functions, such as finger tapping, leg movement, visual inputs, and speech association areas. At the same time, other research detected radio frequency signals emitted by the brain in response to this cortical activation. The neocortex, the "new cortex," we place over the brain is only a few millimeters thick. It detects the cortical activation and radio frequency changes that occur when cortical neurons are activated. The neuronal activation can occur from audible speech, such as speaking a series of words, but can also be created and detected by speech only said to oneself, thoughts, not physically spoken, we term internal speech. The cortical neuron activation creates radio frequency signals detectable by the neocortex we put in place. In turn, the neocortex can create a signal transmitted over the web and detectable as a web carrier signal. In stroke patients the neocortex functions to generate the nerve signals missing when cortical tissue dies, activating nerve endings in the still functioning white matter below the dead tissue. In your case, we are not replacing dead cortical neurons, we are supplementing them. If you agree to the neocortical procedure, we will test the activation process and our reception capability."

"What does the neocortex consist of?"

"It is a Micro Electronic Biologic Sensory Layer (MEBS Layer) a few millimeters thick. It is part biologic, organic material grown from your own skin. Imbedded in this tissue is a thin layer of electronic semiconductor material that can receive and transmit information. In essence, the implant will allow you to transmit your thoughts over a distance, like mental telepathy of a sort. It will technically convert you into a cyborg."

"OK. What the hell is a cyborg?"

"Cyborg is shorthand for cybernetic organism. In your case, a human with organic and bioelectronic body parts. Originally, the term as first used in 1960 by Manford Clynes and Nathan S. Kline, meant a person with organic and biomechanical body parts. So that would mean anyone with a knee or hip replacement. We also include a person augmented with bioelectronic body parts. The neocortex implant has up to now been used after stroke or other causes of cortical injury such as due to primary intracranial tumors or brain cortical injury after surgery. You would be the first to have it placed to augment healthy tissue, not merely compensate for damaged tissue."

"An ethical issue, it seems."

"Yes, something we have debated internally and I have thought about at length."

"And, your conclusion?"

"In a world where fanatics control the minds of many people, any method to gain an edge over the Dark Side, if you will, is a method we have been forced to consider. In the wrong hands, the same methods could have dire consequences."

"Like?"

"Nothing that need concern us here."

"How many of these procedures have you performed?"

"We have now performed the procedure on twenty-five people. Early on, we had several strokes, several subdurals, several parenchymal hematomas and two deaths, but no deaths or serious complications in the last ten procedures. Your risk, however, does include stroke, blindness and death."

Doron laughed. "Well, as long as there is no risk worse than death, count me in."

Arendt admired Doron's humor in the face of volunteering for surgery with significant unpredictable risk. He immediately liked the soldier. The young man had experienced a lot in his 30 years, including the death of both his parents at a young age. Now he was willing to undergo a still experimental intracranial procedure to potentially help his fellow soldiers. "It's not something to take lightly. You will undergo general anesthesia at which time we will drill a burr hole in your parietal bone to insert the neocortex that will coat 40% of your brain surface. Once in place you will not know it is there. We will check you for rejection and treat you for a transient headache, expected for a few days and then it will become a part of you, giving you a telepathic capability undetectable by anyone."

"Does the neocortex give you any control over me? Over my actions?"

"Good question. Can we control you, like in the *Manchurian Candidate*, where the Chinese controlled an American soldier through hypnosis?"

"Yes, like that." Doron's curiosity was piqued.

"No, there is no capability like that. At least not now. If we cannot persuade people to choose life over death, to applaud diversity, to not kill in the name of God, to not believe in heavenly virgins awaiting them after a suicide mission, to recognize a false Buddha on the road... If we cannot persuade people to forego suicide in blind obedience to religious fanatics governing a dictatorial theocracy, to reject beliefs wedded to a twelfth century warped religious ethos... Then there is no hope for our Western civilization, our Judeo-Christian ethics based on reverence for life and not reverence for death, and ultimately no hope for personal freedom over oppression and blind obedience."

"I'm sorry to speak so strongly," Arendt added. "It is not your doing, not your fault. Brave soldiers like you are our best and strongest defense against the crazy world we now live in. Do you have any other questions?"

"How long will I be in the hospital?"

"About three days."

"If you have no more questions, may I ask you one?"

"Of course."

"Why are you so willing to undergo this procedure? To put your own life in danger? To risk stroke, blindness and death when you are still healthy? Our other procedures were all done on sick patients with significant neurologic deficits, trying to improve their physical state."

"When my parents died in the 9/11 attack at the World Trade Center, part of me also died. You cannot kill the part of me that died with my parents. Nothing can cure my hopeless, helpless, longing for the parents I lost at age thirteen." Doron stopped for a moment as he thought back to that time, his voice more distant, quivering slightly, his hand displaying an unconscious trembling. Then he returned to the present, his voice once again steady, his hand no longer trembling. "You need not worry about operating on me. You cannot kill what is already dead. Rather than fear dying from the cortical operation, part of me would welcome it. Perhaps it is a delusion, but I believe I would in some spiritual sense be back with my parents, and I am not even a practicing orthodox Jew. If the procedure helps me and my fellow soldiers deal with terrorists in some manner, under some unforeseen circumstance, that is enough reason to do it, although I suspect I will probably never need to use it."

Arendt put his hand on Doron's shoulder, attempting to comfort, to console him. As he looked at the younger man sitting in front of him, he could also see his own son who was just now turning 13. He realized that many more people than those killed by terrorists were affected by their actions. Many younger generations would be affected, much like the Holocaust. He could only hope that Doron would survive the surgery; that the implant would function as anticipated; that the neocortical implant might one day, in some dire circumstance, help save Doron's life.

Over the next few weeks Doron underwent a battery of tests. He was poked, prodded and dissected through an assortment of MRI studies. Functional MRI exams evaluated the exact sites of his precentral gyrus, his language centers, various cortical association areas, Brodmann's area, Broca's area, visual occipital centers and combinations of these. Simple finger tapping activation studies progressed to spoken word activation, to visual activation and then to unspoken word activation until a signature was created when certain specific functional brain areas were activated. Three dimensional color images of his brain showed the cortical areas activated. Certain unspoken sentences could now be recognized by the detected cortical activation. Just using the electromagnetic radiation given off by cortical activity, Doron learned to activate remote controlled cars and small radio controlled planes without a visible verbal command.

"We have exhausted what we can do with activation studies," Arendt told Doron, after a month. "Are you ready for the neocortex implantation?"

"I was ready a month ago. Let's do it," Doron replied, matter-of-factly.

"Good. I have put you on the neurosurgery schedule in five days. You'll be in the hospital for two days after surgery and we will test the capability over the next few weeks, if not months, and periodically after that. Since you have no neurologic deficits, we can learn more things from your capabilities using the neocortex than most of the surgeries that preceded you."

The day of the surgery, Doron arrived at Tel Aviv General at 6:00 am. He was accompanied by a young woman. The receptionist escorted Doron to the nursing station where anesthesia went over

their plans with him. The receptionist spoke to the woman with Doron. "Are you a friend?" and then noticed the ring on her finger. "Are you his wife?"

"I'm Sarah Herzfeld, Doron's fiance."

"I'm Margot, the nursing supervisor, secretary and chief bottle washer for Dr. Arendt and the other neurosurgeons. Let me show you where you can wait. Dr. Arendt will speak to you after the procedure and let you know how things went and how Doron is doing. He may even talk to you before the procedure."

"Dr. Arendt, this is Margot. Did you know Doron has a fiance? She is here in the family waiting room."

"No, I wasn't aware. We did not want to do surgery on anyone with a close significant other. That would include a fiance. Can you bring her to my office?"

Margot took Sarah to Dr. Arendt's office and left. "Sarah, I am Doron's neurosurgeon. Has Doron explained the procedure?"

"Yes, to the extent he understands it. You will be placing a coating of some sort over his brain
to give him certain capabilities that might help him. Is that right?"

"Yes, pretty much. We had requested a person that did not have any immediate family, including a wife or fiance as it is a risky procedure. Let me go over it, including the risks and benefits. If you would prefer, we won't do it. So we need Doron's and your permission and signed consent to perform it." Dr. Arendt went over the procedure with Sarah.

"If I chose not to have it done, I know it would disappoint Doron and possibly not provide him with some technologic advantage as a soldier. I don't think Doron and I will have a long happy life together. He volunteers for the riskiest military operations. He has never gotten over the death of his parents. Of course, who could get over such a tragedy? So, I give my permission, if you will promise to be careful. I am not ready to give him up. We have not even had a chance to get married. I still have a young girl's dream of living happily ever after with my husband." Sarah looked up at Dr. Arendt with a wan yet hopeful smile.

With Dr. Arendt's promise to be careful, they parted and the operation was performed.

Three hours later Dr. Arendt came back to Sarah's waiting room. "Sarah, the operation went very well and Doron is starting to wake up from the anesthesia. No complications at this point. The next 72 hours still represent higher risk. Starting tomorrow, we'll test the neocortex and run a battery of tests over the next week. Then he can go home, hopefully better than new, with some capabilities, telepathic abilities very few people have. Only those very few who have also had this procedure."

"What would that be?" Sarah asked, relieved at the outcome.

"I am not at liberty to reveal them in detail, but broadly speaking, Doron will have the capability of letting us know if he is in danger, and signaling his GPS location."

An hour later Sarah visited Doron in his room. His head was partially bandaged and he still had an IV. He appeared to be sleeping. Sarah bent down to kiss him and he stirred, opening his eyes just enough to see his fiance through a lingering fog of anesthesia.

"Is it over already?" he said through his sleepy state.

"Yes, dear, it's over. Till your next adventure, or rather, your next trial. They say you have mental telepathy. Can you read my mind?" Sarah asked. Doron, still groggy from anesthesia, did not respond.

"Can you tell how much I love you? How much I need you? You said, they would give you some machine parts, turn you into a cyborg, part human, part machine. Can a cyborg still feel, can your machine parts tell you how much pain I would feel if something happened to you?" Sarah bent down, putting her arms around Doron and holding him for a few moments. "Can a cyborg still feel the warmth of my body lying next to yours?" Doron gently put his arms around her, as best he could. "You're still sleepy from the anesthesia," Sarah said, looking up into Doron's sleepy pained eyes. Sarah stayed with him till 8:00 p.m. when the visiting hours ended. Before leaving, she gave him a gentle longing kiss on the lips, filled with both hope and fear.

Later that evening Dr. Arendt came by to see Doron. "The surgery went very well. No complications although you are still at high risk for 72 hours. How do you feel?"

"A moderate migraine just started a few hours ago, but otherwise I feel okay."

"I expected that. We will give you some pain medicine for that. It generally lasts only about 24 hours. The neocortex we placed is not in your brain, just overlaying the covering, the epidural space outside your brain, only two mm thick. A few years ago, the electronics alone would have been the size of a small room. The biologic components were not yet integrated with electronic

signals and nanotechnology was still in its infancy. Advances in electronics and semiconductors have enabled us to shrink the size of of medical devices and to integrate biotechnology with semiconductor technology. Get your rest, we'll start our testing of the neocortex capability in two days."

Two days later, Doron was asked to think of certain colors, words, read to himself certain passages without moving his lips or verbalizing the words. The neocortex detected these words, converting them into electromagnetic signals in the infrared and radio spectrum that were

converted to signals that could be picked up as internet signals, much like transmitting Facebook information over the internet. Some non-verbalized phrases were more easily detected. Repeating the biblical words of the Shemah three times, "Hear O Israel, the Lord is Your God the Lord is One," would be a signal of eminent danger—a call to rescue Doron if held captive.

Other phrases signaled GPS locations to consider attacking or locating for future surveillance.

The neocortex was all MR compatible. Doron was given a 3 Tesla MRI scan. The detailed imaging could discern the 2 mm neocortex overlying the surface contour of his brain. The neocortex caused a logarithmic increase in functional MRI signals100 fold, allowing much more detailed assessment of neuronal signals and pathways, creating a new venue for future research. Neuronal pathways were imaged and constructed for many newly visualized intracranial connections.

Israel Defense Department Intelligence personnel were in place 100 miles away. Doron could simply repeat the Shemah three times and have a signal picked up through a carrier electromagnetic wave on the internet 100 miles away, giving his location and receiving his call for help.

Doron met with Dr. Arendt in his office one more time before discharge from the hospital. "Well, Doron, you have exceeded our expectations..."

"You mean the neocortex exceeded your expectation..."

"Both you and the neocortex. Such research may one day allow patients with strokes to develop new circuits, limiting their deficits. For the military, your help in testing the neocortex may allow some captured soldier on some foreign battlefield of the future a chance to be found and freed from captivity." With those last words spoken, Arendt stood up, shook Doron's hand, then gave him a warm hug. Arendt held Doron like he would have held his own son, hoping the technology he had placed would never be needed.

Doron then left, got his belongings from his hospital room and met his fiance at the entrance to the hospital. Sarah drove them in their Ford pickup truck to their small home on Mt. Carmel, a suburb of Haifa, Israel. It was early evening. Sarah had prepared a small candlelight dinner for them. Before dinner, Doron showered. When Sarah brought him a towel, though she was fully clothed, he pulled her into the shower, kissing her passionately. Tears from pent up emotion mixed silently with the streaming water, tears of joy, tears of fear for their unknown future. Together they made love with shared reverent silent emotions. Warm caresses complemented tender shared passion, filled with longing and trepidation. As they made love, the lit candles from Sarah's prepared dinner, so bright in the early evening, gradually flickered out, the dinner still uneaten.

CHAPTER 8
DORON AND SARAH
RAISE NADINA

THREE YEARS LATER.
BEN GURION PKWAY. HAIFA.

AFTER DORON ESCAPED from his capture in Iran, he had an Arab friend explain to Nadina that her parents died in Iran. Doron did not know her mother was still alive, but unconscious in an Iranian hospital. Nadina seemed emotionless. Did not cry, never laughed and was diagnosed as autistic, withdrawn into her own world brought on by a traumatic terrorist upbringing.

It was only slowly that Nadina responded to the gentle caring home provided by Doron and Sarah. No longer embedded in an extremist, controlling society particularly degrading to women, Nadina gradually came out of her shell.

Their home wasn't large, only 1500 square feet on two levels. Sarah and Nadina were in the kitchen one afternoon when Doron entered. He could smell chocolate chip cookies baking in the oven.

"Look what Nadina baked," Sarah remarked, as Doron gave his wife a hug and patted Nadina on the head. They had discussed putting her up for adoption but because she was Iranian and seemed listless and depressed it was unlikely she would get a good home. Some of the adoption counselors thought she displayed some signs of autism, making it even harder to place her. After Sarah had spent some time with her, Sarah didn't have the heart to send her off to endless foster care homes, so they kept her.

As Sarah took the cookies out of the oven, Doron looked at Nadina. "Did you bake these?" he asked. "They look and smell delicious."

Nadina let out a little laugh. "Sarah baked...I help," she murmured.

"Nadina helped a lot," Sarah said. "She's a great help," as she squeezed Nadina's hand.

"Why don't we spend the day exploring," Doron said. "Let's go to the Baha'i Gardens. It's the premier attraction in Haifa and we've never been there. It will give us a chance to get some exercise climbing the nineteen terraces." He laughed, looking at Sarah for approval.

Do you want to see a beautiful garden, Nadina?" Sarah asked, beaming at her.

Nadina nodded yes. Doron and Sarah tried to keep Nadina occupied to keep her mind off her tortured childhood and the death of her parents, a tragedy she seemed to have in common with Doron. "You know Nadina, the Baha'i faith was begun by an Iranian. Siyyid Ali-Muhammad was a native of Shiraz, Iran and the founder of the Baha'i Faith. It's the newest religion. Like Judaism and Islam, they also believe in one God."

Doron drove them to the Bahai' Gardens only a short drive from their home, also on the slope of Mt Carmel in Haifa. As they approached the gardens, the golden domed Shrine of the Bab came impressively into view. The Bab was another name for the founder, meaning Gate, representing the gate into the religion. The golden domed shrine stood in the center of the manicured gardens. Below the gardens, in the distance lay the clear blue Bay of Haifa and the Sea of Galilee. The exquisite and impressive shrine was built by a Canadian architect out of Italian stone and Dutch tiles with an architecture combining the best of European and Oriental features.

Together they strolled around the gardens, Sarah holding Nadina's hand. Doing some research, Doron and Sarah had uncovered that six years earlier, when Nadina was only two, a bomb was placed in her stroller at an airport to use her as a suicide bomber, but the plot was foiled. Now the Iranian girl walked through one of the most tranquil spiritual settings on earth, with an Israeli couple hoping they could help her forget the post-traumatic stress of her past and forge a new future.

They walked up the layered steps of the garden, hearing the water running down adjacent streams, breathing in the warm late afternoon air, hoping the tranquil atmosphere would soothe a young girl's hidden demons.

CHAPTER 9
DORON, NADINA AND SARAH:
LIFE TOGETHER

THREE YEARS PASSED. Nadina was home-schooled until the age of 11. At that age, Doron and Sarah felt she had learned enough English and Hebrew to go to the public school in their Haifa neighborhood. She was still somewhat withdrawn and didn't talk to her classmates very much. They realized she was different, looked different, spoke Hebrew with an Iranian dialect, spoke English with a British accent. They mistook her introversion for aloofness. An occasional boy, attracted to her, would try to talk to her and be rebuffed. Her teachers in their meetings wondered if some deep hurt had turned this child autistic or was it just genetics? Something had broken her spirit, something had turned her inward, afraid and alone. Doron had taken her to a child psychiatrist but after half a dozen fruitless sessions, Nadina refused to go anymore and the sessions were stopped. Not wanting any friends, not knowing how to be a friend, she was generally left alone. So, instead of mingling with her peers she spent time in the local library reading what interested her, the books, her only true friends. She was particularly intrigued by Albert Schweitzer, an old white-haired man with a funny moustache who had lived in Lambarene East Africa. Nadina read about his ideas and beliefs. She read about the concept he called "Reverence for Life," and how it had come to him on a boat ride traveling down the Congo River. At the time he was living surrounded by lions, wildebeest, monkeys and crocodiles each trying to survive, all with a shared will to live their individual lives. Having the freedom to learn about this different view and value of life, was a welcome change for Nadina.

This was so different than her own childhood experience which had been filled with subjugation–her mind and spirit imprisoned. Taught to revere death, not life.

One day Doron and Sarah took Nadina to a local zoo and Nadina enjoyed seeing the animals but wondered if they would rather be free and in forests and wild spaces in their native countries. Some of the animals like the seals and hummingbirds seemed content but others such as the lions and panthers seemed somewhat listless as they could not hunt and seemed bored and withdrawn, somehow having a common bond with her.

During one of their trips to the zoo, the air raid sirens went off, scaring the animals. They went and hid in their enclosures as people also found places to wait the sirens out, wondering if any Lebanese rockets would hit the zoo. Sarah held Nadina till the sirens passed, gently providing her with selfless caring affection. Nadina ran from one animal enclosure to the next, wanting to see everything, trying to judge which animals were happy and which were sad in their zoo captivity.

CHAPTER 10
THE OMEGA POINT

IT WAS THREE a.m. when the doorbell rang at Tommy Chu's home in a suburb of Reston, Virginia. The military courier did not like waking the head of the National Security Association at this late hour but had been ordered to do so. No one answered after the first ring and the courier rang again. After the third ring, Lani Chu, Tommy's wife, put a robe over her nightgown and answered the door. The courier apologized for the late night visit. "Is Tommy Chu home?" he asked.

"I'm his wife," she said, annoyed at the late night visit. "Can I help you?"

"I have a package for Mr. Chu but I'm afraid I can only give it to him." Lani noted the courier was not alone. Both he and his partner were dressed in military uniforms and appeared armed. "What is going on? Has the president been shot?"

"No ma'am," the courier said.

"Then why are you here at this late hour?"

The couriers did not reply. Annoyed, Lani woke her husband who was sound asleep. "There are two people at the door in military uniforms with a package for you?"

"Sorry, Lani," Tommy apologized. "I'll take care of it."

"Do you know why they are here at three a.m.?"

"No, but I'll find out." With that, Tommy went to the door.

The courier asked for identification before handing the file to Tommy Chu, the president's head of the National Security Association. On the cover of the sealed 9 x 11 inch envelope were the words, in bold print, "FOR TOP SECRET EYES ONLY, " Stamped in red in three different places. Below this was a separate paragraph, "Examination by unauthorized persons is a federal offense. Violators of this file's contents is punishable to the fullest extent of the law in Federal court, including imprisonment and fines up to $50,000."

Chu opened the file, which consisted of a single sentence: "OMEGA POINT has been breached." He laid the single sheet of paper on their dining room table and made a call to the secretary of defense. While he did so, Lani walked over and read the top secret letter, turning it over to see if there was any other explanatory information. There was none.

After Tommy got off the phone, Lani turned to him. "What the hell is the Omega Point and what does breaching it mean?"

"I can't tell you. You shouldn't even have read the letter."

Lani held up the letter. "Soldiers come to our house at 3:00 a.m., waking us up, carrying guns and you tell me, you can't explain what is going on? If you value our marriage you'll tell me. If I ask the secretary of defense to explain it to me, how will that go over?"

Tommy sat down. He had always admired his wife's inner strength and ability to stand her ground and speak her mind, although right now it didn't appear to be working in his favor. Once he began explaining, it was as if he opened a floodgate of secrets he had kept within for years: "The Omega Point was initially just a research task assigned to DARPA, the Defense Advanced Research Projects Agency, by Pentagon strategists. What they wanted was a means of quantifying the risks of social unrest and ethical framework of a group, society or country graphed against the technologic capability to inflict harm in a conflict. Social unrest and ethical belief is such a nebulous concept, quantifying it seemed impossible until the development of artificial intelligence computer programs that appeared able to at least attempt this quantification.

Multiple iterations of the computer program were created and back tested against previous episodes of social unrest and mass killings and in some cases genocides. They tested it against Hitler's rise to power in Germany during the period of appeasement before war broke out, against the purges and mass killings of Stalin in the 1930s, the Rwandan Genocide in 1994 and the Cambodian Genocide in the 1970s. Through multiple iterations the program

had an 85-95% accuracy in defining a specific point, as social, political and governmental policies intersected military technologic capability at a specific point, the Omega Point. This is the point where the intersection had a greater than 85% chance of leading to a major genocide, a major war or other major flashpoint. So after proving successful in backtesting against many of the major genocides and mass killings of the past, it was applied to the situation in Iran with a specific question in mind. At what point would Iranian social unrest, their extreme autocratic religious viewpoint intersect their technologic progress toward a nuclear weapon to make a major conflict between Iran and the U.S. or Iran and Israel inevitable, above an 85% likelihood threshold? That point was termed the Omega Point. The Omega Point being breached would now imply that a major conflict with Iran or genocide or other flashpoint is almost inevitable and that any negotiation attempting appeasement is a hopeless fool's errand." Tommy Chu turned to Lani. "Now you should understand why the soldiers came to visit. We live in a dangerous world with the nuclear genie being spread to countries that have no ability or desire to keep it controlled. Einstein would roll over in his grave if he knew what his simple equation $E=M(C)$ squared had wrought. I just called the secretary of defense who, I am sure, will call the Israelis to share this information."

Lani didn't say anything, but wished she had not even asked about the Omega Point. She thought of her three young children sleeping soundly upstairs. Then she went to her husband put her arms around him, as he held her and attempted to allay the fears now enveloping her with an inner dread.

Secretary of Defense Schwarzmann was on the phone with Solomon Rabinowitz, the Israeli Prime Minister. Schwarzmann was speaking. "I trust you have been updated on the latest work in Israel and the U.S. on the Iranian Omega Point intersection."

"I am well aware of it; researchers at the Technion keep me apprised of it at least monthly."

"Our computer research scientists have just informed us that the Omega Point has been breached. Are you aware of this?"

"No, I wasn't told. That just adds further risk to a situation with Iran that's already precarious and heading toward a flashpoint."

"The president wanted me to share this information with you, let you know the U.S. Government has your complete support, but that being said, we would not want Israel to take any preemptive action against Iran, even with this breach."

The Israeli Prime Minister spoke. "As you know, we have a stated policy of promising not to be the first country to use nuclear weapons in the Middle East. It was David Ben Gurion, our first prime minister that desired Israel to develop nuclear weapons, not to threaten our neighbors but only as a deterrent to prevent the Holocaust from ever recurring. Today we have nuclear triad capability. As you know, our submarines have ballistic missile capabilities that can deliver a nuclear warhead to be utilized only for survival, in the event Israel suffers a major attack. We have assumed for years that the U.S. nuclear arms treaty with Iran would fail, as it has, and that all future attempts, such as the current embargo against Iran, aimed at halting progression toward nuclear weapons will also fail. So for us, the Omega Point was breached years ago and our current policies are based on that recognition and that assumption. That it's taken the U.S. this long to come to the same realization is more a testament to the proximity of Israel to Iran and the U.S. distance from Iran, as well as the greater size and technologic power of the U.S. Perhaps the U.S. will now appreciate how precarious our situation now is and will help us deal with Iran accordingly."

"I will pass your thoughts and concerns on to the president," Schwarzmann said as the conversation abruptly ended.

Schwarzmann immediately rang the president.

CHAPTER 11
TIME MAGAZINE:
THE ARMAGEDDON ISSUE

IN VIEW OF rising Iranian tensions, Time Magazine came out with a magazine cover that became known as "The Armageddon Issue." On the cover was a picture of a twelve-year-old girl, with the caption, "The last, the very last human." Inside there was an editorial with a question, "Could the last human be a child, a young girl such as Emily shown on our cover? Will there also be a last animal, a last eagle soaring through an Alaskan sky, a last hummingbird in flight, and what will be the last flower, a solitary red rose or a yellow daisy?"

The National Geographic channel sponsored a companion special entitled, "Diverging Paths," with the description, "One path leads to the stars—the other path to Armageddon. Which will humanity choose?" The docudrama depicted the nuclear winter that would ensue after a global nuclear war, where the fires, the ensuing soot covering everything, after multiple nuclear mushroom clouds, blocked out the sun, lowered temperatures at least 20 degrees, while bathing the planet in nuclear fallout and widespread droughts. If prolonged and extensive enough, much like the termination of the dinosaurs 65 million years ago by an asteroid collision with earth, mankind now had the capability of duplicating this same fate, not just for human life, but for all life on earth.

An astronomer was interviewed. "How deep would the abyss be," he questioned, "if life on earth were destroyed, knowing we were on the verge of inhabiting a universe placed at our feet, a universe that appears created mysteriously for our sole benefit?" The astronomer spoke on while images of galaxies, nebulae, star births and new views of the Pillars of Creation from Hubble were displayed. "How unconscionable, how depressing, how deep the travesty, to know that life on earth had been bestowed an unexpected, undeserved, and unimaginably aspiring extraordinary gift: our entire universe to explore, and to have thrown this opportunity away. To know that our possible future leads down these two diverging roads. One leads to a destiny building a starship, called an ark, suggesting the name Noah's Ark, destined to bring life on earth to the stars. One day, potentially, an eagle might soar through the canyons of a distant planet, light years away. The second path leads to destruction of all life on earth."

A biologist was now interviewed, posing this somber thought, "The brain, it has been proposed, was formed as a mutation off the spinal column. Since most mutations fail, is it only to be expected that our brains, this mutation of ours, will lead to our own destruction and failure as a species and doom all life in our own ignoble failure."

Another cosmologist spoke, "What would it feel like to know our potential journey to the stars went unfulfilled, that all life on earth was destroyed due to pervasive unstoppable human arrogance and age old tribal enmities. What hopeless, helpless sadness would there be within the last humans, knowing the miracle which was life on earth had finally and forever been destroyed, due only to our own human failings? How unimaginable to know that this glorious potential future, journey to the stars, this gift laid out for us, perhaps even planned for us, placed at our doorstep lay forever vanquished and unfulfilled and that in the end, all life on earth was destroyed."

The narrator broke in. "Realize that we, humanity, is on a diverging path, a fork in the road to our future. One path heading into an insurmountable abyss, without escape. A question is worth reviewing: When and how was the nuclear genie at the heart of this diverging path, when was it first let out of the bottle?"

A re-enactment of the origin of the nuclear genie was then dramatized.

SUMMER 1950. LOS ALAMOS, NEW MEXICO

"Where are they?" Enrico Fermi asked his colleagues, almost jokingly. Sharing lunch with the famed physicist were Emil Konopinski, Edward Teller and Herbert York, fellow physicists. They laughed at his seemingly jocular wry humor. Fermi took a sip of his Italian chianti, looked up at his colleagues and repeated, "Don't you ever wonder where everybody is?" If life is prevalent throughout the universe, he argued, it should have made itself known in the 13 billion years since the birth of the universe. Life on Earth has filled every conceivable niche, from steam vents at the bottom of the oceans to Arctic and Antarctic glaciers. Given enough time life always finds a way. Yet can there be an entire universe beyond earth, without life, where life did not find a way, a universe seemingly without meaning? The answer lurks deeply hidden within the three simple words of Fermi's question. It is the mark of very insightful people that they can take complex subjects and break them down into the most simple terms. Einstein had done it starting in 1906--thinking about inertia, imagining gedanken experiments, thought experiments, to explore new concepts and ideas. Einstein thought about an object falling in an elevator, with such simple perusals leading to the development of special and general relativity, completely rewriting our understanding of space and time.

On that warm summer day in the summer of 1950, Fermi continued speaking as he performed a series of calculations on a table napkin on the probability of earth-like planets, the probability of life on such a planet and the likely rise of technology that could spread in the universe. Fermi continued, "On the basis of such calculations, I can only conclude we should have been visited by aliens long ago and many times over." Fermi's question, "Where are they?" became known as "Fermi's paradox," leading to many articles, several books and many long philosophical discussions by countless university professors and lay people continuing to this day. Fermi's musings were later expanded upon, formalized and published by Frank Drake as the Drake equation in 1961.

Fermi was not a person whose ideas could or should be taken lightly. He had won the Nobel Prize in physics in1938 for demonstrating the existence of new radioactive elements produced by neutron irradiation, and for his related discovery of nuclear reactions brought about by slow neutrons. Fermi and Edward Teller had both participated in the Manhattan project during World War II, leading to the development of the first nuclear bomb. For all his scientific work, as well as his participation in the Manhattan Project, Fermi has been called the "architect of the nuclear age." Fermi had been at the Trinity test, named by the physicist Robert Oppenheimer after a poem by the sixteenth century metaphysical poet John Donne.

The Trinity test, 5:30 a.m., July 16, 1945, was the first detonation of a nuclear weapon, a plutonium bomb at the U.S. Air Force site at Alamagordo, New Mexico, only 253 miles by car from their pleasant convivial lunch, four physics colleagues shared in Los Alamos that summer day in 1950. The Trinity test explosion, fulfilling the premise and the purpose of the Manhattan Project, was equivalent to 21,000 tons of TNT. The steel tower on which it rested was completely demolished. Fermi along with others from the Manhattan Project viewed the first nuclear-created mushroom cloud, 40,000 feet across, producing several hundred million volts of energy released in a millionth of a second.

Three weeks later, August 6, 1945, a second nuclear device was dropped on Hiroshima, Japan and three days later a third nuclear device on Nagasaki, Japan. This ended the war with Japan but opened a new nuclear Pandora's Box, still playing out. A clear message was sent to the world: "Don't mess with America," although some preferred a different four letter word replacing "mess." This "message," apparently, wasn't understood by Osama bin Laden when he masterminded the 9/11 attack. To help him understand this history, another message was relayed to him, in person, in honor of all those killed in the 9/11 attack, when he was killed in Pakistan by an American SEAL team.

The answer to Fermi's question raised that summer day in 1950, to the paradox it implied, has immense implications for the field of philosophy, for all religions, for atheism, for agnosticism and ultimately for any belief or disbelief in God. Is conscious life, represented by human life on earth just part of teeming conscious life in the universe? This would make conscious life still miraculous but not clearly a miracle; or is conscious life on earth alone in the vast cosmos. If proven to be the case, the singularity of conscious life on earth should rightly be considered an undeniable miracle, begging the idea of a creator. We would be closer to answering ultimate questions. Who are we, why are we here and what is our ultimate place in the universe?

Given the immensity of the universe, the general scientific belief is that intelligent life exists elsewhere but has chosen not to visit and for some unknown reason has also not let their presence be known. Bill Mason on Fox News interviewed an astronomer, Carl Swathmore. "So Carl," Mason asked, "why do you think we have not been visited by aliens?"

"You might be surprised to know, I am a contrarian on this subject, unlike many of my colleagues. I believe alien life has chosen not to visit us simply because they don't exist. I choose to believe that we on earth are the only conscious intelligent life in the universe."

"Do you have any proof or justification for your belief?"

"I can't justify or prove it. But a thousand years from now is enough time to have a final answer. Since most of us won't be alive then, let's do our own gedanken experiment, our own thought experiment to see the implications of my point of view. So let us, for the sake of our discussion, presume my answer is correct and see the implications of such a belief."

"Alright," Mason said, "what are the implications of your belief?"

"If there are no aliens enjoying life on Andromeda or any other galaxy in the universe, then why does the universe exist? I believe we each have a purpose in this world and that the universe has a purpose as well, beyond staring at in the night sky. I believe we are meant to inhabit the universe beyond earth over the next thousand or million years as our developing space-related technology permits. In this scenario, the earth is our birthplace, our cradle, while the universe at large is our ultimate home.

Russian astrophysicist, Nikolai Kardeshev, has characterized advanced civilizations by their ability to control differing levels of energy and power. A Type I civilization can control planetary power, sunlight, storms, control and manipulate the weather and earthquakes. A Type II civilization can control the power of their sun. A Type III civilization can control the power of an entire galaxy. We are now on the verge, within the early stages, of becoming a type I civilization. We are able to harness sunlight in the form of solar panels, use dams to control waterpower, use nuclear power in power plants and now understand the weather well enough to model it. Initial attempts have also been made to control the weather, both by the military and civilian groups. The energy inherent in even an average storm can equal one thousand nuclear bombs, no small feat, therefore, to attempt its control.

There are countries, however, whose ethics are still embedded in the ethos of the Middle Ages, yet are on the verge of nuclear weapons technology. Other countries have technologies inexorably progressing their societies toward becoming a Type I Kardeshev civilization, including the development of weather control technology. The looming inevitable collision at the intersection of these vastly differing world views, the clash of the civilizations they represent, their competing technologies and their conflicting ethics will ultimately determine if the fate of the world is the fulfillment of a remarkable destiny, planned for us, laid at our doorstep, silently awaiting us, the exploration and habitation of the universe beyond earth or a tragic dystopian apocalypse, ending human life on earth, through self inflicted nuclear Armageddon."

CHAPTER 12
EXPLOSION IN IRAN

HAIFA, ISRAEL. ISRAEL ARMY INTELLIGENCE OFFICE.

"SO WHAT HAPPENED in Iran last night? Did we create the explosion?" Doron asked, towering over his Israeli vice chair of Israeli Intel, Tsavi Rosenberg, seated at his desk.

"No, Doron, that was God's handiwork—a seismic event, an earthquake..."

"And just fortuitously under Iran's major nuclear facility," Doron interrupted, looking down on his commander, attempting to judge if he was lying. Tsavi was stoic in his expression of innocence, but Doron was skeptical.

"Do we now have the capability of creating earthquakes and not just storms?"

"I wish we did, Doron. I would just have our physicists, seismologists and geologists create the mother of all earthquakes and explode Iran into the Caspian."

Doron laughed. "You would tell me if we had caused the explosion, wouldn't you?" His demeanor relaxed.

"Yes, I would tell you!" Tsavi exclaimed. "We are all in this together." He looked up, directly into Doron's eyes. "I need your trust and I need you to get well. You're not very useful nursing a broken arm. You need to enjoy some quiet time with Sarah, your new bride. God knows you deserve it."

"Yes, you're right. That's my plan. You'll keep me informed." It was more a statement of fact rather than a request.

They shook hands with Doron while he continued to search Tsavi's expressionless face. He wanted to believe the honesty and integrity of his commander, but remained skeptical, as he departed.

Tsavi waited a few minutes, watching Doron drive off in his Ford Ranger truck and then picked up the phone to call the head of Israeli Intelligence, Yuri Goldberg. "Doron was just here asking about the explosion in Iran. I didn't enjoy lying to him."

"You know you have no choice. If Doron is captured again, the less he knows, the less he can share with our enemies. It is better for him and our country that soldiers or spies or anyone else that may get caught and tortured have as little classified information as possible that could be used against our country. They don't need to know about our supersonic missile technology. One day we may need to use it against all the hidden Iranian nuclear sites."

"That may be true," Tsavi replied, rolling a pencil between his fingers and then breaking it in his palm as he stared blankly into space. "I still don't like lying directly in the face of a person tortured in captivity, who risked his life to protect mine. Intelligence Agency we call it. It should be the DisIntelligence Agency. It's a lousy way to run anything! We are no better than the terrorists that lie to their children and youth with promises of virgins and glory in heaven!"

"We lie to protect those we love. They lie to manipulate people they don't love, don't even care about! That is the difference and it is all the difference in the world. If you look out your window, realize Haifa is only 99 miles from Megiddo, part of the Jezreel Valley. Do you know the name for Megiddo?" Goldberg asked.

"Yes, Yuri, I know."

"And what is it?"

"Armageddon," he replied.

"And that is what we must prevent, by whatever actions are needed. Even if it means lying to one of our brave soldiers. What is best for our country is best for them."

With his frustration and guilt only partially relieved, Tsavi hung up his phone.

CHAPTER 13
MEETING AT THE NATIONAL WEATHER CENTER, NORMAN OKLAHOMA

NATIONAL WEATHER CENTER, NORMAN, OKLAHOMA. OCTOBER 5TH.

AIR FORCE ONE touched down on the tarmac at 4:00 am, three hours before sunrise on a blustery fall day. The rain had begun earlier in the day with thunderclouds darkening the sky. Vice President Tyson was greeted by John Chambers the head of NOAA, the National Oceanic and Atmospheric Administration and at 54 still physically fit and still in love with everything related to extreme weather phenomena. People at NOAA loved his enthusiasm, his wizened leadership developed over many years, and his compassion for those at NOAA and especially those who labored at great risk in many storms in the field. On board was also Tommy Chu, head of the National Security Agency, Raymond Chadry, Secretary of Defense, John Sharp, head of DARPA and Matt Armstrong, a member of the joint chiefs of staff.

"If you planned the storm for our benefit, it wasn't necessary," the vice president quipped, covering her head with a leather carrying case.

"No," Chambers retorted, smiling at the vice president's humor. "Oklahoma gets its share of storms. If lightning develops as we predict, we can observe it from our weather observatory deck, time permitting."

A black chauffeured NOAA limousine took them over to the National Weather Center. Chambers turned to his guests. "Since you have never been to our facility, let me tell you about it as we drive there.

The National Weather Center, the NWC, sits on a 22 acre site within Oklahoma University. The NWC proper is an Oklahoma University building with NOAA as its primary tenant. The five-story building opened in the summer of 2006. The building is 244,000 square feet including a rooftop outdoor classroom and enclosed weather observation deck. The NWC houses about 550 people, including research scientists, operational meteorologists and climatologists, engineers, technicians, support staff and graduate and undergraduate students."

Chambers escorted the group to a large conference room with a large IMAX type screen for projecting real time satellite weather pictures and video produced from a multitude of satellites in low earth orbit.

"Can we start with introductions?" Vice President Tyson requested. "By the way, this meeting includes classified information, so no leaks to any news media. A stenographer will transcribe the meeting for presidential review." Tyson's informal style made people feel comfortable. It also enabled her to get information not always easy to come by in a city where secrets were valued as golden currency, often sheltered close to the chest. The meeting participants sat around a long oak conference table and in clockwise order gave their names and affiliations.

"John Chambers, Head of NOAA."

"Tom Chu. Head of NSA, the National Security Agency." *Unassuming, gentle demeanor but relentless and tireless in securing a peaceful homeland.*

"Raymond Chadry, secretary of defense." *The first Asian Indian born secretary of defense, 42 years old, was born in New Delhi to wealthy parents. When asked why and how an Indian became secretary of defense, the often simply stated administrator's reply was that he did it the old fashioned way, "He earned it!"*

"John Sharp, head of DARPA, the Defense Advanced Research Projects Agency." *Simply put, a genius among geniuses.*

"General Matt Armstrong, member joint chiefs of staff." *Decorated in two wars, a gifted strategist.*

"Natalia Verbrati, Senior meteorologist and mathematician NOAA." *The 27 year old dual PhD in mathematics and meteorology wore faded blue jeans and a loose golden yellow and blue silk blouse, that did little to hide her Italian beauty, high cheekbones, black hair to her shoulders, hazel eyes matching her silk blouse, athletically toned curvy body, complemented by a sensual Italian accent that made many a man wonder, "How could any woman so beautiful be so brilliant?"*

The entrance door opened and Secretary of State Schwarzmann, entered in a huff. "Sorry, I'm late. Please continue."

"Brian Green," Senior meteorologist, NOAA.

"David Chen, physicist, Los Alamos."

Vice President Tyson, leading the meeting, spoke. "I asked Raymond Chadry as our secretary of defense to review for us the U.S. involvement in climate and in particular, weather control. Raymond, you have the floor."

Raymond was given a microphone, but remained seated as he spoke from a prepared statement. "Let me begin my statement with two quotes to give a perspective on the whole concept of weather control. The first is from an Arthur C. Clark novel describing weather modification in a science fiction novel. Since the whole idea of weather control sounds like science fiction, let's start there:

"It had not been easy to persuade the surviving superpowers to relinquish their orbital fortresses and to hand them over to the Global Weather Authority, in what was—if the metaphor could be stretched that far—the last and most dramatic example of beating swords into plowshares. Now the lasers that had once threatened mankind directed their beams into carefully selected portions of the atmosphere, or onto heat-absorbing target areas in remote regions of the earth. The energy they contained was trifling compared with that of the smallest storm;

but so is the energy of the falling stone that triggers an avalanche, or the single neutron that starts a chain reaction." ARTHUR C. CLARKE, Fountains of Paradise, 1978.

"Why start with a quotation from science fiction? Because science fiction writers are visionaries of the future. If you want to know what's coming, what the future holds, read science fiction. Telecommunication satellites, robotics, the internet, genetic engineering, and numerous medical devices first showed up in the works of science fiction writers. H.G. Wells predicted aspects of viral warfare in War of the Worlds written in 1897. Telecommunication satellites were anticipated by Arthur C. Clark, described in Wireless World Magazine in 1945. Robotics were predicted by Isaac Asimov in serialized magazine stories as early as 1940. Genetic engineering was described by Michael Crichton in Jurassic Park in 1993. Intergalactic space travel, human computer interaction described in many Star Trek and Star Wars movies. Aspects of the internet described as early as 1904 by Mark Twain, of all people, in his story, "From the London Times," published in 1904. As with these prior predictions that became reality, I have no doubt weather control will one day go from science fiction to stark reality. The question is not will it happen, but only when, combining major advances in semiconductor technology, drone technology, satellite technology, information computer storage technology, networking technology and artificial intelligence. This will further advance humanity on Earth into a Kardeshev I civilization.

"My second quotation is from a scientific article many years ago, already in 2002 predicting eventual scientific control of the weather:

"Although it is difficult to predict the pace of technological advance, the control of the weather is a plausible outcome of advances in various fields over the time span of a few decades."

"Controlling the Global Weather," Ross Hoffman, American Meteorological Society, Feb 2002, pg 245.

"The possibility of weather modification for military purposes was already realized in the 1950s. Increasingly since that time, the U.S. Army, Navy, Air Force and Signal Corp have been involved in weather modification research and development. Even early on, weather it was realized could serve as a weapon, giving the US a powerful advantage over a less well-armed opponent. It may sound like science fiction, but so did the atom bomb before 1945." *The secretary had served as a navy jet pilot, then secretary of the Navy, then an attache to the prior secretary of defense for five years. At the age of 50 he became secretary of defense when Ismael Gomez became the elected president at the time that immigration reform led to 15 million new Latin American voters.*

Raymond continued calmly reading from his prepared statement. "In 1967 the U.S. Senate passed the Magnusson Bill to fund programs in environmental modification called EnMod, projecting expenditures of $149 million by 1970. During this time these programs transitioned from research only to early operational phases.

"Then in 1978 the U.S. signed the United Nations Convention on the Prohibition of Military or Any Other Hostile Use of Environmental Modification Techniques, known as ENMOD.

"These programs were momentarily curtailed, names changed but many continued under civilian names, still affiliated with military support and review. The benefit of weather control has both far reaching civilian and military implications. The global costs of a large hurricane are in the billions of dollars, not to mention the potential loss of hundreds of lives, destroyed homes, businesses deeply affecting the very fabric of a community, often for generations. If these storms could be modified, many lives would be saved, as well as billions of dollars by averting the overwhelming property destruction inherent in such storms. Because of both the immeasurable civilian and military benefits, there has been bipartisan support for continued funding of weather control technology.

"After Hurricane Katrina devastated New Orleans, it became clear that we were in a cyclical period of increasing numbers of storms, more violent and more costly in terms of destruction of property and lost lives. This has led to renewed congressional support for weather modification. I have asked John Chambers to have one of their NOAA meteorologists review Katrina and what and how weather modification could have limited its destruction and then review to what extent weather modification is currently feasible."

John Chambers turned to Natalia Verbratti, sitting to his left. "Natalia is both a PhD mathematician, a senior meteorologist at NOAA and an expert on Katrina. I have asked her to go over what the storm did and how such storms might one day be modified. Natalia."

Natalia stepped purposefully to a small stage at the front of the meeting hall and put on a small microphone clipped to the collar at the top of her blouse. "Any storm system can be modeled as a set of initial conditions. Mathematically it can be modeled as a set of nonlinear differential equations that include factors as air and water temperature, initial wind velocity and barometric pressure, initial cloud cover as well as a host of other dynamic variables. What is important to understand, is that such large systems are also very chaotic. Despite their size, their eventual path can be significantly altered by slight changes in their initial conditions. Certain perturbations in the system can act like a tuning fork in resonance with the system and have a much larger effect on the system than would be expected by the size of the perturbation alone. As an example of the powerful effects of resonance, here is a video capturing the collapse of the Tacoma Narrows Bridge over Puget Sound November 7th 1940. The bridge had only been built four months earlier. One strong wind could not have collapsed the bridge but repetitive winds blowing back and forth through the bridge struts and roadway occurring at the resonance frequency of the mechanical bridge structure led to its collapse."

Natalia took a sip of water as she clicked on her next video, running her fingers gently through her hair. "On the left screen is a satellite video of Katrina as it developed in the Gulf of Mexico. On the right screen is a computer simulation of Katrina based on its initial physical conditions, modeling the storm on a bank of Cray supercomputers. The storm was initially a category 3 storm but then morphed into a category 5 superstorm with sustained winds of 175 mph and gusts to 215 mph, ultimately killing 1,836 people and causing 108 billion dollars of damage." As the videos played, there was a remarkable similarity in the actual storm and the modeled storm.

"Would you please put on your 3-D glasses now. They should be on your tables. Using our model, we can display 3-D effects not normally recordable in a real storm. Using our model, we can take you through the center of Katrina, down the eye wall, into the eye of the storm." The screen displayed a remarkable video within the eye wall showing house roofs, mobile homes and cars thrust into the belly of the storm and the eventual flooding of Lake Ponchartrain.

"If certain initial conditions of water temperature and wind speed are changed early enough in the model, Katrina could have remained a category 3 and possibly have been directed to miss New Orleans." Natalia clicked her next video. "This computer simulation has lowered the water temperature by just five degrees, with small changes in air temperature and air barometric pressure as well, leading to a grossly reduced overall storm size with the storm veering west of New Orleans toward Texas and Mexico. As remarkable as this video is, U.S. technology is, unfortunately, at least several decades away from such a capability."

Secretary of state Schwarzmann stood up. "Does any country have this capability? Does Israel have this capability?"

"I am not aware of any country with this capability. Over the last ten years there have been an increasing number of articles coming out of Israel related to weather technology that does imply an interest in weather control. It certainly makes sense. Without some attempt at weather control, Israel would be one big desert and by their actions they certainly have transformed that."

John Chambers stepped to the podium. "Thank you, Natalia."

He looked around the room and spotted John Sharp. "Let's hear from the head of DARPA. John, if you would please discuss your view of current and future weather control capability and your assessment of Israeli capability. You have the floor."

John Sharp walked up to the podium. He was 67 years old. In earlier days he had been a professor of physics at Princeton, had obtained a PhD in applied physics at MIT and was recruited into DARPA ten years ago, not so much for his physics knowledge as for his visionary books on the future of technology that had become bestsellers, displaying his ability to think outside the box. DARPA wanted to predict future risks, anticipate future technology before anyone else. He was a distant relative of Albert Einstein and so it was not surprising that he would start with a quote from him. "Albert Einstein once said, 'If at first an idea does not sound absurd, then there is no hope for it.' The impossible is often a relative concept. Most of technology was considered impossible until someone invented or created it. But before it was created, someone had to envision it, anticipate it, so time and energy could then be devoted to its ultimate creation. At DARPA we adhere to a simple basic dictum: if we cannot prove something is impossible, then we assume it is possible. As for our current meeting, this is specifically true in regard to weather control technology." John paused and waited for questions.

Vice President Romano stood up. "So how close are we to controlling the weather?"

Sharp continued. "Today we can model the weather and control certain aspects of it. Thirty years from now our computer technology will be a billion times better than today and so will our modeling capability. We are planning a pilot program. An array of communication satellites around the earth will be outfitted to send laser signals to bodies of water, heating them up. We will also use underwater arrays, strategically placed to synchronously heat up wide swaths of water. Complementing these arrays will be a swath of drones able to function in concert, a network of drones, acting together. This will be done in a concerted effort to redirect small ocean storms or cyclones before they grow to a size beyond our capability to affect them. In areas such as the Gulf of Mexico, we can anticipate placing an array of devices in the Gulf to cool the temperature below which hurricanes will not form or will only develop into a Category one or two storm, limiting their destructive power."

"And what of the Israelis?" Vice President Romano chimed in.

Sharp responded, "There are over twenty small Israeli startup entrepreneurial companies that are now working in the weather technology arena, purportedly because of their need to deal with their Middle East desert climate. They have names such as Chaos, Harpyiae, Anemoi, Weather Tech, Climatron and Geosatellite. One hundred and fifty weather related satellites have been placed by Israel into low earth orbit in the last five years. We are still determining how they are all being used."

Secretary of State Swarzmann, interrupted. "General Carlson, you've met with Israeli Intelligence multiple times. Do you believe the Israelis have any weather control capability?"

Carlson went up to the podium using the microphone. "Although we have had very good relations with Israel, after Obama took office the Israelis, we believe, have secretly created several plans to deal with Iran without our knowledge or support. We know such plans exist but not the details. One plan is a pre-emptive military strike, possibly a nuclear one. The possibility that it may include an attempt at weather modification is not beyond the realm of the possible but implies advanced weather technology exceeding current U.S. capabilities, but perhaps not beyond theirs."

John Chambers stood up and spoke to the meeting attendees. "Before we continue, there is an incredible lightning storm overhead we can observe from our rooftop observatory. Let's break for a few minutes to take advantage of nature's display."

At the rooftop observatory the dark evening sky was lit up by an awesome display of lightning passing from cloud to cloud and in the distance from cloud to ground. The crackling thunder following shortly behind the lightning only added to the powerful display. John Chambers wasn't alone in wondering how mankind could ever truly control nature. As he looked at the display, it was no wonder mankind had created and envisioned the concept that only God was in control of nature. Likewise, through nature, God was in control of humanity. Even he wondered if humankind could ever wrest such control from God.

As they stood in awe of the display, Raymond Chadry, the Secretary of Defense received a call from President Gomez. "What is it, Mr. President?" he asked, walking inside, away from the thunderous booms outside.

"Raymond, there has been a major explosion in Iran. We don't yet know if they have been attacked, or if it was a seismic event. It has destroyed one of their major reactor sites and put the country on alert. I spoke to Rabinowitz, the Israeli prime minister. He says it was not their doing. I don't completely trust him. We need you back at the White House now. You can announce what we know to the other meeting participants. The story will be on the front page of the New York Times tomorrow, but your meeting in Oklahoma is over for now."

Chapter 14
Tragedy Strikes

FOUR YEARS LATER.

FOUR YEARS HAD now passed since Doron's rescue of Nadina and his marriage to Sarah. Doron and Sarah were in their Ford truck riding down the Mt. Carmel slope from their home. The evening air at 7:00 p.m. was still warm but cooling down from the afternoon sun. The Bay of Haifa and the Mediterranean Sea could be seen intermittently as they drove down to the base of Mt. Carmel, heading to a romantic dinner at a favorite seaside Italian cafe. As they drove, they passed the nearby colorful Stella Maria cable car as it took people up and down Mt. Carmel.

"We should take Nadina on the cable car some time," Sarah said, "I'm sure she would enjoy it." She was dressed in a light white summer frock with a locally created red and green lacquered necklace and earrings, adding the only color to her outfit aside from her lipstick. A summer tan set off her youthful Israeli beauty.

Doron turned to look at his wife, grateful that she had accepted Nadina so easily and proud to be the husband of this compassionate, beautiful sabra. They had considered putting her up for adoption but had been told she would be difficult to adopt in Israel. She was not Israeli, they told her, and appeared almost pathologically introverted. The doctors they took her to diagnosed her as autistic. At one point, Doron and Sarah reluctantly had left her at an adoption center but Nadina had looked at them with such sadness and pleading in her eyes no words could have better expressed her desires. Sarah had cried on the way home and continued sobbing while Doron held her through that night, trying his best to console his young wife. Near dawn they went back and picked Nadina up, bringing her back to their, and now Nadina's, permanent home.

They continued their trip to dinner, past the shops and cafes of Mt. Carmel. They passed Zionism Avenue. It was originally named UN Avenue, but in 1975 the UN passed a resolution equating Zionism with racism, so the city renamed the street Zionism Avenue. Although the resolution was later repealed, the city chose not to rename the street.

Along the vibrant thoroughfare, young people were sitting at outdoor tables in small bistros, laughing and conversing in Hebrew, English and Arabic. There was indeed a significant Arab population that made the city a surprisingly friendly open community. All, however, understood that at any moment rockets could land in their midst from Hamas in Arab Palestine to the south or from Hezbollah in Lebanon to the north, destroying their small idyllic world and family. So, because death could come so suddenly, because life was precious but could be so fleeting, they laughed more often, cried more easily, loved more passionately than they might otherwise have chosen to. At one cafe an Arab and a Jew were sharing a rainbow-colored ceramic nargile, a turkish water pipe, smoking not hashish but an aromatic Turkish tobacco blend, fragrantly flavoring the outdoor part of the cafe. A small street festival was filling the sidewalk of one of the streets they drove by, a trio playing a saxophone, 12 string guitar and a large bass instrument, while a small audience listened intently. The bass player wore a yarmulke with long pais outlining the sides of his face that swayed with the rhythm of their music.

Sarah picked her favorite restaurant, Rocco's, an Italian restaurant founded by an Italian from Brooklyn. The place overlooked Haifa Bay, and their outdoor seating permitted a panoramic view of the harbor.

Doron lifted his glass of French cabernet. "Here's to my lovely wife, our life together and our new little family."

Sarah raised her glass, clinking it with Doron's as she smiled.

"And here's to my favorite escaped prisoner!" She laughed, and Doron laughed with her, clinking their glasses again.

They shared warm newly baked bread, toasted to a light crustiness, layered with tomatoes and crisped parmesan and small salads, continuing their toasts. "And here's to lightning and hurricanes," Sarah remarked, remembering the storm that saved Doron's life, as the setting sun's rays sparkled through her hair, giving it a golden tint. And they clinked their glasses together once again.

"And here's to tornadoes," Doron added.

As he raised his half empty glass, Sarah responded. "And here's to earthquakes and avalanches and rain and snow and any other thing God has up His sleeve to bring you back to me!" As they both started laughing Doron gently reached to squeeze Sarah's hand and to give her a kiss, flavored with the cabernet on her lips.

They were oblivious to the other guests, some of whom stared at them. In Israel where the risk of rocket attacks could destroy any occasion, peaceful romantic moments were particularly cherished. Nearby customers watched the romantic couple nearby, appreciating their warmth as they overheard them speak of future hopes and dreams.

Doron and Sarah finished their main course and shared a moist German chocolate torte made that day, feeding each other as they laughed and kissed their way through dinner.

Then they took a walk along Haifa Bay discussing how Nadina was finally starting to enjoy her life, to interact with other children. It had not been autism but a reaction to the militarist Iranian terrorist mindset subjugating everyone, including children, into a cult filled with death, fear and hate.

As they held hands walking past colorful bayside shops, they did not notice the sniper across the street. The bullet was aimed at Doron but as he turned to look at Sarah in the early moonlight, it grazed past him, hitting Sarah in the chest, spraying her white linen dress with blood. She fell slowly, looking at Doron more out of fear for him than for the life ebbing slowly out of her. It was not what either had ever expected. They had accepted the risks to Doron, but he had never expected to lose Sarah. He quickly caught his wife, cradling her in his arms as he knelt with her, oblivious to the shooter in an alley across the street.

The shooter, at first angry at missing his target and about to shoot again, realized, the soldier would suffer more from the death of his wife than from his own death and fled the scene. Sarah spoke with anguish in her eyes for all they would now never share, uttered in a faint whisper, "Please keep Nadina. Protect her. Do this for me and know how much I love you…" He tried CPR but the damage was too severe. He could not pump a heart that held no blood. He cried out in vain, sobbing as Sarah, his young wife died in his arms. He stayed with her, holding her, sobbing uncontrollably, as a siren blared and an ambulance arrived, summoned by a passerby. The mournful scene was now framed by the pale light of the rising moon and a nearby street lamp. Faintly, wafting from several streets over, one could hear the refrain from the street trio playing nearby, the words of Leonard Cohen's song, "Hallelujah," now a mournful dirge. The medics only slowly were able to draw Sarah from Doron's embrace, knowing that only Doron could now be helped, and there was no need to rush to Haifa Hospital, fifteen minutes away. Doron's chest was heaving in deep sobs, tears flowing profusely as the medics gently took his wife from his enfolding arms. As they did so, Doron's eyes were drawn to the moon and heavens, as he cried out to God, "What do you want of me! Everything I love is killed; both my parents and now Sarah!" Doron wanted to die, to die instead of his wife, to ask God to bring her back and take him. There was so much pain welling up inside of him, death would have provided a welcome end to his suffering. Like the terrorists who spoke of death as a heavenly reward, so too Doron now had a death wish in common with them.

Over the next few days, he considered how to end his life. He held a large kitchen knife in his hand even while making dinner for Nadina, pointing it at his chest as Nadina entered the room, causing him to abruptly lay it down, hoping she hadn't recognized the meaning behind his actions.

CHAPTER 15
FIGHT AT MULLALAH'S BAR, EAST JERUSALEM

A FEW WEEKS LATER.
MULLALAH'S BAR, EAST JERUSALEM.

DORON WALKED INTO the bar in the Arab Palestinian neighborhood known for its vehemently anti-Israeli sentiment. He knew wearing his Israeli army uniform was like waving a red flag in front of a bull.

"I'll have a Heinikin," he told the bartender, while searching the crowd.

The bartender nervously served him the Heinikin along with a cold glass. Before he could fill it, two burly Palestinians approached the bar.

"Do they not have enough bars in Tel a Viv and Haifa?" they asked him.

"We usually have to go to Israel to kill a Jew. Too many rockets flying overhead? Is that why you came here?" The two Palestinians laughed. The laughter stopped when Doron poured his beer into his mug, then poured it over one of the larger Palestinians, then smashing the mug into the other one's face.

A third Palestinian grabbed Doron from behind, with little resistance from Doron, while a fourth and several additional men in the bar took turns punching him. They would have killed him, but unbeknownst to Doron, there was an Israeli soldier, Ramul, in the room spying on the Arab bar. Ramul fired a gunshot in the air, which halted the slugfest. Then he quickly called in nearby Israeli soldiers who broke up the fight probably moments before Doron was killed.

In reporting the incident, Ramul noted how provocative Doron's actions were. The conclusion drawn was that he suffered from severe PTSD and a death wish.

After several months in Haifa General, Doron finally left the hospital for his home. Nadina had been staying with a foster family and they brought her back to her home with Doron and a tearful reunion.

The life of Doron and Nadina was now lived without his wife. Ironically, an Iranian child and an Israeli army lieutenant found the only meaning in their lives was selfless caring for one another, each seeming to need the other. Nadina was now 13. She lit Sabbath candles with Doron on Friday evenings, together reciting the Hebrew Sabbath prayers. Together they went to Saturday prayers at the local synagogue. On Chanukah they played dreidle games and lit the Chanukah menorah. Slowly their lives together found some semblance of peace. A peace that would unfortunately prove short-lived.

CHAPTER 16
SARON AWAKENS

SARON LAY IN a coma off and on for three years, initially experiencing amnesia of many of the events surrounding her loss of consciousness. Gradually, the detailed memory of that fateful night returned. She remembered how she lost her daughter in the tornado that killed her husband and freed their Israeli captor. She was told her daughter was probably dead, her body lost in the violent tornado, probably torn apart and scattered over the devastating scene. Saron refused to give up hope of seeing her daughter again.

As she gradually gained her strength, she worked out at Iranian army training bases. She heard the rumors of secret nuclear sites making fissionable uranium and she hoped they were true.

Her beauty attracted many men, but none interested her. Her only desire was to find her daughter and if this Israeli still had her, she would find him, kill him and take back her child to Iran with her.

She prayed at the local mosque for Allah to help her find her daughter and avenge whoever had captured her. She practiced using her knife, her Russian hunting knife, curved like a Bowie knife with serrations to slice through muscle and ligaments or bone.

She practiced judo and karate, defeating many of the men who faced her in local army competitions. Her demeanor was cold and calculating. Her determination was her obsession, her will fixed. Her color returned to a deep bronze complementing auburn hair hanging in ringlets. With dark eyebrows and high cheekbones, her brooding countenance stopped passersby and photographers. She was placed on the cover of Islamic magazines, a knife in one hand and a gun in another, a dramatic captivating symbol of Islamic fundamentalism. To complement her plans, Saron studied Hebrew to help her, when the time was right, to one day sneak into Israel and pretend to be a Middle Eastern immigrant to Israel.

In the evening she would go have coffee or tea in one of the local coffee shops. The Arabs at the coffee bar spoke with pride of the planned nuclear weapons to be created in Iran and the ultimate advance of Islam over Christianity by armed conflict. Her fellow Iranians participated in rallies, listened to fiery rhetoric from President Kafur and the Ayotollah. They lived in a world with limited access to the internet or other forms of free speech. In this closed society and isolated world, hatred of all things Western was taught to their children who marched with guns at age five, filled with the learned hatred that would provide the next generation of suicide bombers.

Many Iranian men stopped to talk to the sultry beauty sitting alone in the local coffee houses filled with smoke, American music and often shrill voices, while she cradled her Turkish coffee, alone with her thoughts. The men approaching her were all rebuffed as she focused on her mission to enter Israel, free her daughter and kill the Israeli army lieutenant she had once before held at knifepoint.

CHAPTER 17
SARON SEARCHES FOR HER DAUGHTER

ONE EVENING AS Doron and Nadina shopped for groceries, a picture was taken of them and found its way into a Tel a Viv paper, showing off the Israeli lieutenant who had saved a little Arab girl's life. The paper somehow passed into the hands of Saron Gazzeri in Iran, who was known to have lost her child in a freak storm. Saron had almost given up hope of ever finding her daughter alive, but looking at this picture, she knew immediately this was her child. As she stared at the paper, she recognized the Israeli soldier. He was the captive she had almost killed, should have killed. The Israeli was holding her child's hand. Rage grew within her. This was the prisoner she had once held captive, her knife at his ribs. If she had only killed him when she had the chance. If she ever had the chance again, she would rectify her lapse. The recollection of her daughter boarding an Israeli copter, came back to her. It had left the scene and must have taken her daughter to Israel. She looked at his picture, cut out the newspaper article and taped it to the wall in her bedroom.

She would find a way to sneak into Israel and rescue her daughter. Then she would punish eternally this Israeli who had stolen her child, raising her as his own! Saron took the knife she always carried at her side, hurling it at the picture of the Israeli lieutenant.

It had taken Saron a year to recuperate from her injuries. But at twenty-eight, Saron could pass for a college coed or tourist. With her red hair, she did not even look like an Iranian. Several weeks later, a friend helped her get a black market Israeli ID. She packed a knapsack, had her cousin drive her to the southern border of Israel and at night stole across the border.

She walked along Ben Gurion Avenue from Jaffa Road, stopping briefly for dinner at a café in the German Colony. Nearby was the splendor of the Baha'i Gardens, but this was lost on Saron. She knew enough English to converse with the receptionist at a small hotel on Ben Gurion Avenue where she rented a small studio. The living arrangements went well enough to make her comfortable. She let her hair grow out and wore nondescript jeans and simple blouses, but her red hair although helping to hide that she was Iranian, was also not typical of an Israeli, so she told people she was a tourist, planning to enroll at the Technion to study engineering.

She then went to a hair salon, had her hair colored black, against the suggestion of the hairdresser, who loved her red hair. Then she went to a tattoo parlor and had several nonpermanent tattoos placed, one around one eye, highlighting its features and one on her arm, of Albert Einstein along with several relativity equations, including $E=MC2$ to go along with the persona of a technical student planning to attend the Technion.

Her daughter, Nadina, was now 13. She would be in elementary school so Saron visited the elementary schools in Haifa. After two weeks she found her daughter in the school playground of the Carmel School in Ahuza, a suburb of Haifa. She wanted to run to her daughter, to grab and hold her, but did not want to give away her presence. All in due time. Her daughter had grown in the year she had been away, was more outgoing, appeared much happier. When the school session was over, Saron saw the Israeli soldier pick her up from school. Nadina took his hand and went into his truck. She lost them in the bustling street traffic.

The next day she rented a car and followed them to their house a short way up the Carmel slope. Over the next few weeks Saron watched them interact, seeing her daughter act totally different than the introverted, depressed child she had been in Iran. What had caused her to change? she wondered.

While they were gone, she found a window unlocked and searched the house, hiding in a closet when they returned. She listened and watched as they interacted only feet from her. Doron did homework with Nadina, read stories to her. Nadina helped Doron cook their meals. At first Saron felt the Israeli had brainwashed her daughter, but eventually came to realize, he had somehow managed to bring her daughter out of her state of fear and depression. It did not matter. She would still kill him and rescue her daughter. For the next few weeks she observed them grocery shopping, riding bikes, walking the streets of Haifa, going to playgrounds. The more she saw, the more depressed she became, that it was not her, Nadina's mother, that had brought out the true personality of her daughter.

CHAPTER 18
SARON FINDS NADINA

HAIFA, BEN GURION AVENUE.

DORON DROVE NADINA to school. There was a wrought iron fence encircling the playground at the school. After Doron left, Saron finally had the chance to speak to her daughter, through the bars of the schoolyard, during a play session at her school.

"Nadina, it's me, your mother!" she called to her daughter.

At first Nadina didn't recognize her. Then she walked up close to her and recognized her mother, in spite of her disguised appearance.

"I thought you were dead! Killed in the storm! How did you survive? How did you get here?"

"I was in a coma from a head injury but survived. Your father is dead," she stated matter-of-factly. He had never respected either one of them.

"I want to take you back to Iran where you belong."

Nadina looked up at her mother. "I don't want to go back to fighting an endless war and being taught to hate Israelis. Doron saved my life. Then his wife was killed by an Iranian terrorist and still he tried to help me, when he should have hated me for also being Iranian."

"Nadina, you have been brainwashed by the Israelis, you don't know what you are saying." Saron's eyes pleaded with Nadina. "I am your mother. You need to be with me."

"You tried to turn me into a suicide bomber, for your cause, not mine. You let me watch as you tortured Doron and turned me into a vegetable that could no longer talk or feel. I thought that was all life held for me. In Israel I found people who don't hate everyone, who showed me love and cared for me. People let me walk in gardens, breathe fresh air." Her voice rose in anger. "Gave me a reason to want to live again!"

Saron looked at her estranged daughter. "In a few days, I will come for you. You need to respect your mother. You will come with me back to Iran where you belong." With that Saron left. Tears fell from her tattooed eyes, as she wondered what had transpired within Nadina to so transform her child.

Two Arabs observed the meeting. They had been observing Nadina for some time. They were uncles of Nadina. They were not there to free Nadina, but, after seeing her happily interact with Doron and Sarah, before her death, decided to kill her for being defiled living with an Israeli soldier, for so dishonoring her father and their Muslim beliefs-- an honor killing.

A few days later while Nadina was at school and the house was empty. Saron broke into Doron's house and unlocked a window, giving her access to the house at any time. She hid in a closet in Nadina's room while a housekeeper brought her home from school. Nadina went to her room in the evening while the housekeeper slept downstairs. Saron came out of the closet, momentarily surprising Nadina. Saron spoke to her daughter throughout the evening, pleading that she leave with her, but Nadina would not agree. She wanted the new life she was living in Israel with real friends and an awakened interest in life. Saron hid her growing rage, and departed.

A week later Doron returned from another mission. Nadina hugged him as soon as he entered the house. "You told me how your parents were killed—then your wife was killed. I have suffered also. Please don't die and leave me!" she pleaded with Doron.

Doron looked at the Iranian child sitting next to him, filled with anxiety. He had tried his best to get himself killed in an Arab bar and this child was beseeching him not to leave her. Within his psyche, he recognized that without him, Nadina would either be sent back to Iran or to endless foster homes, all likely to revert her back into the autistic state she just came out of, or even worse, lead her to her death.

"I'll try to hang around at least till your next birthday, in July when you will be thirteen. How's that?" Doron questioned.

"No, that won't do. I need you till I'm 80!" she responded emphatically.

"When you are 80 I'll be 110! No one in Israel lives that long and certainly no one in my family!" Doron grinned, a bit puzzled.

"I don't care. That's what I want and that's what you need to promise me." Nadina looked up at Doron awaiting his response.

"Alright. Alright. Do you know Moses lived to 120?"

Nadina shook her head.

Doron continued. "At the age of 120 Moses climbed Mt Nebo, where God showed him the land of Canaan, the land God promised to Israel. With his life fulfilled, Moses then passed away. If he could make it to 120, maybe I can at least make it to 110. Is that a deal?"

"That's a deal," Nadina accepted, as they both smiled at one another.

With that Nadina gave Doron a kiss on the forehead and let him tuck her into bed, not knowing Saron was again in the closet listening and observing though a small hole in the closet door.

In the street outside, Nadina's uncles perused the exterior of Doron's house casing it for a future entry.

With Doron's promise to live to 110, Nadina fell into a restful sleep. Three people were, nonetheless, simultaneously planning Doron's death. Saron, Nadina's mother, who was restlessly sleeping in Nadina's bedroom closet, was planning his demise. Nadina's two Iranian uncles were outside Doron's home and that very night were simultaneously planning not only Doron's death, but Nadina's as well.

CHAPTER 19
IRANIAN CENTRIFUGES ATTACKED

OVER A THOUSAND centrifuges were spinning deep within Alborez Mountain on the western side of Iran. Several minor shocks occurred, suggesting earthquake tremors. Several weeks later a massive explosion occurred. The time was 3:00 a.m. on a sultry Wednesday night. Only ten people were killed since few people, apart from security guards, were present within the nuclear facility at that late hour. The automatic centrifuges themselves never stopped. They spun with a constant hum, audible throughout the facility. The explosion turned the facility and the centrifuges into worthless rubble, now silent. Iranian nuclear physicists and security police were brought in to investigate. The physicists thought it was an earthquake. The Iranian security police were not convinced. However, if they called it sabotage and yet had not prevented it, they feared reprisals from their own government, imprisonment for not having better safety measures or even worse, facing the firing squad. To prevent any risk of government reprisal, the security police and the physicists agreed together to call it an earthquake.

Unfortunately for them, a few weeks later, another hidden mountain nuclear facility also exploded deep within a separate mountain without any preceding seismic-like tremors, making espionage now the leading culprit. Multiple earthquakes perfectly centered beneath the Iranian nuclear facilities were now at the bottom of the culprit list. So the security personnel who had maintained it was an earthquake accident, were rounded up and summarily shot at dawn by a firing squad as a warning to all others that hiding the truth from the government would not be tolerated. The physicists were too vital to the Iranian nuclear program to be executed but were warned that their lives were safe for now but balanced on a knife edge. They could still be replaced. Who was behind the explosions? Was it the Americans or the Israelis, the Iranian leaders wondered, but for the moment nothing could be proven.

Inside Israel, people danced in the streets, rejoicing. The average Israeli had no idea how any of Iran's centrifuges had been destroyed. The religious minority believed God was at work. There were others that believed Israeli military technology, some new unknown powerful weapon, was at work. Very few believed it was random earthquake activity. The government and military leaders in Israel, of course, denied any participation.

"So how did you guys pull it off," Shlomo Rabinowitz, a new member of the Israeli Army Tactical Weapons Unit, asked his friend Lieutenant Sammy Cohen.

"I can't tell you the details, or I'd have to kill you, Shlomo," Sammy replied, grinning.

"Don't tell me the secret of the weapon, just the general technology used," Shlomo asked again.

"The Israeli military has been aware of Iran hiding their centrifuges at the base of mountains to protect them against typical air to ground ballistic missile attack."

"So what did they create?"

"They developed a missile that is fired into the base of the mountain, heats up to 5000 degrees in minutes as it burns its way through rock and rubble to detonate anything from TNT, small nuclear war heads or non-detectable fusion bombs that leave no radioactive trace. That is all I know and all I can tell you. As a new member of our tactical weapons unit, you have a right to know what I know. But don't even tell your wife. The Iranians suspect us even when we do nothing, so they don't need any further provocation."

Several hundred rockets were fired into Israel from Lebanon as a response and 95% of these were shot down by defense systems provided by the U.S. Ten people including several children were killed by rockets landing near Tel Aviv. The launch sites in Lebanon were taken out by Israeli jets, with 25 Lebanese citizens killed. For a while the cafes, restaurants and boutiques in Tel Aviv were empty, but after three weeks people came back as though it was just an afternoon rain shower that had now passed. Israelis had learned to live in the midst of intermittent bombing and were to some degree remarkably desensitized to it.

Due to these events, the security around the remaining mountain centrifuge sites was reinforced. The perimeter guards, surveillance cameras and small patrolling drones were doubled. New radar systems were installed to monitor the overhead skies. Doron was sent on a mission to survey a new potential target in western Iran. Nadina was staying with a foster family. While perusing the mountain site, he was spotted by one of their new drone cameras. Three Iranian soldiers had guns pointed at him, before he even knew they were there. They would have simply shot him except they knew their commander would want to interrogate the Israeli soldier, torture him if necessary to find out how Israel had managed the surreptitious attacks on their deeply hidden centrifuge sites.

Doron was placed in an outdoor fenced jail—one like Isis used to burn their victims. During the night Doron sent a thought signal to Israeli Intelligence with an associated GPS signal defining his whereabouts.

At sunrise, an Iranian military interrogator, Roccan Yamuli, woke Doron with the end of his machine gun. "We will kill you, that is a given," his interrogator informed him with a British accent. "You can die quickly with a bullet or more slowly doused with gasoline. That is your choice." Roccan was forty, trained to squeeze as much information as possible out of people before killing them. He was a devout Muslim, reciting morning prayers with devotion. Many an afternoon was spent torturing prisoners, liberal Muslims, including women and children, and many non-Muslims. He followed scriptural beliefs taught to him by radical Imams in unquestioned fiery sermons. He turned to Doron.

"What were you doing here?"

Doron did not reply. He did not look at Roccan, only stared at the ground. He was thinking of how he would choose to kill Roccan if he ever got the chance.

"What type of weapon are the Israelis using to sabotage our mountain sites?" Roccan glared at Doron, raising his rifle, pointing it at Doron.

Still there was no reply.

"I will give you two days to change your mind and then we will burn you alive. Personally, I would prefer you don't talk and give me a chance to watch you burn." Roccan laughed as he spoke, glaring at his silent prisoner in abject scorn.

Doron spent his evenings in silent prayer. He asked God why he had so let him down. If He was all-powerful, why had he let his parents perish in the 9/11 terrorist attack? Why had he had been freed from his last capture during a violent storm, only to hold his young wife Sarah cradled in his arms as she died? "What do you want of me?" he cried out to an emotionless mute sky. He was caked in dirt, several weeks of unshaven beard now grown, torn and bloodied, camouflage fatigues only partially covering his body.

As his thought deepened into a dream state, he climbed stairs to heaven to accost God for all the wrongs dealt him, the heartache he had endured and still felt, a numbing aching memory. "What is it you want of me?" Doron cried out again. "Have I not suffered enough?" He sought out God in his dream, wrestling with the formless face of God. "Just kill me," he begged, as he wrestled with the apparition of God, a God he could not defeat, and likewise a God that chose not to kill him, for some unknown reason chose not to end his suffering...

He was shaken out of his dream by the sound of nearby gunfire.

Flashes of light briefly lit the scene. His first thoughts were that Israeli soldiers were killing his captors. As one of the Iranian soldiers lifted his gun to shoot him, the Iranian was stabbed by one of the invading troops, but no one came to free him. After two hours, the fighting and gunfire ceased.

It was 3:00 a.m., too dark to see what and who remained. He heard voices but nothing he could recognize.

It was after sunrise that he learned what transpired as a black garbed, black cloaked, hooded soldier, his chest covered diagonally with a strap of bullets and a Muslim emblem of Isis approached.

"This is what you saved me for?" he asked of the silent God, he had just fought with. Three other Isis soldiers appeared. The four Isis soldiers walked slowly to his prison cage. He didn't know why, but for a moment he thought of Nadina, the innocent Iranian child being watched by his cousin, Rifka, and her husband, Raoul, and wondered if she was safe. He was expecting to be killed and thus fail to keep the promise he had made to his dying wife, to look after Nadina, to protect her, and likewise failed in his promise to Nadina. One of the Isis soldiers entered the cage and approached him swinging his gun, using it as a bat. Doron grabbed the rifle as it was swung and in a swift move used it on his attacker, knocking him down. Before he could turn the business end up, three other Isis fighters lifted their rifles at him, clicking bullets into chambers, as they yelled at him in English, "Drop the weapon, or die!" Knowing he could not outshoot three of them, he dropped the rifle. The Isis soldier that had fallen struck him in the side of the head and then his chest and stomach, kicking him as he fell. Then the Isis soldier left. Doron repeated the Israeli code words in his mind to transmit a message to Israeli Intelligence and hopefully summon a rescue mission. This was the same code that had freed him previously.

One of the other Isis soldiers spoke to his comrades as they walked away. "We will televise his picture to the world and then we will televise burning him to the glory of Isis."

True to their word, they televised his capture. Televised his imprisonment in a metal cage.

They told him to plead on television for mercy, to beg for mercy. He refused. They fed him the scraps from their dinners just enough to keep him alive. This went on for a week. Several Iranian women and children were also in the encampment. The children playing, oblivious to the prisoner in their midst. Then, suddenly, a ten-year-old child, bitten by a hornet developed hives, then developed wheezing. No one knew what to do. Standing next to the child and mother was another ten-year-old child, also hysterical with fear, with hopeless helpless pain, the first child's twin brother. They had no epinephrine to reverse the allergic reaction. Doron called to one of the women, the child's mother, that he was trained in emergency respiratory therapy; if they would let him, he would try to save the child's life. The mother was hysterical with grief, but at first the Isis soldiers refused Doron's offer. As the child's condition progressed into full blown laryngeal edema, they finally let Doron out, four rifles pointed at him.

"I need a knife," Doron requested. The child's mother gave him a small knife. Then he grabbed a Starbucks straw laying on the stack of last night's dinner fare. He had several people hold the child down, who was now gasping for air and starting to turn blue with cyanosis. Doron quickly cut a hole in the trachea just above the cricoid cartilage and put the plastic straw through the opening, creating an airway below the obstructing laryngeal edema. The child's mother looked searchingly at this Israeli soldier, her mortal enemy, now the only hope to prevent her child's death. As soon as the cricoid was penetrated, immediately the child breathed in a gasping life-saving breath through the straw. After a few gasping breaths the child's purple cyanotic color, started pinking up. A military jeep arrived and several Isis soldiers drove the child to the nearest hospital two hours away. The Isis soldiers then threw Doron back into his cage kicking him to show nothing had changed. He was still targeted for death by gasoline.

At the hospital, the child was immediately given intravenous benadryl, epinephrine, solumedrol and a saline drip. Within a few minutes the reaction had subsided, the straw removed and the knife tracheostomy surgically repaired with several sutures. When the mother was questioned as to who had saved the child's life, there was no reply.

Two days later, Isis still planned to kill their prisoner, lest any word got out that an Israeli soldier had saved the life of an Isis child. As the mothers present realized what was being planned, they took matters into their own hands. Three of them formed a ring around the soldier, and chained themselves to the metal cage. To kill the Israeli, they would have to kill them all. The Isis soldiers considered doing just that, but they couldn't televise that to the world, so they left to plan their next move over the next day.

The Isis women knew they had little time to lose. Late that night, while some women kept the guards occupied, several other women made it into the cage and freed the Israeli. Doron escaped into the woods and was finally able to communicate with Israeli intelligence who sent a copter to pick him up. Israeli Intel said the metal cage had blocked his previous radio transmission, preventing his radio frequency signal from reaching them. Doron was in poor physical shape, starved and beaten by the Isis fighters. His left arm from the distal forearm into the wrist and hand was severely infected, the median and radial nerves likewise severely damaged. Shortly after entering the copter Doron lapsed into unconsciousness.

For their part in the escape, the women involved were summarily shot, including the mother of the child whose life Doron had saved.

CHAPTER 20
DORON UNDERGOES PROSTHETIC SURGERY

DORON LAY UNCONSCIOUS for two weeks. His forearm was infected with a gram negative bacteria causing local gas gangrene and sepsis. The infection had also destroyed many nerve endings in his left forearm. The forearm muscle tissue atrophied from simultaneous diminished vascular supply and loss of neurogenic stimulus. With Doron still unconscious, a decision was made to amputate the wrist and hand to save Doron's life. The team of surgeons considered trying to salvage the hand and forearm but the damage from the infection and injury was too severe and this plan was rejected. When Doron awoke, his left hand and wrist were gone. Doron was in shock. "Why couldn't you have tried harder? How can I function without my hand?"

"We tried to save your hand and forearm until it was clear that to save your life we needed to amputate. It was not an easy decision. I'm sorry but we had no choice."

"It was certainly not our first choice," Dr. Ishmael Abramowitz, his surgeon, told him. "We have already planned to fit you with a hand and wrist prosthesis."

"I don't want a prosthesis!" Doron screamed. "I want my hand back!" The surgeons answered with silence. "If I had succeeded in doing what I intended at that Arab bar in East Jerusalem, we wouldn't need this conversation!"

Six weeks later Doron's forearm had significantly healed, for his next staged operation. Doron underwent a five hour operation. Forearm tendons were now connected to titanium and biosynthetic microelectromechanical sensors in a prosthetic wrist and hand. At first the tendon to his thumb and middle finger didn't work properly. When he tried to move his thumb, his middle finger would stick up as though he was giving someone an obscene gesture, which he went out of his way to share with his surgeons. "After receiving a new hand, this is how you show your appreciation," Ishmael Abromowitz, his surgeon quipped. Two more operations were needed to correct the finger dysfunction and fine tune the function of his digits. After this was accomplished, they tested the strength of his grip. At first they gave him a rubber ball, which he squeezed. Then they gave him a baseball, which he squeezed till the seams exploded off, the inner twining and cork center fell apart to the floor. When Doron realized his grip was stronger than ever, the first smile appeared on his face since the events at Mullalah's Bar.

"The strength of your grip, I should warn you is ten times the strength of an Olympic weightlifter's hand, so be careful," his attractive therapist warned him. He reached out to shake her hand with his new left prosthetic hand. "I don't think I'll be shaking your new left hand." Instead, she shook his right hand.

After the forearm and hand function was perfected, the electromechanical tendons and mechanical digits were covered with a type of polypropylene material matching his skin color. To the casual observer, Doron had a flesh-colored, normal-appearing hand and forearm. After this was accomplished, Doron looked at the therapist and surgeon. "Now that I see what you've provided me, I no longer regret losing my hand." He raised it, opening and closing it, to confirm its functionality. "Anyone want to arm wrestle?" he asked with the hint of a grin, as he raised his head to look at his surgeon and therapist. "You doctors gave me a neocortex to aid me. My neurosurgeon said that made me a cyborg, a cybernetic organism with organic and biomechanical parts. If that was what I was then, what does this make me now?"

"A more advanced cyborg," his therapist replied. "Eventually we will do away with all body parts except the brain and people will become complete cyborgs."

"What if you also do away with the human brain, the human mind?" Doron asked.

"Then you are no longer human. You are a robot. It is your mind, the tangle of neurons in your brain that makes you human, not any of the mechanical parts, not any of your muscles, not even your heart."

Doron listened but as he did so, he was also slowly moving his hand and forearm, learning how to use his new electromechanical parts, understanding their potential, accepting, welcoming, incorporating these new body parts as an integral part of himself.

CHAPTER 21
A METEOROLOGIST FROM NOAA VISITS THE TECHNION

THE TECHNION, HAIFA ISRAEL.

THE TECHNION, KNOWN also as the Israeli Institute of Technology was founded in 1912 and is the oldest college in Israel. For recreation, the school provides an Olympic-sized swimming pool. Natalia Verbrato, had never expected to visit the Technion but enjoyed the scientific intellectual atmosphere of the institute that had produced three Nobel laureates.

Natalia was swimming in the Technion's pool. She had been a swimmer in college, even winning a few meets. She found the pool a refreshing respite from the hot dry air outside. Her long strokes and lithe body were quickly noticed by the young students using the pool as well. As Natalia got out of the water, shaking the water out of her hair, there were many eyes on the Italian beauty, as she reached for her towel. John Chambers, her boss and the head of NOAA, had sent her to the Technion to learn more about Israeli weather technology with a visit to the two-year-old Technion Center of Applied Meteorology, TCAM, pronounced TeChAM. She understood her real job—spying on Israel--which left her with mixed feelings.

Chamber's request was posed secretly at the request and funding of the Department of Defense. Many questions had been raised regarding Israeli technology and weather-related events. More than a dozen small entrepreneurial companies had been spawned in Israel in the last few years dealing with weather technology and most had come out of the new Technion Center.

"We would like you to find out what the true Israeli capability is to alter weather patterns and create storms," Chambers had told her. "You have the charm and intelligence to get people, particularly men to talk." He smiled at her, trying not to be overly dramatic or sexually explicit. All you have to do is give them a little of your Italian charm," he added, as his smile broke into a subdued laugh.

Natalia thought about it for a few days. What had she become? What had she unknowingly signed up for? So now, she realized, she was an Italian meteorologist and mathematician functioning as an American spy in Israel.

Chambers had given her a short biography of the Israeli army lieutenant who had been freed by a hurricane and ensuing tornado and gave her Doron's contact information, suggesting she call him when she got settled in Israel.

At first, she had not planned to call him. She visited several of the new entrepreneurial weather-related companies, but although they were friendly and showed her some of their technology, she sensed they were very protective of their patents and their privacy. They seemed unwilling to share most of their capabilities. She thought that maybe if Doron would accompany her, they would be more forthcoming. Then one evening in her apartment near Mt. Carmel, there was a news story about the army lieutenant that had lost both parents in 9/11, that had been captured and tortured in Iran for two years before miraculously escaping and saving the life of an Iranian child, whom he was now raising. Several years later his wife had been killed by a sniper, leaving him further traumatized. Maybe she could find a way to cheer him up, to help him and he could, likewise, help her learn more about the weather technology being developed here in Israel.

Natalia gave Doron a call. At first he told her no, he would not meet with her, but after a few phone calls from Chambers to the Defense

Department and from the US Secretary of State to Israeli Intelligence, Doron was ordered to meet Natalia. Their first meeting was at Moishe's Cafe Klatsch on the side of Mt. Carmel.

Natalia arrived first, dressed in a pale blue and white blouse and and matching skirt, her hair slightly curled from a recent shower, simple but elegant. Not much was needed to complement Natalia's full Italian lips and breasts.

Doron arrived a few minutes later, dressed in a short sleeve army shirt, tousled dirty blond hair framing dark brooding eyes. Now at age 33, he had clearly recovered from his last ordeal at the hands of Isis. He was still depressed from his secret missions into Iran and the death of his wife, but lack of any physical interest in Natalia produced an opposite affect on her. She was often annoyed by the many cloying men smothering her with attention. Doron's lack of interest in her physical presence, his reserved demeanor and ruggedly handsome appearance attracted Natalia to Doron from the start. She felt like taking this forlorn soldier, with his sad eyes and a life of hardship under her wing and giving him a reason to enjoy life once again.

She asked Doron about the storm that saved his life.

"The storm was unusual," he said. "We don't get many storms here in the Middle East. On the shores of the Caspian, storms do occasionally arise and can be severe. It was not created by Israeli Intelligence. We can't create storms." Doron was only partially lying. Israel couldn't create the storm that saved him, but Israel had helped convert the shelf cloud into a tornado and had directed its winding path onto his prison home. Israel, he had been told, had no interest in sharing its technological advancements, which was now a military advantage in dealing with Iran. He looked at Natalia, admiring her intelligence, thoughtful probing questions but was not physically swayed by her beauty. He had lost the only person who had ever physically attracted him. He had lost his soul mate. He looked up at Natalia and past her, through the glass front of the cafe, observing the young students from the Technion biking past the cafe.

"Has Israel done anything to control the weather patterns allowing desert sands to transform into vineyards along the slopes of Mt. Carmel. The creation of the BaHai Gardens is as beautiful as anything in Europe or California." Natalia looked up at Doron but his stoic look revealed no information about his truthfulness.

He again did not respond.

Natalia continued. "I have read about some of the new companies that have been getting venture capital from Silicon Valley. There are at least ten of them that are working in weather-related fields. Startup companies such as Climatology Inc, Chaos, Greentree, Computational Meteorology, Magnetic Meteorologic Modeling, MMM, AI Inc., and a host of others. Many are based out of the Technion here in Haifa. Google, Apple, Intel, IBM, Microsoft, Facebook and Twitter, I am aware, have helped fund many of them and have research centers at the Technion investing, it appears, heavily in these companies. There are now more Cray supercomputers at and around the Technion than at MIT!" Natalia laughed.

Doron responded. "The Jewish people enjoy learning. You don't spend forty years wandering the desert studying the Bible without ingraining learning in your descendants." He gave Natalia the hint of a smile.

"Could you take me to visit one of these new venture companies. How about Chaos Climatology? I did my PhD in mathematical modeling of the climate. I would be curious to learn how they use Chaos theory in their research."

"I'll see what I can arrange," Doron replied. "I can't stay any longer. I promised a little girl a ride on the Carmel Cable cars."

"Could I join the two of you? I still have a few questions and I would enjoy that experience as well. I am also a new tourist. You can be my guide." Natalia gave Doron a convincing look as she ran her hands through her hair.

At first Doron said no, but while Natalia tried to convince *him* with her charm and warmth, Doron decided Nadina might enjoy a woman's company and reluctantly agreed.

Doron drove them to pick her up Nadina. "This is Natalia, a meteorologist from the United States," Doron told Nadina.

"What is a meteoronomist?" she asked.

"Meteorologist," Natalia said. I study the weather, try to tell when it will be sunny or rainy or stormy. If you knew when it was sunny you would know when to play outside or hide from a storm." Her warmth readily brought out the curiosity in Nadina.

"Can you change the weather?" Nadina asked, not realizing how appropriate her question was.

"I can't but there may be some people in Israel who can." She stole a look at Doron who remained nonplussed. "I hope to meet some people who have learned to stop the rain, move the clouds and move a storm. What weather would you like them to provide?"

"I like sunny weather. No more rain or storms." Nadina was very somber. Nadina had not forgotten the storm that had almost taken her life.

Together they boarded the round orange-colored Carmel Cable car at the base of Mt. Carmel. Thirteen-year-old Nadina held Doron's hand, as the three of them gazed out at the stunning vista of Haifa Bay as the cable car headed up Mount Carmel.

A long time ago, Doron had promised Sarah they would take Nadina on this trip, but never expected to do it without her. He tried not to show Nadina the loss he felt as the cable car moved up the small mountain.

"I like seeing for miles, like now," Nadina remarked, looking out at the setting sun across the Mediterranean, a few ships out on the bay and the lights from the city gently glowing below them.

The city of Haifa and the coastal seaside stood out in relief, with small shops dotting the sea coast. At the top of the ride they explored Stella Maris and visited the nearby Stella Maris Carmelite Monastery, the so-called Star of the Sea. "The monastery was begun in the 12th century during the Crusader occupation and became the Carmelite order," said Natalia.

Together they strolled by the Old Lighthouse, the shops of the Stella Maris region, stopping to admire the striking vista of the Bay of Haifa.

Natalia bought Nadina an ice cream cone and together they sat while she finished it, before venturing into the nearby Stella Maris Church. The attractive church was built out of Italian marble. Within the dome of the church were paintings from the Old Testament including a scene of Elijah swept up in a chariot of fire. Doron was glad to have Natalia along as it helped bring out the personality of Nadina, helping her enjoy their excursion all the more.

Then they toured the Bha'i Gardens halfway up Mount Carmel. Although Doron lived in Tel Aviv only a short drive to Mount Carmel, he had never visited the Bha'i Gardens. Nadina had now given him a reason to do so. The garden terraces are a monument to the followers of the Bha'i Faith and surround the Shrine of the Bab, the resting home of the Iranian founder of the faith. The gardens, designed by an Iranian architect, Fariborz Sahba, have elements of the Persian Gardens of Shiraz, Iran, the Nishat Bagh Gardens of Kashmir India and English gardens.

Finding such lush gardens in Israel with its inherent Middle East desert climate is a testimony to the carefully constructed irrigation system and for some reason never given by the Israeli engineers, also seemed to have surprising rain showers almost centered on the gardens.

They started at the top of the gardens, slowly making their way down a set of stairs flanked by two streams of running water flowing down the mountainside alongside the stairs, like small brooks adjoining a river stream. Everything was either green or colored with a myriad of flowers. Rows of elegant, tall but narrow cedar trees gave the setting a majestic appearance. Other small trees and a few palms gave it a tropical feel more reminiscent of Florida than the desert climate of Israel.

Nadina ran around the trees, splashed her hand in the streams, ran through the fountains, much happier than Doron had seen her since Sarah's death. At the Shrine of the Bab, halfway down the terraced gardens encircling it, they stopped to rest and admire the scene. From this location they could look down on the Bay of Haifa, glistening in the afternoon sun. The view was so serene, the setting so quiet and peaceful, it was hard to imagine they were in Israel. They continued their exploration of the gardens led by Nadina who appeared to want to run around every tree in each of the gardens, splash her hand in every pool and run through every fountain. Then they returned to their car left parked at the entrance to the Stella Maris cable car station, though Nadina was lagging, obviously reluctant to leave this wonderland.

"Thank you for taking me on this tour of the Bha'i Gardens and the Cable Car Ride," said Natalia. "I enjoyed meeting Nadina. You not only saved her life but appear to be making her a very happy young girl."

"Nadina liked you immediately and she is usually very introverted with strangers. We both enjoyed your company. I'll call you after I make the arrangements to visit Chaos Climatology." Doron held out his hand but Natalia reached to give her escort a hug, an Italian warm hug, wanting to let him know she was available for more than just a friendly handshake.

In response, Doron gave her a dispassionate hug, not reciprocating the warmth of Natalia. Doron only let her kiss brush his cheek. The death of his wife Sarah had now been several years ago, but still felt like just days ago, the pain still there. He had no wish to find someone new, no matter how enticing the offer. The idea of kissing someone else sickened him, no matter how beautiful the woman. The Israeli soldier's heart was still filled with the memory of Sarah. Doron knew it would be a long time, if ever, before he would or could find a place in his heart for another.

CHAPTER 22
NATALIA AND DORON VISIT CHAOS CLIMATOLOGY

A FEW DAYS later Doron picked up Natalia for a visit to Chaos Climatology one of many new start-up venture companies just south of the city of Haifa located at Hof HaCarmel. As they rode to the company headquarters, Natalia noted branch headquarters for Google, IBM and Intel all within a few miles of each other.

Chaim Rabinowitz, the company president led them into a small conference room, where they all took offered cups of coffee. Covering an entire wall was a painting of a huge thunderstorm as seen from space, with a vortex ending at a small point on earth, Natalia recognized the point as Haifa and Chaos Climatology.

"So tell me a little about your company," Natalia asked. "Why name it 'Chaos Climatology'?"

Chaim was a physicist, 25 years old, wearing a white tee shirt with Schroedinger's wave equation written in broad strokes across the front, and above the equation the words, "And God said.... Below the equation were the words, "And then there was light!" Blue jeans and bright red and blue Nike sneakers, made Chaim look like a college student. His pais and short trimmed beard made it evident he was also an Orthodox Jew.

"All weather systems are chaotic," Chaim remarked. "People describe the "Butterfly effect," meaning if a butterfly flutters its wings in Peking on Monday, the weather will be affected in Madrid or New York or Haifa on Thursday, and at times the affect may be significant. Small changes in initial conditions can produce dramatic ultimate final effects."

"So how can you hope to make weather predictions if everything is so sensitive to initial conditions?" Natalia questioned.

Chaim glanced at Natalia, dressed in only a pale yellow summer dress—yet drawing a double take. He could readily understand why a woman such as Natalia could cause a man to ignore the precepts of the Bible. He nonetheless returned to Natalie's question. "That's just the point. We at Chaos are not interested as much in predicting the weather, as we are in changing it. For the same reason that small changes in initial conditions can change a weather pattern, so can small changes done at the right time, in a repetitive manner affect the future weather pattern, possibly changing a severe storm into a less severe storm, from a direct hit to a large coastal city, such as New Orleans to only a partial hit. We don't need to completely control the weather, just modify it enough to limit its damage." Chaim gave Natalia a flirty smile.

"So is that how the storm that saved Doron's life was directed?" Natalia looked up at Chaim for a straight answer, without a returning smile.

"We are aiming for such a capability, but are at least ten years off from such a thing. We did not affect the storm that freed Doron, although we would have, if we could." Chaim spoke convincingly, without hesitating, but Natalia was not completely convinced. "One of our researchers is giving a talk on our technology right now; perhaps you would like to sit in?"

"Of course I would," Natalia replied, hoping to learn more about this company and the science behind them.

In the nearby auditorium, Stan Lee, one of the company's physicists, was giving a talk on how they had configured the Navier Stokes Equation on nonlinear fluid dynamics to mirror the pattern of a storm by knowing the initial conditions of temperature, pressure, initial wind velocity and water temperature. By repetitive measurements and several Cray supercomputers analyzing the data they hoped to model any storm system in real time.

As they took their seats in the back of the small auditorium, a computer animation on a large front screen showed one of the prior storms over the Florida panhandle, and then a remarkably similar model on a split screen. Stan continued his presentation. "If we change the initial conditions of water temperature just a few degrees, barometric pressure or wind velocity, just as in the "Butterfly Effect" we can elicit significant changes in the eventual storm. The question of most importance then becomes, how can you change these initial conditions over a large enough area to cause a significant effect?" Natalia and Doron listened, fascinated by the very concept of the weather control Chaos was attempting to achieve.

In a separate room in the basement, another researcher was using a storm creation device to display a miniature storm in a wind tunnel. Rising out of the water was a storm, with the look and feel of a hurricane, shelf cloud and tornado. Then by changing water temperature, wind velocity and barometric pressure he transformed the storm into varying strengths, mirroring the predicted computer models, the very capability the company president, Chaim Rabinowitz, had just denied.

Nearby, at a blackboard, Stan Lee was seeking to prove a theorem relating the Navier Stokes Equation, topological manifolds and a Mandlebrot Chaotic attractor.

Silent until now, Natalia said, "I'm not sure you're going in exactly the right direction with that equation..." Natalia had recognized his error. "Do you mind if I help?" she offered, as she walked up to the front of the classroom. The audience wondered who this stranger was. Who did she think she was, venturing onto the hallowed ground of top numbers geeks?

Stan sheepishly handed her the chalk. Natalia rewrote the equations in a simplified form showing that one of the partial derivatives had been left out, correcting the proof. After five minutes she handed the chalk back to Stan. "Thank you, miss... whoever you are... I didn't catch your name," Stan asked.

"Natalia. Natalia Verbrati. I'm a mathematician and meteorologist at NOAA."

The audience stood up and gave her a round of applause, and a few whistled as she returned to her seat. After the lecture, Doron drove her home, joining others in admiring the intellect of his visitor.

CHAPTER 23
US MILITARY VISIT THE TECHNION, HAIFA ISRAEL

THE MILITARY PLANE landed in Tel Aviv at 3:00 a.m., in the darkest part of the night, greeted by Moishe Tanner, the Israeli Ambassador to the U.S. The five Americans on board were escorted to an unmarked black limousine and taken to a small hotel near the Technion in Haifa. Included in the contingent were the U.S. secretary of state, Arnold Schwarzmann, Tommy Chu, head of NSA, John Sharp, head of DARPA, Raymond Chadry, Secretary of Defense and previously, a four star general, and John Chambers, the head of NOAA.

"We'll have breakfast now; then I suggest you get some rest after your long trip," Moishe Tanner advised. "We have a long day planned tomorrow." Israeli time was seven hours later than eastern standard time, making it 10:00 a.m. eastern time in Israel. "After breakfast let's meet again at 5:00 p.m. We'll take you to a conference room and give you the update you have requested of our companies in the field of weather technology. Then we'll visit several of them tomorrow."

In the middle of breakfast Tanner received a call from Yuri Goldberg, head of Israeli intelligence. Tanner stepped outside to take it. "So how was your initial meeting with the U.S. contingent?" Yuri asked.

"Fine. They were tired from their trip. We're having breakfast together now. Then I've suggested they rest, take a long nap, give themselves a little chance to adjust to the time change."

"How is your family and how is Dovid, your eldest? Having a bar mitzvah soon, I hear."

"Cut the pleasantries," Tanner interjected. "You didn't call me to discuss my family. What is it?"

"I know we need to share some of our latest weather-related technology, but certain things are off limits. We've been over this ad nauseam. You understand what we can share and what needs to remain secret. We cannot divulge our full capabilities. If we did, the U.N. would vote to sanction us against our use of this technology and we would probably lose U.S. support. So be careful what you say. Be careful what rooms at the Technion you enter!'

"I understand," Tanner replied. "I will share what is largely already public knowledge and just a touch more, so they will feel we have shared some secrets, but not the details of companies not yet public, of capabilities not in the public domain."

"Good. I'll meet you at the Technion tomorrow evening at ten p.m. to go over how things went. Good luck and be careful. The wrong knowledge in the wrong hands could place our very existence at risk!" With that said, Yuri hung up their private line.

Natalia Verbrata, who was already in Israel, joined the visiting U.S. group at breakfast. Tanner addressed the U.S. contingent while they ate an Israeli breakfast from a self serve buffet. This included shakshouka, eggs poached in a tomato and vegetable sauce, freshly baked bread, tahini, Israeli salad, hummus, orange and apple juice and coffee.

"Let me have one of our scientists talk to you--Ruven Rosenberg. He knows more about weather technology than I will ever know. You may recall Ruven. He made the evening news when he saw a lightning flash hit the Wailing Wall a few years ago when he was just 13 years old. Don't let his slight stutter fool you. Ruven got his PhD in mathematics and computer technology at the age of 16. He then won the Field Medal in mathematics at age 18. He branched into weather control technology, not in spite of everyone telling him it was impossible, but because of it. He now is a technology officer for Chaos Technology, one of our Israeli companies working in the weather control field. But let me stop and let Ruven speak for himself. His voice may be a little slow, he may stutter a little, but there is nothing, let me assure you, that is slow about his mind. Play him in chess at your own risk. Ruven."

A tall freckled 18-year-old took the microphone. There was an occasional stutter, but a surety in his thought that made people take notice and focus on his words. "How Israel came to be interested in weather technology should be obvious. Half of Israel is a desert climate. Without planned irrigation this land would be unusable. Initially we started with kibbutzim, agricultural communities creating farms in the desert. Specialized drip irrigation methods invented in Israel were employed throughout the nation. These methods were also used in creating the remarkable Baha'i Gardens in Haifa with specialized water conservation methods for the gardens and fountains."

"There are many technology centers scattered around Israel and it has the highest number of scientists and technicians per capita in the world. Intel, google, Microsoft, IBM, Cisco, Motorola and GE all have research centers in Israel.

"The Ben-Gurion University Technology Park opened in 2013. A research incubator program was envisioned as part of the Ben-Gurion University of the Negev and begun the following years, expanding in the technology supported and amount of support.

"Similar programs were also begun at the Technion in Haifa. Branches and alliances have developed in the U.S. and elsewhere, including the Jacobs-Technion Cornell Institute and the Guangdong Technion-Israel Institute of Technology in China.

Ruven continued, "It was probably inevitable that the growth of computer modeling would tackle weather technology. Initially this modeling was to further weather prediction. Weather prediction it turned out has its limits as weather forecasting met the limits imposed by an understanding of chaos theory. What does this mean? Weather is inherently *chaotic*. This was first realized by the mathematician Conrad Lorenz in 1961. He changed the initial conditions in his weather model in one term from 0.506127, rounding it off to 0.506. Just a rounding error. That simple minimal change, drastically modified the weather prediction two months later. Long term weather forecasting was doomed by what he called the *butterfly effect*.

"What chance of predictability is there," Lorenz asked, "if the flap of a butterfly's wings in Brazil sets off a tornado in Texas?""

On the screen there was a video of a sunny day in New Orleans. This was replaced by a butterfly flapping its wings on a sunny day in Beijing, China. And then a scene was displayed from Katrina, the storm that devastated New Orleans. Ruven continued. "This may seem like an exaggeration, but it makes its point.

"A few years ago in our technology centers, we set up a hatchling, if you will, of incubator companies whose founding vision was to delve into the so-called impossible. Some of these companies at the time seemed outlandish, outrageous, more in the realm of science fiction than current reality. One of the founders at the original meeting, Yitzchak Rabin, likes telling this anecdote that helped him spark the initiative. He was at the University of Pennsylvania working on his PhD when Robert Schrieffer, who won the Nobel prize for the theory of superconductivity, described how he came upon the theory. Robert was riding the A train in New York when he came upon an idea to solve the problem. He spoke sheepishly to his mentor, John Brittain, who had already won one Nobel prize for the invention of the transistor."

Schrieffer told him, "I came upon this idea while riding the A train in New York City, an idea that solves our problems with our theory, but it seems impossible, as it violates all our previous concepts...."

Brittain looked over his work, and glanced up, interrupting the apologies of his young PhD student. "Don't worry about what it violates. This is the answer." So, like Brittain looking over Schrieffer's work, not only do we not reject seemingly impossible ideas, we welcome them. As Einstein has said, in another context, "If at first an idea does not seem impossible, there is no hope for it."

Ruven continued. "Some of these weather-related incubator companies gave themselves ordinary names such as, 'Climatron' and 'Weather Tech.' Others have more exotic names such as 'Anemoi,' the Greek god of the wind, 'Harpyiae,' Greek god of the Whirlwinds, 'Zephyrus,' the Greek God of the West Wind, 'Eos,' The Greek god of the dawn and 'Hera,' the Greek God of the Air. Another company is called simply 'Chaos,' a company I helped start—basically a bunch of PhD mathematicians and computer geeks analyzing ways to use chaos theory in new ways. Our plan? Make the chaotic nature of weather prediction an advantage and not a hindrance. We expected these early stage incubator stage companies, some not much more than an idea at the time, would have trouble getting start-up funding, but after a billion dollars of funding by U.S. high tech companies, U.S. agricultural and seed companies as well as Chinese venture capitalists, we stopped the funding. These companies have all aligned with microelectronic sensor companies, microdrone companies, makers of miniature drones, and computer technology companies to cross pollinate one another with their respective technologies." Ruven looked over at Tanner, who nodded in gratitude. Ruven then took his seat.

Tanner again took the podium. "Hold your questions for now. To best show what one of these start-up companies has so far accomplished, we'll visit one, Harpyiae, at nine a.m. tomorrow, Israeli time, so get some rest and sleep as you adjust to Israeli time."

The next morning they reconvened in a conference room at the Technion, where they enjoyed a working breakfast. Tanner took the podium again welcoming the U.S. contingent to Israel. "Let me have one of our meteorologists, Uhurul Naral, give you a video background presentation." Uhuru as her friends called her, was a striking 25 year old black woman that had come to Israel from Zambia as a six-year-old child after her parents were killed by Boko Haram terrorists. An Israeli couple visiting Zambia at the time, adopted her. Uhuru showed a few Utube videos of extreme tornados from a satellite perspective and from the ground. As pictures of large supercell storms and tornados were displayed, the audience felt powerless, insignificant in the face of such awesome seemingly uncontrollable natural power. Uhuru continued. "What these companies desire to do, is find better ways to predict the onset of a tornado, find ways to redirect the path of a tornado and lower its strength. The cost of a tornado's destructive power in human life and financial loss are both incalculable."

What was not lost on the visiting group, what was not yet described and was their main reason for coming to Israel--the questions in all their minds: "What capability did Israel have for actually creating or redirecting a tornado? Ultimately, what capability did Israel have for controlling the weather?"

The group left the conference room and drove to a large building at the north corner of the Technion, surrounded by a 6-foot iron fence, with security guards at the door. Natalia Verbrata noted the names of some of the multiple start-up companies described in the prior presentations. There was also a sign on one of the doors denoting the nearby presence of the Israeli Defense Intelligence also within the building—something she hoped to check out later, if given the chance.

They were greeted by a petite 25-year-old, Roslyn Tannenbaum, the head technology officer of the Harpyaie. The group entered the balcony of a theatre with seats overlooking a large tank. Within the tank were several small buildings. "You may get a little wet. Put on these rain jackets and wear these goggles as a precaution—you'll soon see why and use these ear plugs."

With that said the group took their seats. A rain shower began within the confines of the tank. A cloud formed above the rain and soon transformed into a supercell type storm with an anvil and shelf cloud accurately modeling a real storm. This transformed into a thunderstorm and then twisted into a very concise perfectly formed tornado, taking out several buildings. Lightning flashed and thunder boomed for several minutes and then the storm ended within a minute of the building's destruction.

Rosyln then spoke. She had an Israeli British accent having grown up in a London suburb. "Many groups have modeled hurricanes. The University of Iowa, for example, has created such a model. We have taken their modeling several steps forward. By placing microsensors in microdrones within and around the hurricane, capable of withstanding 200 mph wind speeds, we have used *the butterfly effect*, the effect Ruven told you about earlier, but in reverse. Early on in our research we realized that the earlier in the path of a storm you alter wind, temperature or pressure, the easier it is to change the path of a storm. However, the earlier in its path you choose to make these changes the less certain will be its path. We have three Cray supercomputers working in parallel with an IBM Watson computer doing real time iterations in our modeling, making a thousand real time on-the-fly changes per minute in the physical parameters that control a hurricane and tornado, capable of redirecting the path of a hurricane on a small scale. We do not have the capability to do this today on the scale of an actual tornado, but that is one of the *impossible* tasks in our company's future investigation. What you will now see is a demonstration on the scale we have currently achieved."

Roslyn nodded to one of the technicians. The tank was replaced with an identical tank. Another storm was created heading toward several buildings, as the sounds of many computers whirred and about 50 microdrones buzzed around and through the created tornado. A supercell storm cloud again developed. A tornado then formed, headed into the model town, but slowly veered away from the town center, to the edge of the town, harmlessly dying outside the buildings of the town. There was a low murmur coming from the group, in awe of what they had just seen. "The microdrones adjust their own temperature and wind speed to affect the path of the tornado. If done early enough during storm and tornado formation, it can affect the path of a tornado, but only on the small scale just displayed." The room was buzzing, with the visitors talking to one another, marveling at what they had just witnessed. The question on everyone's mind was: "If Israel could achieve this weather control on a small scale, did they have any such ability on the scale of a natural disaster, a large hurricane, or a category 5 tornado?"

Roslyn spoke to the group. "We don't have time for any questions now. There is a courtyard outside where we have lunch set up. Let's break for about two hours and then we'll meet back in the conference room and I'll answer your questions, along with my colleagues."

CHAPTER 24
NATALIA MAKES A SECRET VISIT

NATALIA, INSTEAD OF going out to the courtyard, backtracked to the door marked Israeli Defense Intelligence. The door was locked. She moved behind a nearby post and waited. After about five minutes, someone came by with a security card, gaining entrance. Before the door closed, she put her foot in the doorway, waited a minute and snuck inside. Within, there was another amphitheater, twice as large as the one where she had just been. The lights were low and another demonstration was taking place. With everyone watching the demonstration it was easy for her to unobtrusively take a seat in the overhead theatre type seating as the demonstration continued. The size of the structures and the size of the modeled storm was twice the size she had previously just witnessed. A capability their speakers had previously denied. One of the buildings in the town model had a red light glowing within it. A supercell storm developed with a shelf cloud and a tornado forming, but rather than randomly demolishing buildings, it slowly appeared redirected in its path, as a multitude of lights flashed from microdrones flying within and outside the tornado and eye of the storm. A wall of computers hummed nearby, then the tornado advanced to the building with the red light hovering over it until the roof flew off and the building exploded outward, with little damage to the adjacent structures.

Natalia thought, if Israel could do this to a real tornado, they would have quite the military, as well as quite the commercial capabilities. They could charge an enormous fee to aid in protecting towns and cities in tornado alley in the U.S., the Bahamas in the Caribbean and other high risk spots around the globe. What if they now had the technology to have veered Katrina away from a direct hit on New Orleans, billions would have been saved as well as many lives. As she was getting up to leave, the lights came up and a security guard grabbed her, asking for her security clearance. "I am with the U.S. delegation visiting Israel. I was looking for the bathroom and somehow ended up in here." Her plea of innocence was not well received. She was escorted to a private room where fifteen minutes later Yuri Goldberg, head of Israeli Intelligence and Moishe Tanner, the Israeli U.S. Ambassador, appeared along with Roslyn Tannenbaum, who had guided the previous demonstration.

"You put us in a very awkward position," Yuri Goldberg stated, restraining his anger. "We welcomed your visit and shared aspects of our technology, but like the U.S. we cannot share everything our research is developing or is capable of. Even the knowledge Roslyn shared, in the wrong hands can create untenable problems for Israel, let alone place at risk the capabilities you have just witnessed."

Then Roslyn spoke. "In Israel we live with the constant risk of being bombed, the risk of war. I have three children, two girls and one boy all under the age of five. I would like to see them live a full life without war, without the constant threat of violence. If we can prevent Iran's nuclear program without war, the whole world will be the better for it and all our children, even those in Iran will be safer. Revealing the demonstrations you have witnessed, will only help defeat the forces in Israel seeking to control Iran without war."

Natalia looked up at her interrogators. None of whom knew that aside from being a meteorologist at NOAA, she also worked for the CIA. "Before we came to Israel, we pledged to keep secret what we would be shown." Natalia thought about what she had just witnessed and the pervasive risks faced by Israel. "I will share what Roslyn showed me and the others previously only to those with appropriate high level security but out of respect for Israel, the security of Israel and that of the U.S., I will refrain from sharing anything about the demonstration I just witnessed." Natalia told them what they wanted to hear, but knew her first allegiance was to the CIA. They spoke for another hour and although realizing the risk they were taking, Israeli Intelligence knew they had no choice but to release her back to her fellow U.S. contingent.

Back in the conference room, Roslyn Tannenbaum answered questions while Tanner and Goldberg stood by.

"What is Israel's capability to affect the weather?" asked John Chambers, the head of NOAA.

Tannenbaum spoke. "On a small scale, as you have just seen demonstrated, we can model any type of storm, any type of tornado you can envision. To take this ability out of the laboratory requires dealing with immense size and destructive power. Although the total energy of a tornado is low compared to the large hurricane that spawned it, the energy within a tornado is very concentrated. Tornadoes are the most powerful force in nature for their size. The average energy of a tornado is about 10,000 kilowatt-hours. A typical hurricane has the energy of 10 billion kilowatt-hours, equivalent to a hydrogen bomb. The energy density within the tornado is six times greater than in a hurricane, giving it overwhelming destructive power. An EF5 tornado will totally devastate any community including concrete reinforced structures. Our start-up companies have proposals to deal with hurricanes and tornadoes, to redirect them to less populous areas and to reduce their power. But this work is only in its very early stages."

"What is Israel's capability to create a storm or tornado as a military weapon?" Raymond Chadry, the U.S. secretary of defense asked.

Tanner responded, taking over from Tannenbaum. "We have no capability to create a massive storm or tornado denovo. We are working toward methods to affect a storm in progress and redirect it, but no more." Natalia realized this wasn't completely true, and perhaps not true at all, based on what she had just seen, but remained silent.

"How has Israel, such a small country, managed to exceed even the U.S. in such sophisticated technology, from military technology to microelectronic sensors and weather technology?" John Sharp, head of DARPA asked.

Yuri Goldberg replied, "Being surrounded by people who not only don't like you, but openly threaten to annihilate you, frequently hurl missiles into your largest cities–these constant threats of annihilation have a way of focusing your attention. Maybe it is also part of the overall Jewish phenomenon."

"What is that?" Sharp asked.

"It is a phenomenon that 30% of American Nobel Prize winners in science and 25% of all American Nobel winners are Jewish, out of a population representing only 2% of Americans."

"And what would you propose is the explanation?" Sharp said.

"It may be our struggles for survival over many generations, our roots in Judaism always questioning and searching for God and perhaps something deeply rooted in our DNA passed on between generations."

"Do you have any time frame in which you anticipate true natural weather control capabilities coming to fruition?" Sharp asked, changing the subject to his most immediate concern.

Goldberg said, "To deal with a sizable storm or tornado would require thousands, if not tens of thousands of microdrones, with microelectronic sensors relaying information real time to computer models that can relay information also in real time to change wind speed and temperature and pressure, causing small effects early enough in a developing storm to lead to larger effects over time. This capability will probably require 20-50 years of research. That is our best estimate. We are certainly not there today."

"Then what about the lightning strike on the Wailing Wall? What about the tornado that freed your Israeli lieutenant from his capture? Did Israel have anything to do with those events?" Secretary of State Schwartzmann asked.

"We wish we could do half the things people accuse us of," Goldberg replied. "Yes, we have companies working toward these goals but they are many years away from achieving them. The U.S. will be informed if and when our companies are capable of achieving such results."

"How will they inform us?" questioned Schwartzmann.

"Our companies all want to be IPOs on the NASDAQ, probably eventually bought out by U.S. conglomerates, while advertising their capabilities in local newspapers along the U.S. hurricane alley," Goldberg said, with a hint of a grin.

The next day they again met and also convened with the technology heads of several other companies—some dealing with microdrone capabilities. One company showed a video of two of their drones. One flipped a long thin metal needle caught by another drone and balanced it in mid air, something they adapted from a Swiss drone company which they had purchased. They were shown microelectronic sensors that could detect climate parameters and effect atmospheric temperature changes using drone capabilities. They were also shown Israeli missile technology that could self-correct missile paths during flight.

The following morning the visiting contingent took a military flight back to Washington, amazed by what they'd seen but also not convinced that Israel had been completely truthful, that Israel had not developed weather control technology beyond their admission.

CHAPTER 25
NATALIA VISITS CIA HEADQUARTERS

CIA HEADQUARTERS, LANGLEY, MCLEAN VIRGINIA.

NATALIA VERBRATI ENTERED the CIA headquarters, glanced reflectively at the memorial wall now holding 135 stars carved in stone. She walked past it on her way to a conference room. The wall stood as a silent memorial to those CIA officers making the ultimate sacrifice for a nation who often had no knowledge of these heroes living their secret lives. Natalia took a seat in the conference room facing five members of the CIA, debriefing her about her recent Israel trip. A small light lit up her face as her CIA colleagues sat, barely visible, in a subdued light.

"Thank you for your written report, Natalia," remarked Samri Abad, the CIA director. "We would like to hear your thoughts in person to best understand what you uncovered on your trip."

Natalia knew the CIA wanted to make sure there was no additional information they could glean from a direct interview.

"You stated that Israel had a number of early stage companies working on weather technology. How advanced are they?" the CIA director asked.

Natalia looked up at her colleagues, feeling more like a witness in a courtroom interrogation than a colleague in for a friendly chat. But that, she knew, was just CIA protocol. Rather than "trust but verify," a motto followed at the State Department, at the CIA, it was simply verify everything, trust no one, even if it's your mother with her right hand on a Bible! Natalia squinted to see her colleagues in the dim light. "It was surprising to see the breadth of incubator companies working on weather control technology. For such a small country they have a surprising per capita commitment to technology, cybersecurity, microelectronic sensor technology and weather control technology in particular. Very impressive."

"As a meteorologist, what is your assessment of their capability?" Paul Stark, the second in command at the CIA asked.

"There are over twenty incubator companies working in different growing fields of meteorology, all having some relationship to weather control technology. Some are exploring better weather forecasting, some exploring weather manipulation, changing parameters of temperature, wind and pressure to gradually redirect a storm in early stages before it reaches an uncontrollable size. There seemed to be less research being done to actually create a storm denovo, less ability to create any significant tornado, if you will, and direct it at a target. I did watch a display showing the creation of a small tornado from a supercell storm that destroyed a building in its path. They did display an ability to direct the small modeled storm and subsequent tornado. They did not display or admit to any ability to affect a large natural storm or tornado. They denied any such ability on direct questioning."

"Do you believe them?" the CIA director asked.

"I believed them, in part because I don't believe it is currently possible. What they are pursuing is using chaos theory in an unexpected way."

"Please elaborate in simple terms. I'm just a simple guy," Ralph Long, a 40 year CIA operative asked. He was, however, neither simple nor simpleminded.

"Chaos theory applied to the weather, leads to the realization that small changes in initial weather conditions, lead to large unpredictable patterns just a few weeks later. This is why weather prediction fails after a few weeks. But what if you affect the initial conditions repeatedly, constantly using computing power to forecast the weather after every small change?

The chaotic nature of the weather will cause weather patterns to change. These patterns are currently unpredictable. But if you wait for chaos to change weather parameters, until they promote your intended affect and then use physical means to bolster these conditions when in your favor, you may be able to affect an ultimately large change in the weather conditions that may lead to redirection of a storm."

"Does Israel even have the computer power to make these weather predictions on the fly, let alone the ability to affect temperature of the air or water, wind speed and pressure in any significant weather event?" Sandra Cole, another CIA colleague, asked Natalia.

Natalia hesitated for a moment. "Israel, I believe, has the computational power to do it. They have three Cray supercomputers and an IBM Watson computer system that could do the computations on the fly. As of today, Israel does not have the ability to affect the physical parameters in a large weather system and certainly not fast enough and often enough to input the computational information." She knew she was at least partially lying. She had seen a created storm directed away from a building. That was not on the scale of a real storm but not insignificant either. She would leave certain things unsaid.

"Does the U.S. or Israel have the capability to input the physical changes to these parameters to redirect or create a storm or tornado?" the CIA director asked.

"Israel doesn't have it; we don't have it. No one on planet earth today has it in terms of civilizations. This would require a Type I Kardashev civilization capable of controlling the energy of a planet, including its weather. We are not there, although we have tried. Israel is not there. No one is there."

"Will we or Israel or anyone else ever get there?" the CIA director asked.

"Much of the technology we have today was said to be impossible 50 years ago. Many things that will be possible, even obvious in 50 years, seem impossible today. In the next ten years, the answer is no. In the next 20 years, probably no. In the next 50 years, maybe yes. In the next 100 years, probably yes. In the next 1000 years, definitely yes."

"Are there any more questions of Natalia?" the CIA director asked. There were none and the meeting disbursed.

As Ralph Long left, he thought about Natalia's responses. She had answered most questions with little hesitation but hesitated before answering one of the questions, possibly an innocent hesitation, but possibly not.

Natalia walked out past the CIA memorial wall, wondering if she had done the right thing.

Hiding some knowledge to protect an ally, from whom? She didn't sleep very soundly that night.

A year later she unexpectedly received a gift from a start-up company in Israel, named "Harpyaie," Greek God of the wind; 1000 shares of company stock.

CHAPTER 26
IRANIAN LEADERS MEET SECRETLY IN SEMORAH, IRAN

SEMORAH IRAN.

SECRET MEETING OF Karuf Akiladar, the president of Iran, Ayatollah Ruhollah Khomeini, Iran's supreme religious leader, General Raj Mustabib, the military command leader and Kralen Retalaban, nuclear physicist and head of their nuclear development program.

Tea was served and small Iranian pastries.

They waited for Khomeini to start the meeting. He was turbaned, with a grey beard and weary looking but piercing eyes. "How far along is our nuclear program in making fissionable material?" he asked Retalaban.

Retalaban was trained at MIT in nuclear physics and then did a stint at Berkeley in nuclear engineering. After working at Los Alamos with a top level security clearance, Iran recruited him with a $1,000,000 annual salary and a belief in returning Iran to the prestige it deserved as the leader of the Arab world. Retalaban was as knowledgeable in nuclear development as any US nuclear physicist and was treated as a demigod in Iran, an invaluable asset in Iran's search for power and respect.

"We will have enough fissionable material for our first bomb in two years," he replied. Retalaban was 40 years old, dressed in western jeans, a casual pale blue shirt. A western haircut, handsome, clean-shaven, a Berkeley campus look. The Iranian leaders did not care how he dressed, but only how quickly they achieved their nuclear ambitions. "We have

3000 centrifuges spinning 24 hours a day, seven days a week to make the fissionable material."

Khomeini looked at him as though sizing him up. "I want the bomb by next year's Ramadan," he spoke matter-of-factly, staring solemnly at Retalaban, then took a sip of tea. "After the annual hajj to Mecca next year, I would like us to test our bomb, honoring the pilgrims to Mecca that will join us in prayers."

"It cannot be ready by then," Retalaban respectfully replied. "That is only eighteen months away."

"Double the number of centrifuges to six thousand. If you achieve it, we will double your salary and you will have the added gratitude of the Iranian people."

Retalaban shifted nervously in his chair. At MIT he was considered a gifted theorist among the gifted doctoral students and had gotten a 100 on the PhD qualifying exam, previously unheard of, yet he was unsure if this newly requested feat was achievable.

Khomeini then turned to President Akiladar whom he had handpicked for the presidency as his puppet. The election results were rigged, causing a popular uprising which was forcibly put down while the U.S. did little, their President Lopez trying diplomacy to no avail. "Keep open our willingness to discuss our arms program with the Americans."

Akiladar nodded in understanding. He smiled broadly at the supreme leader.

"If the Americans ask why we have a nuclear program, tell them it is to provide nuclear energy to our people. If they ask why we don't use our oil, tell them so we can sell them our oil out of our benevolence and raise the price to them over the Russians and Chinese." A wry smile appeared as his eyebrows rose in condescending pleasure.

The supreme leader continued. "If we can bankrupt them or the Europeans by their addiction to our oil we will have less need to one day use a nuclear bomb on them to destroy their lewd ways and create an Islamic theocracy. At the UN, follow the same path. If the Japanese no longer need their nuclear fuel, buy it from them. Tell them all what they want to hear as we continue on our path to nuclear parity. They will respect a nuclear Iran in ways they do not respect us now!" The supreme leader looked out beyond the people with him in the conference room, as though already envisioning his hajj to Mecca to share the victory of Iran over the West, the shared victory of Islam over the Jews and Christians.

"Diplomatic duplicity," became the buzzwords describing the method Iran utilized to blatantly lie to the West at the negotiating table, while secretly advancing its nuclear program.

While Europe tried to engage Iran, Washington's warnings of duplicity fell on deaf ears.

Europe's desire to not be drawn into any conflict with Iran, as well as their desire for cheap oil, led them to trust Iran just as they had trusted another ruler with global ambitions decades earlier—Adolph Hitler.

CHAPTER 27
NADINA

WITH RARE EXCEPTIONS, such as their trip to the Bha'i Gardens when Sarah died, Nadina fell back into a state of withdrawal and depression, resembling her previous semi-autistic state. When Doron wasn't around, teenage Nadina, now 14, started attending parties in the woods around Tel Aviv, filled with hard grunge rock music and drugs.

It was there that she started smoking hashish and tried a tab of ecstasy. Out of depression, the loss of her biologic family and now the death of Sarah and her own unknown recurring demons, a "helpful friend" showed her how to inject heroin into her arms. It helped her sleep and forget the loneliness, the lack of identity and feelings of worthlessness. Doron was oblivious to what gradually became a frequent pastime of Nadina. Although drug use in Israel was much less common than in the U.S., it was not insignificant either among Israelis or the Palestinians, each living under constant stress, feelings of abandonment and alienation. Nadina had her own well-earned entrance qualifications into this world.

On some afternoons, Nadina would ask Doron to let her take public transportation to the Baha'i Gardens. Reluctantly, Doron agreed, hoping her visit would rekindle the happy spirit in Nadina, just coming out of hiding when Sarah died. At the gardens, Nadina befriended some of the Baha'i who came to recognize their frequent visitor. She would wander the garden slopes with headphones repeatedly playing one song, "Queen of Carmel." The song, a gentle tribute to the gardens soothed the turmoil in her heart, somehow quieting a young girl, as she explored the spiritual setting of the Baha'i Gardens. The Baha'i, likewise, took her under their wing. At Nadina's request, they told her about a fellow Iranian, the Bab, the founder of the Baha'i faith. They shared with her his Iranian heritage and the tragedy that was his life. A life that seemed in many ways to mirror hers.

They told her of his martyrdom, about his execution and the execution of thousands of his followers. They told of his imprisonment in Maku, a bleak castle set upon a rocky cliff with no greenery. It was to create a tribute, in reverence to the Bab that the Baha'i Gardens were envisioned, filled with all the beauty, greenery, the spiritual uplifting presence so lacking in the Bab's Maku prison home.

Occasionally while at the gardens, Nadina would find a private spot and take a tab of ecstasy or inject heroin into a vein, wanting to find peace at any cost. One evening, she sat on a grassy knoll, in the open, laying out her needle and drugs in front of her. First, she listened to "The Queen of Carmel." As it ended, a local radio station played "Angel," written by Sarah McLachlan.

By the failing light of the setting sun, Nadina put a tourniquet on her left arm, and was trying to inject a syringe filled with heroin, but her arm was shaking, her youthful body sobbing because of an inability to find a vein. It was then that three Baha'i accidentally came upon her. Two men and one woman. Tears began to flow out of Nadina, as she tried to hide behind closed eyes. The Baha'i knelt on the grass with Nadina. One of the Baha'i held her hand, gently taking the syringe from her and releasing the tourniquet. Another put his arms around her and softly laid her head gently upon his shoulder as she cried big sobbing tears into his open arms. The third Baha'i held her other hand and said a short prayer, "Dear Lord, let this child, one of your most precious children, find a path to peace, find in you the love she needs." The Baha'i stayed with Nadina for several hours, giving a young teenager the time she needed to collect herself, while lingering sobs from Nadina still shook her body. The heartfelt sobs reflecting the teenage girl's tortured past, the pain, the agony, tortured memories of bombs placed over young girls' chest by her own parents, revisiting tormenting childhood memories. The young girl's nightmares and fears were released, replaced by a hope for a new life, at the foot of the shrine of the Bab, on a grassy knoll in the Baha'i Gardens. The setting sun cast a lingering reddish hue on the Shrine of the Bab, the light from the setting sun glowing serenely throughout the gardens and Haifa Bay in the distance. When Nadina had calmed down, with little said, the three Baha'i drove Nadina to the front door of her home, leaving her, as Doron let her inside.

◆ 145 ◆

CHAPTER 28
AMBUSH AT DORON'S HOME

WHEN DORON WASN'T on a secret mission and was available to do so, he often drove Nadina home from school. One such evening, after driving her home, they made dinner together, macaroni and cheese, a small salad and jello for dessert with a glass of chocolate milk to wash it down.

Then Doron helped her with her homework. Afterwards, Nadina stayed up in the downstairs living room watching a movie and promising to go to bed in her room upstairs, after it was over. Doron, tired from a long day, went upstairs to bed in his room.

Though she'd waited agonizing months for what she would consider the perfect moment, Saron had never given up on taking Nadina, even if she couldn't win her over. Saron was already upstairs, hiding in Nadina's bedroom closet waiting for the girl to go to bed. While Nadina watched a Disney movie, Yosuf and Gamliel, her uncles broke into a backdoor leading into a pantry and from there, made their way to the kitchen.

Yosuf, 23, 6 foot 3 inches, bearded and broad shouldered at 240 pounds, whispered to his brother. "I'll grab Nadina. If we aren't forced to kill her now, she can be our plaything later and then we will kill her. You hide behind the stairs. I'll let her scream enough to wake the soldier. When he comes down the stairs, shoot him and we'll take Nadina as our reward to enjoy

this evening. You understand?" Yosuf turned to his brother, 31-year-old Gamliel, both well indoctrinated into Jihad, determined to kill another Israeli and enjoy the fruits of their labors, now innocently watching a Disney movie, "Frozen" while munching on popcorn. Their friend, Raman, was in their car parked outside, waiting impatiently to drive them off.

Yosuf entered the room with Nadina's back to him, as she lay lounging on a frumpy but soft-cushioned couch. With an unchallenged motion, he grabbed the 14-year-old, putting his large hand roughly over her mouth muffling her attempt at a scream, popcorn flying off the couch, her respite from endless violence abruptly over. Yosuf lifted Nadina into the air, her legs squirming wildly as he held her up close to his body. Her brown eyes bulging in fear, her arms trying to pummel him without effect.

Aside from the TV there was little light in the room save for a full moon casting an evanescent soft light in the room through two large windows.

As planned, Gamliel went behind the stairs leading to the upstairs bedrooms, waiting, his hand holding a gleaming Browning HiPower pistol.

When his brother was well hidden, Yosuf let Nadina let out one scream as she kicked the popcorn bowl onto the floor, her legs flailing wildly. This was enough noise to waken Doron who grabbed the Baretta he always slept with, off his nightstand. From the top of the stairs, he could see Nadina held by an Arab intruder.

When Doron first moved into the house, he had placed reflecting mirrors at each corner of the room, positioned to leave no part of the downstairs hidden.

The light of the moon was just barely sparkling off one of the mirrors, but it was enough to warn Doron of someone else in the room, near or behind the staircase. The specular reflection suggested metal, a knife or gun. If he moved down the stairs, he'd be shot or knifed. He had no concern for his own life. He'd already given terrorists many chances to kill him, not to mention walking into a bar filled with vehemently anti-Israeli Arabs while wearing his army uniform, practically begging them, daring them to kill him. But it was Nadina's life that now hung in the balance, dependent on decisions he would make in the next few seconds.

In his youth Doron had been a gymnast on the trampoline and floor but that was years in the past. Instead of going down the stairs, he jumped off the balcony toward the couch doing a 270 degree flip, landing on his back, horizontally on the couch, his back parallel to the floor, looking straight into Yosuf's startled eyes, two feet from both Yosuf and Nadina. Yosuf lifted his knife to fend off Doron or kill Nadina, but it was too late. The Baretta went off twice before Doron landed on the couch, entering Yosuf's forehead and top of his skull, part of which blew off.

Landing on the couch, cushioned Doron's fall as Nadina fell to the floor knocking Doron's Baretta from his hand, off the couch and then rolled several feet. Doron slid behind the couch to cradle Nadina, using his body as a shield. The Israeli was now defenseless as Gamliel ran out from under the staircase firing his Browning Hi-Power at Doron and Nadina crouching behind the couch.

Doron told Nadina to lay flat and crawl toward the front door. Doron then dove for his Baretta, expecting to be shot but planning to kill the lone assailant left, with any life still remaining in him. When he reached his gun, he was surprised no more bullets had been fired at him, but even more startled by what he now witnessed. The intruder was falling forward, a knife in his back. As Gamliel fell, a dark brown, black haired, tatooed woman came into view, visible to Doron in the pale moonlight like a ghostly apparition, rising slowly over Gamliel as he fell.

Saron had heard Nadina's scream and gun shots, and she'd leaped from Nadina's room into the scene just in time to use the Russian Zuni knife meant to kill Doron, to destroy her cousin and protect Nadina.

Nadina, meanwhile, had crawled to the front door. She made it outside only to have Raman catch her just as she thought she'd escaped. He pulled his own pistol, a Glock, and went inside the house. His left arm held Nadina, also covering her mouth.

Doron and Saron stood near each other, close enough for Doron to remember the scent of the terrorist who had danced around him provocatively, while, blindfolded, he had tensed for his death blow. The hair color was different. The tattoos were new, but the scent of the woman was unmistakeable. The terrorist who had planned to kill him, had now saved his life!

Ramon saw his two dead compatriots, presuming they had both been killed by the Israeli, not noticing the blood on Saron's right hand. Saron knew Ramon, speaking to him in Persian. "Let me kill the Israeli. He took my daughter and I came to avenge his actions. I was in a coma dreaming of this moment. I have waited for two years to kill him. Let me also avenge the deaths

of Gamliel and Yosuf, my cousins, and I will reward you later." She walked over to Ramon, who had always been jealous of Saron's husband. As she glided her hand sensually over Ramon's back, he hesitated then gave Saron his gun as he envisioned his anticipated night with Saron.

Saron took two steps away from Ramon, pointing the gun at Doron, who now also expected her to finally fulfill her plan to kill him. He stood there unafraid. He knew Saron would not harm her daughter. He had done his job.

Nadina tried to talk, to scream, but was held too tightly by Ramon. As Saron pulled back the trigger of the pistol pointed at Doron, she suddenly turned toward Ramon, shooting him squarely between the eyes, killing him instantly.

Nadina then ran to Doron, expecting her mother might now kill him. "Ramon can now go get his 40 virgins, but he can't have me!" she blurted out, almost silently to herself.

Saron then pointed the gun at Doron. "I could kill you now for taking my daughter and that is all I dreamed of while in a coma. That is what I came here to do. But you have now saved my daughter's life and although I don't approve, she now treats you like her father. If I go back to Iran, they will kill her for living with an Israeli. They have already tried to do so tonight. Back in Iran, they will also now kill me for killing Gamliel and Ramon. You walked into an Arab bar asking to be killed. If I killed you, I would just be giving you what you have wanted since your wife was murdered. But it will also alienate me from Nadina. You have already saved her life more than once. So instead, I will let you live to protect Nadina, as I will be without a country." With that, Saron lay the gun down and Nadina ran to her mother crying. Saron cried with her, grateful to finally have a chance to hold her daughter and feel her daughter's heart beating against hers.

CHAPTER 29
DORON RAISES NADINA

DORON AND NADINA continued their life together. Doron tutored her in calculus and science for several hours after she got home from school. Nadina would occasionally find Saron waiting for her in her room.

"I will talk to Doron so you can join us on walks through Haifa. I don't think he will mind." Nadina looked at her mother for approval.

Saron had found a place to live in a boardinghouse a mile away. "I don't think he would approve. I did try to kill him once, and am not sure myself that I won't try again, if he doesn't kill me first." She was sitting on her daughter's bed, thumbing through a magazine, turning up to look at her daughter as she finished her sentence.

"You said yourself you needed him alive to protect me! I do need him! He has done more to keep me alive than you or my real father ever did! I see that now. If you want to be with me, you have to get to know Doron. He has suffered greatly. His parents were killed in the 9/11 attack, his wife killed while they were out for dinner, his hand amputated from infection after saving an Iranian child's life. Now he takes care of me better than you or my father ever did!" Nadina scowled at her mother. "The next time we go for a walk around Tel a Viv, I will ask Doron to let you join us. If he says it is OK, I'll message you when to meet us. You better go now while it's still light out." Although still objecting, Saron left by way of the window in Nadina's room.

The next day Nadina, now 15, spoke to Doron on their ride home from school. "Would you mind if my mother joins us for our walk tomorrow evening?"

Doron turned to look at Nadina. "You know, if you want to leave and go with her, I won't try to stop you. She is your mother. I thought she had died in the hurricane. I did not even know she was alive."

"I don't want to go with her and live a life in fear. To go back to Iran and be killed. To be treated as an infidel, for what? For having the gall to have my life saved by an Israeli? My friend, Nashoma, was killed for the terrible unforgivable crime of going to a soccer game! I would be lucky if they just killed me and didn't first torture me and put it on national TV. Here in Israel I have the freedom to walk without wearing a Chador or Hijab, the right to wear makeup, the right to go to a concert or soccer game. I have taken some time to learn about religions that aren't radicalized to the point of preaching hatred and death to nonbelievers. I now know what I choose to believe! I believe in reverence for life, like Albert Schweitzer, not reverence for death! I have found a religion that probably saved my life, here on the banks of the Carmel Hills in Haifa, the Bhai Faith. So I want the freedom to explore this faith further. To explore the social media of the internet that gives me the freedom to be who and what I choose to be. Not a slave to the state.

"Doron, not only have you saved my life twice, but what you have given me is a father I never had in Iran. Don't make me leave for a miserable future filled with fear, torture and probable death!" Nadina turned to look at Doron, sad eyes pleading her case, tears flowing down as she lowered her head in anguish. At fifteen, Nadina had already shed a lifetime of tears, lived a lifetime of harrowing near-death experiences.

Doron went to her, held her in his arms, silently letting her exhaust her tears in his arms. Then he lifted her chin. He thought back to the promise he had given to his wife, Sarah, as she lay dying in his arms, to protect and raise Nadina. Looking at her, he spoke softly. "You can stay with me as long as you desire. I will protect you as best I can. You are now old enough to make your own decisions and to start learning how to protect yourself. I will take you to the gym to work out, have you take lessons in self defense, judo and karate. I will teach you to shoot a gun at a firing range so that you can ultimately protect yourself."

"Can my mother join us on our walk through the streets of Haifa tomorrow night?"

Doron laughed. "I don't think your mother would want to be seen walking with a Jew."

"She has no choice. If she wants to walk with me, she has to walk with you. So is that a yes?"

Doron hesitated, but said yes, thinking Saron would probably not show up.

CHAPTER 30
SARON JOINS
DORON AND NADINA

THE NEXT EVENING after dinner, Doron asked Nadina, "Ready for our walk?"

"My mother isn't here yet. She said she would think about it."

"I am not surprised, she probably didn't want to be seen with me! You know she has lived her life as a terrorist trying to kill people like me. I have spent my life trying to defeat people like her and when necessary, I am sorry to say, kill people like her--who happens to also be your mother! Not a likely combination to share a pleasant stroll in the park."

As Doron opened the front door to leave, standing in front of him was Saron, dressed in jeans, with her head covered in a Hijab, a headscarf. "I wasn't e-expecting you to come," Doron remarked casually, hiding his shock.

"I try not to do what is expected," Saron replied, smiling at the Israeli's wary eyes.

Together, the three of them walked through the neighborhood of Doron's home in Haifa. Doron and Saron flanking Nadina, each holding her hand. Some of his neighbors also out on the pleasant evening stopped to watch the trio walking by, surprised by the sight of the Arab and Jew joined together, flanking an Iranian girl, each holding one of her arms.

They walked through a nearby park, watching in silence as Nadina fed some ducks on a pond.

They stopped for ice cream at a local shop, listened to a small jazz band play songs at a street corner. Together, watched a group of young bicyclists go by on a tour of the city. "I would like to do that someday," Nadina remarked.

"First you have to learn how to ride a bicycle," Doron remarked. "Maybe your mother would like to teach you?" Doron turned to Saron.

"I don't know how to ride a bicycle either," Saron responded.

Nadina piped in, "Well, then Doron, you will have to teach both of us."

Doron laughed. He could just imagine trying to teach Saron how to ride a bike. And Saron letting him teach her ... anything.

Over the next few months, the three of them spent many days together. They went to a local gym where Doron taught Nadina to train on nautilus equipment, run on a track and do gymnastics. Saron joined them on some of these trips. At the gym with her hair down and in gym shorts Saron attracted quite an audience, observing her striking green eyes and red hair, tattooed arms and lithe body, offset by her tawny, golden brown complexion. More than one male asked if she wanted any help training, which she refused. Then they started running outside in the streets and hills around Haifa, first a quarter mile. Then as Nadina showed an interest in running further, they increased their runs to a mile and then five miles. After their runs they would each shower separately at Doron's house and go out for breakfast or brunch.

In the evening, when alone with Nadina, Saron tried to convince Nadina to leave with her. "You cannot stay here living with a Jew," Saron said.

Nadina turned to her mother, pleading her case. "Where would we go? Back to Iran so we would both be killed? Syria, Lebanon? No place would be safe for us. Doron has saved my life, treats me like his daughter. He is a better parent than you ever were. You were ready to have me die as a suicide bomber when I was just a baby!"

Saron knew deep-down she was right. She thought of grabbing Nadina and forcibly taking her away. But she had no place to take her.

She knew Nadina would just run away at the first opportunity, so she was forced to stay in Tel a Viv at least for now and keep an eye on her.

Against her mother's wishes, Nadina continued living in Doron's house. Nadina help cook meals. She hurried through her homework as soon as she got home from school, leaving time for their adventures outdoors.

One day at the local gym, they began experimenting on the high bar. Doron showed off his gymnastics skill, the same skills he used to kill one of the home invaders six months earlier. Nadina tried the high bar and after a few tries was able to do a flip which she easily repeated several times. When they weren't looking, Saron decided to try it as well. At first Saron took her time getting used to swinging on the bar, flipping her body front and backward. As she practiced, Doron moved into position to spot her, if she tried a flip. After a few swings to gain momentum, Saron tried a flip but didn't succeed. Doron caught her as she was coming down, preventing a neck injury. Doron lay her gently on the ground and Saron slightly shaken stared up at Doron from her recumbent position. She noticed for the first time the grayish tint to his blue eyes, the slight furrows in his brow, his strong features, the faint wrinkles and sad eyes all bearing deep emotion not well hidden. A number of gymnasts and others working out came over to see if Saron was all right. Some also noticed a strange chemistry between the two, hidden behind a shroud of animosity. Embarrassed and nonplussed by Doron's help, Saron did not bother to thank him, but Nadina let him know she was grateful for it, for her mother's sake. Saron then did two more flips, this time successfully.

Gradually over the next year, Saron came to respect the soldier for having saved her daughter, for giving her a home and helping her create a life. Then one day Saron told Doron of her life.

Learning as a child how Israel had been given the Arab land by the U.N., and learning to hate Israel and the Jews who inhabited the formerly Arab land. To Doron the land had, even longer ago, once belonged to the Jewish people and when the Holocaust left the Jews without a home, the U.N. gave them back their land to provide a home to millions of displaced Jews. Saron did not agree with this point of view, but recognized the theocratic government in Iran had done little to help their own people and that women in particular were subjugated cruelly under their leadership. So they came to an agreement that the Iranian theocracy in power would be better off replaced by a government that did not view terrorism as a road to help the Iranian people. A global jihad only harmed the Iranian people and the drive for nuclear weapons on the part of Iran could only lead to eventual nuclear destruction.

"Why should I believe the Holocaust ever occurred? I have been told my whole life it was fabricated by the Jews to get our land."

Doron looked at Saron, amazed at her disbelief.

That evening Doron visited a neighbor, an old friend, Yitzhak Rabinowitz who had majored in political science and taught political science and philosophy at Tel a Viv University.

"How can Saron believe the nonsense that the Holocaust didn't occur?" Doron asked, bewildered.

His friend looked at him and almost laughed. "I would laugh at the absurdity of the belief that the Holocaust never occurred, except for the fact that in Iran that is what is taught. Iran is a closed society and it has been that way since the radical Mullahs came to power after the Shah was ousted. The Iranian leader, the religious leaders, radical Muslim extremists for the most part, restrict the books that are available to read. They restrict the access to the internet and all social media. They limit what is taught in school to their sense of history and their perverted world view. In such a society, the mind of the people, the society as a whole, is imprisoned, particularly the women. That is why your friend has no knowledge of the Holocaust. In Iran, if you voice any views different from the government, attempt any civil dissent, they put you in jail or kill you."

"So how can I show her the history they 'forgot' to teach her in school?"

"My advice would be to stop seeing her. She has a world view 180 degrees different from yours. You will never change it."

"Well, what if I want to try? What if I want to counter the false narrative of history given her in Iran? What if I want to let Nadina grow up unafraid of the truth? Let them know how Israel came into existence after the Holocaust. Let her see what it is like to live in a society where you are free to explore social media and are free to learn uncensored history."

"If you insist, you can start by taking them on a trip to Yad Vashem. You told me Saron was a terrorist and almost killed you. I don't know how she will respond to seeing our Holocaust History Museum. "

CHAPTER 31
YAD VASHEM

TWO DAYS LATER Doron drove Saron and Nadina to Yad Vashem. Saron let her hair down and wore a white cotton blouse and a pale green chiffon skirt and flat shoes. For the first time, she did not wear a niqab or other Arab headdress. Surprisingly, she liked how it felt to be without it. Her red hair, green eyes and Irish Iranian complexion brought glances of wonder and surprise. Nadina, now 15 years of age, wore a similar white blouse, jeans and sneakers. Her black hair and brown eyes were in sharp contrast to her mother's red hair and green eyes, but her high cheekbones and the beauty of her facial features matched the beauty of her mother, albeit in a more subdued, gentler manner. There was no doubt, Nadina was her mother's daughter.

To get into the museum they had to walk through an aqueduct inscribed with biblical words from Ezekial, "I will put my breath into you and you shall live again, and I will set you upon your own soil." The museum is triangular, prism-like, slicing into the western slope of Mount Herzl. As they walked into the museum, Nadina turned in a circle, looking up at the high concrete walls and the sky shining down from above. They took time to enter small rooms cut into the concrete side walls of the museum. They stopped at exhibits of pictures and videos displaying life in the Jewish European ghettos before the Nazi destruction, then the images of the mass murders of countless men, women and children. Nadina noticed images of hungry children her age, huddled together on the street. Saron noted a picture of a father holding his young child, his back turned to a Nazi soldier holding a rifle about to shoot him and his child. Doron's eyes glistened with tears, admiring the paintings done by innocent unsuspecting children shortly before entering gas chambers.

As they walked through the museum, Saron quickly realized that everything she had been taught about Jewish history had been a lie. The true history was here in the museum's videotaped archives, in the pictures on the walls, in the paintings and the poetry, in the words of the victims of the Holocaust. This was a record of murder not of a few people but a genocide of most of European Jewish life. This was murder out of blind hate, unfortunately, not unlike what radical Islam planned for the remaining Jews, the relatives of the survivors of the Holocaust. She looked up and read a story of a mother given "Sophie's choice," by the Nazi soldiers surrounding her. "Choose which child of yours will die, or we will kill them both." The Nazis not only desired to kill all the Jews but were inclined to torture them in as cruel a fashion as human ingenuity could devise.

Doron, Saron and Nadina together listened to a videotaped story recollected by Judith Kleinman, who was asked by her Nazi captors when she was only 6, living at the time in Nazi-occupied Venice, to choose if she wished to stay with her mother or go with a strange neighbor. Sensing something was amiss, she picked the stranger. The choice saved her life. She never saw her mother again but survived, eventually reared in a convent in Germany. Judith eventually made her way to Israel at the end of the war, only then learning that both her mother and father were killed in Nazi concentration camps.

Saron sat down on a nearby bench, feeling sick. Was this genocide any different than what Iran was now planning for the Jews and their descendants that had survived the Holocaust and had emigrated to Israel? After resting for a few moments they exited the main museum into daylight and a sunken square courtyard, surrounded by limestone and a grove of trees.

Doron turned to Nadina. "I hope the museum was not too depressing for you?"

"It is very depressing," Nadina replied. "Very sad. It seems for some people life has no value. But the most distressing part of the museum is the realization that the whole country of Germany, except for a few very brave people participated in supporting the Nazi killings. I heard there is a children's museum, dedicated to the children killed in the Holocaust. Can we visit it?"

Saron looked over at her daughter, realizing fourteen-year-old Nadina was no longer the introverted autistic daughter she had raised in Iran. She had clearly changed in her five years in Israel. As hard as it was to admit, the change was all to the better, and none of her doing.

Doron turned to Nadina. "The children's museum is nearby. We can walk there, after we get some lunch here, if the museum hasn't ruined your appetite, and your mother gives her permission."

Saron turned to her daughter. "We can go, if you are up for it."

Nadina nodded affirmitively.

Saron continued. "I would also like to see the children's museum, since this history was hidden from me in Iran. "Now I can see what people mean when they use the term 'revisionist history'."

Doron bought their lunches and sat on a veranda overlooking the museum. A young girl, Rivka, came over and spoke to Nadina. Together they played in the grass. Rivka let Nadina hold her ten-week-old puppy, Ralphy, a beagle mixture, his long ears flopping happily as he ran between them in the afternoon sun.

On the way, they walked past a railroad car on a track depicting the trains carrying Jews to the death camps. Doron took the time to explain to Nadina and Saron what the railroad car represented. "The railroad car sits at the edge of a track now going nowhere, a grim reminder of the nightmare, and the lies that had been perpetrated, as the Jews were told they were going to work in the concentration camps, that work would make them free--instead they were transported to their deaths."

They made their way to the Children's Memorial Museum, hollowed out of the limestone rock of Mount Herzl. They walked down limestone steps into a large subterranean cavern. There were memorial candles. As they entered, Nadina saw pictures of hundreds of children on the circular wall surrounding them. Children, many of whom were her age. A plaque on the wall described the killing of 1.5 million children during the Holocaust. Then the light dimmed and memorial candles lit the room with a shimmering golden light as the names of the children killed and their age at death were recited in a memorial tribute.

As they stood in the shimmering light an explosion shook the walls of the museum, some limestone debris fell in the center of the room, some of the children's pictures fell off the wall as panicking visitors hurried out of the museum, the three ran outside with the rest of the visitors. Warning sirens were blaring as it became clear there had been a missile attack from Lebanon. Most of the missiles had been stopped by Israeli counter missile defense systems, but two had landed. One in a suburb of Tel Aviv and one near the Children's Holocaust Memorial. As they left the museum, Nadina saw a child lying face down on the grassy knoll where she had just played with Rivka. It was Rivka, unconscious, her puppy jumping in panic around her, licking her face, tugging at her arm, trying to revive her. An ambulance took Rivka with her parents to a nearby hospital. On the evening news in Iran, people were pictured giving out candy to passersby celebrating the missile attack. The next day, a news report indicated Rivka was alive, had suffered a concussion but would survive. Two days later the three of them visited Rivka in the hospital, Nadina telling Rivka she would pray for her recovery and hoped Ralphy was ok.

Saron decided to read more of the history of the Jewish people, a history denied her in Iran.

"Why are you so interested in philosophy and Jewish history?" Doron asked her one evening as they sat together at home.

Saron looked at Doron, hesitant to reply. "I never expected to have this interest, until I realized how much has been hidden from me by the controlling religious leaders in Iran. By hiding many of the books I am interested in reading, by trying to control my access to certain writings, certain viewpoints, they have only made me hunger for this knowledge, like a poor starving mongrel in the street hungers for scraps of food."

Saron was never one to do anything halfheartedly and enrolled in a philosophy program at Tel Aviv University with a minor in artificial intelligence. She was the only Iranian enrolled in the school. She read books on the nature and origin of evil, from the Enuma Elish describing evil in ancient times as a cosmic battle, to Greek Tragedy and Greek philosophy, to the description of evil in the Hebrew and Christian Bibles. Then she went on to read works by Hobbes, Montaigne and Milton. Months passed as she went on to read Doestoevsky, Conrad, Freus and Camus. In her second year at Tel Aviv University she read Nietsche, Blaise Pascal, Wiesel, Abba Eban and post World War II philosophical and scientific thought on both the philosophy and science dealing with the mechanism by which evil takes root in closed, authoritarian societies.

Doron and Nadina attended Saron's graduation where she was asked to speak as the valedictorian of her class. "That an Iranian should be standing here, as the valedictorian of an Israeli university class at Tel Aviv University, is more than surprising, more than remarkable. It is even more remarkable, when one realizes that I am not just Iranian, but a Moslem, and only a few years ago was an Iranian soldier, a full-fledged idealogue in Iran's Jihad against Israel, the U.S. in particular, and Western civilization in general. At one point my daughter at the age of five was almost blown up as part of a suicide bombing mission." Saron turned to look at her daughter in the audience, acknowledging her with a nod as Nadina stood motionless.

"I didn't choose to change. My daughter, Nadina, was captured by an Israeli soldier in Iran and brought to Israel, raised in Israel for the last six years. I came to Israel three years ago to rescue my daughter and kill the soldier who had brought her here. I felt only hatred for Israel and in particular the Israeli soldier who had taken my daughter from me. When I came here, I discovered my daughter's life had been saved during the rescue in Iran. Nadina was kept here because my husband was dead and I was presumed dead, unconscious in an Iranian hospital.

"So instead of being held prisoner, I discovered a daughter happier than she had ever been in Iran, where I was told she was autistic. She is anything but autistic now. Several of my relatives in Iran came to kill my daughter and once again the same Israeli soldier saved her life. I had a choice, take Nadina by force to Iran, where we would both be killed, or stay in Israel, which had helped her overcome autism, depression and even drug addiction, giving Nadina a chance at a happy fulfilling life."

Saron looked out at her audience of largely Jewish youth. "How ironic it is, how unexpected to be standing in front of you. So why did I decide on studying philosophy? To better understand the roots of the hatred, terrorism, the extreme Jihad spread by Iran. Two primary causes immediately come to mind; first, an authoritarian state, a closed society, not allowing certain books to be available to be read, imprisoning or murdering any opposition and secondly, a religious theocracy wedded to the ethos of the 12th century. By comparison, in Israel I have been given the freedom to study philosophy and do my own research on the roots of evil, the nature and origin of extremism. I found no more full-fledged display of extremism and the government glorification of hatred and global Jihad than in my own home country, the theocracy of Iran. It is my belief that, like myself, the people of Iran would welcome a government that pursues a path to peace and economic prosperity rather than a fruitless attempt at world domination, replete with its hatred of the West. It is my hope, that my recent studies in philosophy, the liberating experience of freedom, and awakened thirst for knowledge, may one day allow me to help Iran make a transition to a true search for peace."

With that, Saron sat down, as her audience stood up cheering and clapping in unified appreciation. The president of the university asked her to stand once more, as the applause continued, congratulating her again on her achievement and a most remarkable speech.

All the graduating students then came up to receive their degree. Saron appeared proud when the college president handed her the diploma. Then everyone threw their tasseled graduation caps in the air in a joint celebration. At the edges of the celebrants were uniformed Israeli soldiers ever ready to deal with a terrorist attack, a reminder that no event in Israel is presumed safe. Fortunately, there were no untoward events that late May day.

To celebrate Saron's graduation, Doron, Saron and Nadina, now 17, had dinner that evening at a restaurant in Tel Aviv, a vegetarian restaurant picked out by Nadina. "Congratulations on your graduation," Doron said, holding up a glass of wine and toasting Saron, Nadina held up her glass of water, joining the toast.

"So what are your plans now?" Doron asked, turning to look at Saron as they ate dessert.

"To get a combined PhD in philosophy and artificial intelligence," Saron replied, matter-of-factly. "Tel a Viv University has offered me a full scholarship for a PhD degree in philosophy and the Technion said I could also take courses there in Artificial Intelligence as part of a joint program."

"That sounds like a lot of work. What would you do with such a degree?"

"Studying philosophy can teach more about the roots of evil, fanaticism, radical Islam, Jihad, but this knowledge can't help anticipate the risks of future conflicts. Along with these courses, I plan to study artificial intelligence (AI), hoping to use AI to generate mathematical models of the roots of evil, to create probabalistic predictions of future outcomes. Using AI, I believe there is a predictable point, some have called it the Omega Point, where a society like Iran can be predicted to use nuclear weapons, when developed, to usher in Armageddon, ignoring and possibly even welcoming its own destruction."

With that, Saron placed a bite of her chocolate creme brulee on her fork, slowly placing it in her mouth, savoring its creme taste, as Doron silently stared at her. A knife fell to the floor at an adjacent table, as Saron's words had apparently startled a nearby couple overhearing her. Nadina finished her rainbow sherbert, but Doron left his slice of key lime pie half-eaten.

CHAPTER 32
COFFEE HOUSE CONVERSATION BETWEEN DORON AND SARON

A FEW WEEKS later Saron called Doron at his home while Nadina was at school. "Can we meet at Gilda's, the coffee shop near you? I have something to discuss?"

"Is it about Nadina?"

"No. It has nothing to do with Nadina. I'll explain when we meet."

An hour later they met at Gilda's and sat together in an unobtrusive corner.

"I need you to secretly get me back into Iran." Saron was glancing down at her coffee cup as she spoke, not looking at Doron.

Doron startled by the request, stared at Saron as he spoke. "I have not had good experiences with you in Iran," Doron said, thinking of Saron's knife skirting his ribs as she'd danced provocatively around him during his captivity in Iran.

Saron ignored his remark. "I have been in touch with one of the Iranian resistance movements that would like to see Iran get rid of the religious leaders and replace them with a secular government interested in breaking relations with Al Qaeda and Hamas, even accepting Israel's right to exist and negotiating a path to peace and a solution to the Palestinian issue."

"And you want me to believe you? Why should I believe you? What if your relatives are waiting for me and you or members of the Revolutionary Guard? What if it's just a trap?"

"We already killed two of my cousins when they came to visit. You may have seen some of the protests against the Rouhani regime on TV. Fifteen hundred Iranian protesters were killed by Quassim Sulaiman in 2018. In 2019 he was killed by a Trump drone attack. Outwardly there was a mass funeral show for the West but many Iranians privately rejoiced at his death. Then after the Iranian military admitted to shooting down a Ukrainian jet with many Iranian citizens aboard, the protests against Rouhani started anew. When he died, his replacement, Karuf Akilidar has had trouble controlling the dissidents. He is hesitant to kill Iranian citizens and suffer even stronger trading sanctions against Iran."

"Why does this group want you to go back?"

"They want us to help plan a rally for freedom in Iran. To cause overwhelming public outcry against the militant theocracy, force their removal and their replacement by a secular government."

"Us, did you say us?" Doron asked.

Saron replied. "They want to make us, you and me, the poster children, so to speak, of a new movement. Iranian and Israeli together seeking peace and coexistence."

"As soon as the Revolutionary Guard finds me, they would kill me!"

"And they would kill me too, just as surely. So for now we'd just work secretly with this, the largest dissident group."

Does it have a name?"

In English, "Sacred Mission."

"Why not, 'mission impossible'?" Doron replied, in mock humor.

Saron laughed, then looked up at Doron. "There is tremendous unrest among the Iranian people right now. The American Iranian sanctions have sent the economy into recession and depression. The Mullahs have run out of the Obama bribery money that never did anything but help fund the Iranian proxies, Al Qaeda and Hezbollah."

"So why should I believe anything you say?"

"I have an encrypted video of several of the dissident meetings. You can show it to Israeli Intelligence for their opinion. The resistance movement wants us to work with them on methods to expand their support. Your intelligence officers can recognize some of these people from the resistance protest marches on TV."

"I can't promise anything but if you have the video, I'll have it reviewed and then get back to you."

Saron slipped Doron a thumb drive, then they separately left the coffee shop. A day later Doron delivered the thumb drive to Tsavi Rosenberg, the vice chairman of Israeli Intelligence.

CHAPTER 33
DORON MEETS WITH ISRAELI INTELLIGENCE

THREE WEEKS LATER, Doron was asked to attend a meeting in the office of Tsavi Rosenberg, the vice chairman of Israeli Intelligence. With them in the office was a person Doron did not recognize.

"Doron," Rosenberg said, "I invited Yuri Goldberg to join us. Yuri is the head of Israeli Intelligence. He tries to stay out of the news and limelight and does not generally meet with our soldiers, which is why you may not recognize him. Doron and Yuri shook hands.

"Tell us everything you know of Saron Gazzeri," Yuri requested.

Doron laughed. "How much time do you have?" He looked at Rosenberg and Goldberg. They did not return his smile.

"As much time as you need," said Goldberg .

Rosenberg poured coffee for Doron and Yuri. Doron took the coffee and added some cream and two sugars, taking his time, collecting his thoughts, thinking back to his imprisonment in Iran, before speaking.

"I first met Saron in Iran when she and her husband held me prisoner in a small wood-framed house on the shore of the Caspian. I never got a very good look at her, but sensed her presence as she danced around me holding a knife to my ribs. I still have some scars from that memorable first meeting."

"And this is the woman, an Iranian terrorist who held you prisoner, that now wants you to take her back to Iran?" Yuri asked incredulously.

Doron nodded affirmatively then slowly wove the tale, explaining the remarkable turn of events in his relationship with Saron and her daughter, Nadina. "During the storm that saved my life and freed me from captivity, the rescue helicopter at my direction saved Saron's daughter, Nadina's life. I saw Saron and Gazzeri lying unconscious after the storm and presumed them dead, and in Israel heard no more about them. Gazzeri, Saron's husband was actually dead, killed in the storm. Saron, however, survived but was in a coma for months. She recuperated for several years before making her way to Israel, planning to rescue her daughter and attempt to kill me once again."

"Let me repeat my first question," Yuri quipped. "And this is the same woman who wants you to take her back to Iran?" Yuri gave Doron a puzzled look. "I heard about your visit to Mullalah's

Bar in East Jerusalem. Why not just go back there? They will kill you without the necessity of a trip to Iran."

"Yuri, let Doron finish telling us about Saron," Tsavi admonished, giving Yuri a stern look.

"Alright," Yuri said. "So, Doron, what happened when Saron came to Israel?"

Doron took a slow sip of coffee, then put the cup down as he continued. "My wife, Sarah, and I raised Nadina from the age of eight. When we found her she was completely withdrawn. We were told she

was probably autistic, but we weren't convinced. Over a few years, she gradually came out of her shell. She became enamored of the BHai Faith. Then my wife was killed and I was left to raise Nadina alone. Having to raise her probably helped save my own life. Nadina took the death of my wife Sarah as badly as I did. At one point she experimented with drugs and fortunately with the help of several Bhai' priests, gave this up. Then Saron showed up one evening as well as two of her cousins and a third Iranian, all planning to kill me and Nadina. Saron was hiding in my house, in Nadina's room that night. I killed one of her cousins and Saron killed the other. At that point Saron had the opportunity to kill me, but instead killed the third Iranian intruder, one of her cousins, saving both my life and the life of Nadina."

"And why didn't she kill you when she again had the chance?" Tsavi asked.

"Saron told me later that if she took Nadina back to Iran, they would kill Nadina for having lived with an Israeli, and an Israeli army lieutenant made it that much worse. She came to understand that I had not kidnapped Nadina during the storm, but saved her life, bringing her to Israel to recuperate. Observing Nadina in Israel, eventually convinced Saron to accept a difficult truth for her. Nadina was happier in her new life in Israel than she had ever been in Iran. Now that Saron had personally killed her cousin, an Iranian military agent, the Iranians would want to kill her for her deeds. So, now even she was safer in Israel than in Iran. So she needed me alive to help her and Nadina survive in Israel."

"How long has she been in Israel?" Yuri asked.

"About four years now. The three of us, Saron, Nadina and I have explored parts of Israel together, including Yad Vashem and the children's museum there. Growing up in Iran, Saron had been fed typical Iranian lies, denying the history of the Holocaust. It is hard to refute it after visiting Yad Vashem. Hearing the words of survivors, seeing their pictures, particularly the children. Maybe more Iranians need to experience Yad Vashem, especially the children before they are indoctrinated with hate. I think it was her visit to Yad Vashem that motivated Saron to study philosophy. She enrolled in Tel Aviv University and in two years graduated with a bachelor's degree in philosophy and was the valedictorian. The only Iranian to have ever done so!"

Probably the only Iranian terrorist to have ever attended the school," remarked Yuri.

"So after a few years of knowing her and her daughter, you think you can trust her?" Tsavi asked. "Once you are in Iran with her, it would be easy for her to kill you or have you killed. We cannot send a storm your way every time you get in trouble. We were lucky it worked out the first time. The storm itself could have killed all of you!"

Doron decided to change the subject. "Have you reviewed the thumb drive I gave you?"

Neither Yuri or Tsavi spoke. Instead Tsavi turned on a computer monitor. "Here are images of several members of the resistance movement at one of their meetings. On the split images on the screen we have put some images from recent resistance rallies in Iran. Images of some of the protestors were enlarged and compared to some of the members of the Iranian resistance movement. "As you can see, the members of the resistance movement at their meeting are allparticipants in resistance rallies, and a few of them are now imprisoned in Iran. We have been following some of these people for many years. Saron's story has backed up our review of who these resistance members are and their participation in many resistance rallies."

Yuri turned to Doron. "So let's say you manage to get into Iran without being killed by the Iranian Revolutionary Guard at the border and without being killed by Saron in Iran. Say you meet with the Iranian resistance and they don't kill you. What will they want you to do to help them?"

"I don't know. But what aid could we give them to help support the resistance movement in Iran?"

Yuri thought a moment before speaking. "I think we should speak to the Americans. Discuss this with them. We can all try to put together a united working plan for you. When you meet with the resistance you can then use this plan to help them, hopefully, once and for all, replace the religious theocracy now in power. Since you came here from the U.S., we have assigned you many of our most dangerous missions. You never complained, never objected. Now you're proposing an even more dangerous plan for yourself. Personally, if I were you, I would not do it."

"Doron, if you insist on attempting this mission, I will set up a meeting with the Americans to create a plan for your meeting with the Iranian resistance. Thank you for coming."

After Doron left, Yuri placed a call to Arnold Schwartzman, the secretary of state.

CHAPTER 34
ISRAELI INTELLIGENCE MEETS WITH U.S. MILITARY AT THE PENTAGON

ARLINGTON COUNTY, VIRGINIA ACROSS THE POTOMAC FROM WASHINGTON, D.C.

MEETING AT THE Pentagon from the U.S. were Raymond Chadry, secretary of defense, General George Macy, Pentagon strategist, Arnold Schwartzmann, secretary of state, Chris Ryan, the head of DARPA, Tommy Chu, head of the National Security Association and Vivian Tyson, Vice President of the United States.

Coming from Israel were Tsavi Rosenberg, vice chairman of Israeli Intelligence, Yuri Goldberg, head of Israeli Intelligence, Monica Bergson, Foreign Minister of Israel, Myra Shmolin, Brigadier General, Israeli Defense Forces and Shimon Rivlin, member of Mossad Central Institute for Intelligence and Special Operations.

Vivian stood up to address the meeting. "As I understand it, we are meeting to help the Iranian Resistance movement. Is that correct, Yuri?"

Yuri stood up to respond. "One of our soldiers has become friends with an ex-Iranian terrorist now living in Israel. They have been asked to return to Iran and help the resistance movement gain power. Due to the U.S. embargo on doing business with Iran, the Iran economy is in a shambles. The Iranian people are tired of living in poverty to support a government more interested in sending money to support global Jihad than to deal with poverty and lack of jobs in Iran. So, right now there is as strong a populous desire for change as there has ever been."

Secretary of State Schwartzmann stood up. "So how does an Israeli soldier figure into this?"

Yuri leaned over to Tsavi. "You know more about Doron than I. Why don't you answer?"

Tsavi stood up. "Doron is a joint U.S. Israeli citizen and a lieutenant in the Israeli Army. Saron was a hardened Iranian soldier, militant and terrorist but is now living in Israel where her daughter is living as well. What caused this radical transition would take too long to describe in this meeting, but we believe this is not a subterfuge but a change in her world view. Saron has great support in the Iranian Resistance movement. Some in this movement believe the storm that saved Doron's life is a sign that, basically, God wants to broker a peace in the Middle East, and He has chosen Doron and Saron as His messengers of peace."

Vice President Tyson stood up. "And how much did Israeli science help God in this incident?"

Yuri Goldberg, head of Israeli Intelligence stood up. "When we met with many of you recently in Israel we showed you our capability in weather control. As we stated then, we are working toward developing weather modification of an actual storm but are nowhere near that now.

"We are here to devise a plan for Saron and Doron to present to the Resistance Movement not to argue over Israeli technology. What we want is a revolution of ideas and culture in Iran."

Chris Ryan, the head of DARPA stood up. "Your statement is a good lead into a discussion by our next speaker, Sam Foster, a political science professor from the University of California at Berkeley. Sam wrote a book entitled, "How to Start a Revolution." Since that appears to be our mandate, let's hear from him. Sam..."

Sam Foster had grayish blond hair in a ponytail, wore jeans and a casual shirt almost like he just came from Woodstock. He took the microphone. "I would not ever have expected to be speaking to this group, probably mainly conservative-leaning people. Politics, as they say, makes strange bedfellows. So here I am.

"To change the cultural allegiance of Iranians you have to understand the cultural, political, legal and media situation in Iran. The first thing you would need to do is find ways to express opinions contrary to the autocratic theocracy in power that they won't or can't block. You need to take control of social media, such as Facebook, Google and Twitter for starters—that is, you need to prevent these means of communication from being blocked. Unfortunately, how you do that requires a higher pay grade than mine.

"You also need to share your message on Iranian TV. Everyday news broadcasts are now completely controlled by the Iranian government. Another quandary beyond my pay grade.

"Iran is not a free society for a reason. The government is not interested in open discussion of their politics or actions. To keep it that way, they imprison dissidents or kill them. You would, I suppose, not be surprised at how well this quashes any resistance. The fact that there is a sizable resistance movement in Iran at all is a testament to how downtrodden, hungry, poverty stricken hopeless and helpless many Iranians feel. What you want is a cultural revolution among the people in Iran against their government. Cultural revolutions are constantly being organized in the West, including the U.S.–constantly testing the political structure and power base, but that is not what you asked me to discuss this evening. You need to know this is a worldwide phenomenon, not just a product of Iran."

Raymond Chadry, the secretary of defense stood up. "What about the power structure in Iran, the military that helps keep the government in power and protected from the unrest of the people?"

"Good point. The military currently supports the government but any cracks that you can create in this support would be beneficial to the resistance. If you can find a way to get the military to support the resistance, you would have radically changed the power structure in Iran. Without military support, the Iranian autocracy would crumble by an inability to control popular unrest.

How you would achieve this, is again, above my pay grade."

Chris Ryan, head of DARPA stood up. "I would suggest we meet with representatives from a host of social media companies and see how they can ensure their media is open to resistance movement sites. Keep the government from closing them. I would also suggest we find out if any of the supporters of the resistance are friends with the higher echelon military and see what could be done to have them come over from the 'Dark Side.' Any thoughts from the Israeli contingent?"

Shimon Rivlin, member of Mossad stood up. Mossad, Israel's covert intelligence agency, had been involved in multiple covert operations since 1956, including, assassinating Nazi war criminals hiding in South America, assassinating individuals involved in the Munich Olympic athlete massacre in 1972 and Operation Entebbe, which contributed to the daring rescue of 102 kidnapped airline passengers. To keep their members secret, they rarely attended any meetings outside of Israel.

Rivlin spoke. "We have several contacts in the Iranian resistance that have support from a very few of the Iranian military. Several of these people have had friends and relatives assassinated by the Iranian autocracy. So the ruthless treatment of any dissidents by the Iranian autocracy has caused some cracks in their support. You can't just kill everyone that disagrees with you without creating some animosity in your populace and this includes some of the military and other support personnel. These people know to keep their thoughts and feelings private. Their first allegiance is to staying alive. We are talking about four or five out of a few hundred in the upper echelons of the military. Bribery might get you a few more but not the numbers needed for a coup."

Vivian Tyson, vice president of the United States, stood up. "I will set up a private meeting at the White House between the major social media companies. See what the president can do to gain their support in securing an open web for communication of ideas. If the people of Iran were free to choose their government, if they weren't held hostage by the tyrannical regime, we believe they would overthrow it for a freer society, a growing economy and a change from being a pariah on the world stage to a country partnering for growth. Obama gave over $350 billion to the Iranian government, saying with a straight face, it wasn't a bribe, and look what it got him? At worst, we could have used the money in a more direct way, bribed quite a few of the military with it, achieving a lot more support than their foolhardy attempt at negotiations." With that said the meeting broke up into small groups for further discussions and then disbanded. No mention of the meeting was provided to or leaked to the news media.

CHAPTER 35
MEETING AT THE WHITE HOUSE

ONE MONTH LATER the meeting planned by Vice President Tyson was held at the White House.

In attendance were Ismael Gomez, President of the United States, Raymond Chadry, secretary of defense, General George Macy, Pentagon strategist, Arnold Schwartzmann, secretary of state, Chris Ryan, the head of DARPA, Tommy Chu, head of the national security association and Vivian Tyson, vice president of the United States. Also in attendance were technical representatives from Facebook, Google, Apple, Microsoft, Intel and Twitter. Two Israeli attendees were technology experts from the Technion Israel Institute of Technology, Mordecai Rothman and Evan Jacobs.

Vice President Tyson spoke. "The reason we are here is to ask the help of our largest social media companies to protect the freedom of communication in Iran. Amid the current Iranian protests, the government pulled the plug on the internet. Due to the embargo on Iran, gas prices increased 300% as they did in 2019. Rioters set some banks, government buildings and gas stations ablaze causing multiple arrests and the largest internet shutdown in Iranian history. We are not asking you to violate the freedom of speech of any group but to protect it. There are many different groups in Iran. Some support the autocracy in power, some do not. All deserve to be heard. The Iranian regime in power has tried to block the freedom of speech of anyone that disagrees with them. This is their prime means of staying in power. We are asking you to protect the Iranian people's right to communicate between themselves and with the rest of the world through an unfiltered internet."

Michael Chan, a technical chief from Google spoke. "None of us control the internet. We just use it like everyone else."

Chris Ryan, head of DARPA said, "DARPA was an offshoot of ARPA, the Advanced Research Projects Agency started by President Dwight Eisenhower in response to the Russian Sputnik launch. ARPA's main mission was computer science and developed early networking operating systems. The network was called ARPANET. So the internet's initial creation was due to a military security concern. Today computers communicate through radio waves sent between radio transmitters and receivers and broadened in 1977 to transmission of radio waves to and from satellites. The global interconnection of computer networks became the internet. The way to navigate this network became known as the World Wide Web. Today, we need your help to make available to your users an internet that cannot be controlled by an autocratic government such as Iran."

Leroy Jamison, one of the chief technical officers from Microsoft said, "Iran can block any of the local servers, essentially blocking the Internet in Iran. How would you propose getting around that?"

Tommy Chu, head of national security spoke. Servers are shortly going online in the neighboring countries of Bahrain, Qatar, Turkmenistan, Azerbaijan and Iraq. Radio wave signals will also use cell towers scattered in Iran to provide internet access to local Iranian computers.

"But you still won't be able to prevent the Iranian government from blocking internet access, will you?" Intel director, Jamie Stowers, interjected.

Chris Ryan from DARPA answered. "We thought that would be the case. We discussed the problem with internet technology experts in the U.S. and Israel. We told them securing the internet from blockage was impossible. The U.S. technology leaders agreed, including our own experts at DARPA, and it was our predecessors at ARPA that helped create it. A couple of months later the Israelis solved the problem. Mordecai, care to expand?"

Mordecai Rothman, a full professor and PhD in computer science and applied engineering at the Technion in Israel was also the chief technology officer at Cybernetics, a cyber security and internet access firm in Tel a Viv. "When the question was posed to us as being impossible, that intrigued us, as we have a company saying, "What is a synonym for the impossible? The future. The most disruptive technology is one deemed impossible by others. Certainly, the very creation of the internet was a massively disruptive technology as all of you likely are aware. We have tested the internet access against Iranian attempts at blockage and so far it has stayed up with a 98% uptime. Not a bad achievement."

Ismael Gomez, President of the United States stood up and spoke. "So why do you think

your country could solve this problem and the country that invented the internet could not?"

Evan Jacobs, another PhD from the Technion stood up. "We have the greatest respect for your country, for U.S. technologic prowess and past achievements. We are only a very small country, but we have one incentive you do not have. Unfortunately, our people are daily under the threat of annihilation by our neighbors and in particular, Iran. Such constant threats have a way of focusing your attention to issues of national security such as the internet blocking problem presented to us. Instead of your country's vast resources being focused on scientific achievement, more and more it seems to be focused on dealing with issues of social unrest. Fortunately, we don't have such a problem in Israel."

"Maybe we should have you try to solve that problem for us as well," President Gomez remarked.

"I know you're being facetious in saying that but without wanting to appear presumptuous, I have given it some thought," Mordecai Rothman stated. "May I share those with you?"

"Please," President Gomez replied.

Everyone wondered what Rothman had in mind, as he stood to speak. "I very much enjoy American science fiction and one of my favorite stories is the H.G. Wells masterpiece *War of the Worlds*. In that novel the martians invade the earth and seemingly nothing can defeat them. "They have scientific technology beyond anything on earth, much like the U.S. has compared to the rest of the world. Then suddenly, they are defeated by an internal bacterial disease that kills them from inside. No country today has the power to destroy the U.S. from the outside, but like the Martians in *The War of the Worlds,* the U.S. is at risk of being destroyed from the inside, a more insidious risk, I would maintain, to America's dominance of the future than perhaps it has ever faced before. Whatever you can do, Mr. President, to address this risk would bode well for America, certainly as well for Israel and the world at large."

In the days that followed, the multinational companies decided that if they instituted these changes for Iran, they would be asked to do the same for Russia, for China and North Korea. If this plan was uncovered, there would be a tremendous backlash against them and they would lose the ability to compete, particularly in the huge Chinese market against the Chinese multinationals such as Alibaba and Ten Cent. So for a while there was a stalemate. Then Vice President Vivian Tyson gave each of them a private call.

"We in the administration appreciate your concerns, but this is not a financial matter, a matter of competitive advantage but a national security matter. And understanding this, we need you to be aware that failure to institute the protocols to maintain the internet in Iran will cause us to institute legislation to break up each of our huge multinational companies on the basis of being a monopoly. So you have a simple choice--accept the need to support our security interests or risk having your companies broken into pieces that I suspect will have significant consequences in your ability to compete with foreign multinationals. I should also mention that I will be running for president in the next election in six months, and should I win, I will certainly remember who my friends were, who put America first, and who put short term gains against national security, and ultimately long term peace and prosperity."

Tyson was clearly playing hardball with the U.S. multinationals and they didn't like it. They were used to getting their way. But Vice President Tyson was still the black girl who grew up in a poor shantytown in Alabama, whose great grandparents were share croppers on land once farmed by slaves, many of whom were her distant relatives. She firmly stood her ground. An agreement was reached to institute the anti-internet blockage protocol in regard to Iran, but not require it against any other country for at least three years. With that agreement, the U.S. multinationals all stepped into line supporting the administration's internet protocol regarding Iran. The Iranian autocracy could no longer block the internet usage by the Iranian resistance or any Iranian citizen for that matter. This was major blow to Iranian destruction of the resistance movement and their control of the free exchange of ideas in Iran.

The resistance movement in Iran celebrated this achievement, one of the steps with which they desired to support their cultural revolution. But they were still far from accomplishing this revolution. They knew the autocracy would not let go of power without a fight to the death.

CHAPTER 36
IRAN AND NORTH KOREA MEET

SEMORAH, IRAN.

RACHMAN SOLIDAR, THE Iranian Supreme Leader, awaited the landing of a private plane on the tarmac. Soldiers lined both sides of the path to a black limousine. It was a ceremony to impress the visiting guest. Surprisingly, it was not for a Muslim, not for a Russian head of state or a hopeful European trading partner. Fifty-three-year-old Solidar rubbed his white beard in anticipation. He was all smiles as he greeted the North Korean president and her accompanying contingent of five members of the Korean president's inner circle.

The leaders were all given headphones that used voice recognition technology and voice translation technology. The Iranian words were recognized by the technology, translated into perfect Korean of the president's chosen dialect. The company behind the technology was MVT, Miracle Voice Technology, an Israeli company, 30% owned by IBM that aided the company with their Watson computational ability. Zahir Rosman, the president of the company, was a Moroccan Jew. The company's insignia was erased from the headphones to not give anything Israeli credit in Iran. But although Iran denied Israel's right to exist, they did recognize, at least in private, among their physicists, military and scientists, that Israeli technology and many physical laws and theories were first described by Jews. The meeting was in fact a discussion of technology first theorized by another Jew, Albert Einstein.

Einstein had written a now famous letter to President Franklin D. Roosevelt in 1939 warning the president of the possibility of an extraordinary new weapon, a nuclear bomb.

"In the course of the last four months it has been made probable — through the work of Joliot in France as well as Fermi and Szilárd in America — that it may become possible to set up a nuclear chain reaction in a large mass of uranium, by which vast amounts of power and large quantities of new radium-like elements would be generated. Now it appears almost certain that this could be achieved in the immediate future."

Einstein did not work on the Manhattan Project. The Army denied him the work clearance needed in July 1940, saying his pacifist leanings made him a security risk, although he was allowed to work as a consultant to the United States Navy's Bureau of Ordinance. He had no knowledge of the atomic bomb's development, and no influence on the decision for the bomb to be dropped. According to Linus Pauling, Einstein later regretted signing the letter because it led to the development and use of the atomic bomb in combat, adding that Einstein had justified his decision because of the greater danger that Nazi Germany would develop the bomb first. In 1947 Einstein told Newsweek magazine that "had I known that the Germans would not succeed in developing an atomic bomb, I would have done nothing."

Had Einstein known that countries such as Iran and North Korea would use his research and insight to develop their own nuclear bomb technology, and Germany would not succeed in its development during World War II, he might have tried harder to keep the genie in the bottle. But scientific knowledge, physics in particular, never stays dormant, never goes backward, but only grows in its understanding of nature, and unlike religious theocracy, does not dwell in the anachronism of the past.

North Korea had nuclear technology that Iran desired. What did Iran have that North Korea wanted? Some money and a lot of oil. Where did the money come from? In January 2016, the last year of the Obama administration, the same day five American hostages were released from custody in Iran, a U.S. jetliner delivered $400 million in Swiss francs, euros and other unmarked currencies to Teheran's Mehrabad Airport. The Obama administration denied the payment was a ransom, although they paid the same day the hostages were released. The shipment was kept secret until the story broke, released by the Wall Street Journal on the following August 2. Needless to say the optics of the deal made it appear a ransom payment. And that was how it was spun in Iran. If that was not distasteful enough, this payment was then followed, two days later, by the payment of $1.7 billion to Iran also in foreign currency. The Obama administration claimed the payment was the settlement of a 37-year-old arbitration dispute between Iran and the U.S. The $1.7 billion represented payback of $400 million plus interest for a $400 million payment by the Shah of Iran for military equipment never delivered. So in the space of a few days the U.S., under the Obama administration, paid the number one global sponsor of terrorism $1.7 billion dollars in foreign currency. Part of this was still available to Iran in their negotiations with North Korea. The Iranian press and military simply stated that it was a ransom payment, and this was probably the most truthful statement ever to come out of Iran, the Obama White House denial notwithstanding. To quote the U.S. press, "IF IT WALKS LIKE A DUCK..."

To complement their monetary gain, were vast Iranian oil reserves and the initial lifting of Iranian sanctions, allowing Iran to more fully develop and sell these reserves. Iran has proven oil reserves, at least according to their own government, of 150 billion barrels, ranking them 4th in the world. This is about 10% of the world's proven petroleum reserves.

In return for Obama's monetary transfer, Iran nonetheless continued to chant "Death to America," and characterize the U.S. as the "Great Satan." The appeasement of Iran had not even temporarily stopped Iranian support of terrorism and their constant verbal assaults on the West.

Rachman Solidar, the Iranian Supreme Leader, sat on a small

cushion opposite the new North Korean President Li Jung Chang, who had succeeded Kim Jong-un after his death. Like her predecessor, Kim Jung-un, Chang had previously studied physics. There were rumors that she carried a vial of the VX neurotoxin in her purse, that she had managed an immunization against its lethal effects, and that if she didn't like a paramour or husband, she would dab it behind her ears like perfume, which would take care of the husband or paramour after a few whiffs. For this reason, Chang was sometimes given the moniker the Black Widow. The "Kiss of the Spider Woman," it was widely reported, was certainly not like any other.

"So why did you invite me to visit?" Chang asked, while sipping her favorite oolang ginger tea. Chang was 33, hair curled in gracefully at the nape of her neck. Black and red, her favorite colors, complemented by her Asian exotic beauty, gave her an aura of sensuality, intrigue and danger. As Chang looked down at the tea, she continued. "I see Iran has been shipping more oil. How convenient to have billions of barrels to sell to the West. I am certainly jealous of Iran's good fortune." Chang glanced up at Akilidar, enveloping him with the visage of the beguiling temptress.

Solidar turned toward his guest. "I am always glad to visit with you and share our stories of dealing with the 'Great Satan.' But I did not invite you here just to exchange pleasantries." The supreme leader looked up at Chang, to make sure he had her attention. "We have billions of gallons of oil that you are jealous of. And you have something we are jealous of."

"And what pray tell is that?" Chang asked.

Solidar spoke slowly, emphasizing each word. "Your nuclear bombs. Your technology to construct a bomb, your delivery system and missile technology."

"Since most countries hate us equally," Solidar went on, "we need to solidify our friendship to stand united against them, particularly the 'Big Satan'."

"And how do you propose we do that?" Chang asked, feigning ignorance.

"We can supply North Korea with millions of dollars worth of oil, in return for the technology we seek, plus our pledge of economic ties and peaceful relations."

"Millions for North Korea will not do it," said Chang, as she nonchalantly took another sip of Oolang tea.

"Did I say millions for North Korea?" corrected Akilidar. "I meant millions for North Korea but additional millions for your personal Swiss bank account. You must have misunderstood."

Chang looked up at Solidar, smiling. "You make a very tempting offer. One that I will consider seriously." She was silent for a moment, pausing to take another sip of the oolang ginger tea. The taste of the ginger lingered, refreshing. She then toasted her host, clinking their Chinese tea cups together, in a presumed tentative agreement.

As Chang stood up to leave, Solidar approached her to give a parting hug, then thought twice about it. "I trust we have come to an agreement," he stated with a slight stutter. He stood, awkwardly, several feet from Chang.

Chang smiled provocatively at Solidar. She noticed how Solidar's jugular bulged as he spoke. Although not a vampire, Akilidar sensed both fear and blood, and she did have a fondness, a taste for both. "In due time," she whispered. "In due time."

The next day, a phone call was placed from a private cell phone in a small private home in Iran by the Iranian who had brought the ginger tea to the two heads of state. It reached a member of the Saudi government in Riyadh, sharing the details of the tentative alliance and agreement. From there another phone call went to a member of the government in Jordan.

CHAPTER 37
CHEMICAL CLOUD

WEST BANK. ISRAELI OCCUPIED TERRITORY

THE SYRIAN WAR continued, even after Isis was defeated. Assad's successor, Adnan Qabbani was as ruthless as his predecessor. With his opposition showing some strength and ignoring U.N. conventions, Qabbani used chemical weapons against his own people. The chemicals formed a cloud of poison gas over southeast Syria. Unfortunately, due to unpredictable wind shifts it drifted over Lake Tiberius, and appeared headed toward the West Bank. This land was under Israeli and Palestinian Authority control. It is bounded by Israel and Jordan and a population of close to 3 million Palestinians and 400,000 Israeli settlers and about another 220,000 Israelis in East Jerusalem all now under risk by the chemical cloud.

Head of Israeli Intelligence, Tsvi Schachman, met privately with Israeli President Shamuel Shapiro and several representatives of Israeli weather control companies. President Shapiro, turned to the others. "Can we use our weather control technology to turn this cloud into the Mediterranean?"

Tsvi Schachman, the head of Israeli Intelligence said, "If we attempt to do this, many of our secrets that we have tried to hide will be divulged. We will be blamed for every weather event in the world. Are you prepared for that?"

"If we don't try, a few hundred thousand Palestinians will die, not to mention thousands of Israeli settlers in the West Bank."

The head of Israeli Intelligence again responded. "We will be saving many of the people who want to kill us."

"We will also be saving many women and children. We have no

choice but to try to change the path of the chemical cloud. Can we do it?" He turned to the CEOs and engineers from an array of Israeli weather technology companies.

The CEO of Anemoi said, "The computational models suggest the safest method is to concentrate the cloud into a tight vortex, a tornado and use our tornado modeling and weather technology to direct it along an unoccupied narrow path below Nazareth and above the West Bank—then steer it around Israel into the Mediterranean."

"Any other thoughts?" President Shapiro asked, running his right hand nervously across a balding head.

B spoke. "If we let it rise in the atmosphere, the next rainfall will send it randomly, possibly to the West Bank or even on an Israeli population center such as Tel Aviv!"

C added, "There is a wind now blowing toward the Mediterranean. Using our models we can try to maneuver this wind with our drones, helicopters and jets. It will take at least a week, if we are lucky, to evolve the cloud into a focused storm."

"Start evacuating as many people as you can."

It took ten days to convert the gentle wind into a revolving vortex, without the rain that would have dropped the chemical agent on the population below. The vortex was diverted into the Mediterranean but 2% of the chemical landed, nonetheless, on the West Bank. Several hundred affected people, mainly Palestinians, were taken to Israeli hospitals close to the West Bank.

One of the Palestinians was a suicide terrorist, who blew up the Israeli hospital to which he was taken, killing 190 people, mainly Israelis, including ten doctors and fifteen children.

Disgusted by this action, 200 Palestinian doctors went on strike for two weeks, and were joined by 2000 Palestinian women, until finally, the Palestinian leaders apologized to Israel and out of the nightmare a peace settlement between Israel and the Palestinians was agreed to, with a Palestinian recognition of Israel.

The agreement spanning ten years included the creation of a Palestinian State out of the tail of Israel near the Gulf of Aquaba. This area would be double the occupied territory. It would be irrigated, fertilized and climatized with Israeli weather technology over ten years into a resort oasis. In return, the Palestinian West Bank territory would be cut in half and the Palestinians would leave Gaza. If this could be accomplished successfully, at the ten year mark

Saudi Arabia, Jordan and the Palestinian Authority would recognize Israel. In the West Bank a memorial to the Israeli doctors that died trying to save Palestinian lives was erected with a ceremony attended by the Palestinian Authority as well as Palestinian and Israeli physicians.

CHAPTER 38
TRIP TO NEW YORK CITY

NADINA WAS INVITED to join the Bahai' faith but not at the Shrine of the Bab in Carmel, Israel.

The Bahai' in Israel had promised to not proselytize in Israel out of respect for the Jewish faith, even if by personal request. Nadina, they said, could join the Bahai' faith in a ceremony at the USA National Bahai Center in Evanston, Illinois, a suburb of Chicago. Doron and Saron asked Nadina to think about it for a few months, and when her desire had not waned, they offered to take her to the U.S. for this ceremony.

Doron spoke. "If we go to the U.S., I would like to first visit the monument to the 9/11 World Trade Center terrorist attacks. That is where my parents were killed. I have never seen the memorial in honor of all those killed that day." He suggested they fly to New York City, visit the memorial and then fly to Chicago for the ceremony at the National Bahai Center in Evanston.

The trio flew into La Guardia in New York, took a taxi to a relative of Doron's parents still living in Washington Heights in upper Manhattan. The next day they took the A train heading toward downtown New York City, expecting an uneventful ride. Saron and Nadina decided to read the advertisements and graffiti and wandered down several train cars, while Doron sat alone in the train car they had first entered. They had seven stops to go. When they got to 59th street, three Muslims entered the cab where Nadina and Saron were seated. Saron had her hair down, not covered by a Naquib, looking more like a native New Yorker than the terrorist she had once been. Nadina, now 16, was blossoming into a beautiful young woman. The three Muslims sauntered by.

"What are you doing in New York?" they questioned Nadina.

"We're visiting the memorial for the 9/11 attack," Nadina replied.

One of the Muslims replied. "We are going to go there too. Our friends did not finish the job. We are going to take out a few more Americans," the largest one said with pride a half smile on his face. He looked at Nadina mockingly.

"You can join us and go to heaven with us," he offered.

Saron noted a wire sticking out from his shirt. A suicide bomb.

"Of course, if you don't come, we could blow up the train now, and you could join us in heaven this instant," he offered. He looked around at the other people on the train. About fifteen people were in the shared train car--women, men and a half dozen children going about their lives, oblivious to the danger in their midst.

One of the terrorists chimed in. "We could find a place to spend the night. You and the three of us, before we go to the 9/11 memorial. I hear there is a celebration planned in several days. A good reason to delay our trip there. Of course, to be polite, your mother could come along, She looks like she could please a man..." He looked from Nadina to Saron, admiring Saron's stunning beauty.

Saron's head had been bent down, ostensibly staring at a newspaper she was holding. In her hand, beneath the paper was her 8-inch Russian Zooni knife she had once held against an Israeli's ribs. Against all odds, she had never killed an Israeli with it, but now, ironically, she was debating which Muslim terrorist would feel the blade first. As she looked up into the eyes of her assailants, they would have been wise to recognize the steely determination in her eyes, an upturned eyebrow, the complete lack of fear in her demeanor. Surrounded, like a caged crouched tiger, she was now at her most dangerous.

One of the terrorists reached for Nadina, attempting to pull her toward him. Saron thrust the blade through her paper and cleanly sliced through his hand as he screamed, she then stabbed the other assailant, the one with the suicide bomb, passing her long claw-like blade cleanly through the electronic mechanism of his bomb, and from there into his chest. Saron nonchalantly wiped the bloody knife on the crouched back of the assailant whose hand she had just sliced through. During this momentary lull, the third assailant turned to flee, grabbing Nadina as he did so with Saron in pursuit, her knife flashing in her hand, still dripping blood. Screaming passengers ran out of the train as it slowed for the next stop. The assailant with the bomb fell to the ground; his shirt opened, exposing the bomb no longer functional, showing the passengers they'd been saved from a suicide bomb by a dark red haired woman, possibly a Muslim herself.

Doron was sitting in his train car, oblivious to what had just transpired a few cars away. Sitting across from him was an elderly Muslim woman by herself, when four teenagers came in and sat next to her, shouting profanities. "Why don't you go back into the hole you came from!" they yelled derisively. "We don't want you here!"

Doron watched for a few moments. "Then one of the teenagers grabbed her purse."

"Give it back to her," Doron told them.

"Who's going to stop us? You and who else's army?" They turned toward him, laughing as they judged their next victim. One of them noticed the Jewish star around his neck. "You're Jewish? Why would you defend a Muslim?" The four of them stood around him, while he remained seated.

Rather than verbally respond, in one smooth motion Doron jumped up, punching one cleanly in the jaw with his titanium prosthetic hand, breaking his mandible, sending the assailant sprawling. Then he kicked a second in the head with a sideways kick that sent him flying. The third pulled out a knife. As the knife thrust forward, Doron grabbed the assailant's arm and turned the knife into his assailant, sending him to the ground, bleeding profusely. The fourth assailant, about 13 years old ran out the door as Nadina appeared, resisting the burly Muslim who was rushing her along, gripping her by the neck. Doron waited till they ran alongside him, separating the assailant from Nadina by a karate chop to the forearm. Doron fended off one, a wild punch rocked him, but Doron took his turn to punch the Muslim in the mid-section. This caused the assailant to bend at the waist. The terrorist pulled out a gun, pointing it at Doron. As he aimed, Doron put his prosthetic hand over his heart just as the assailant fired. The bullet hit the prosthetic hand and made a loud metallic sound as the bullet flattened in his hand, falling harmlessly to the floor. The bewildered gunman hesitated for a moment, giving Doron a chance to grab the gun out of his hand. Doron then kneed his assailant in the head to the cheers of the nearby passengers still left, who had not yet managed to run into other cars.

As Doron kicked the assailant out the subway door, Saron appeared, just in time to see Doron once again save Nadina's life. As Doron started to speak, Saron cupped Doron's face in her hands, her knife falling to the floor with a clanging noise as it slid slowly past the startled passengers, a few drops of blood still dripping off the serrated blade. Saron gave Doron a deep sensual kiss, surprising him as he stood motionless. After their kiss, Saron stood still, gazing at Doron momentarily with a look of gratitude and compassion for the man who had just saved her daughter's life once again, yet fearful for this impossible relationship. Saron's look and kiss was now indelibly imprinted in Doron's memory.

A teenaged young woman seated nearby, could sense Saron's passion. Goosebumps crawled up her arms as she observed the couple, and she led the applause from the remaining subway passengers appreciative of their heroics; the romantic kiss turned into a quiet reverence. At the next stop, Doron escorted the attacked Muslim woman off the train, returning her purse. Doron, Saron and Nadina then left the train at the 9/11 memorial exit, having experienced, at least for the time being, enough of the New York City subway rapid transit system.

Saron and her red hair was now mentioned in several newscasts, so she put on her Naquib to disguise herself. She was nonetheless hailed as a hero by New Yorkers watching the news that night. At the 9/11 memorial, Saron, nonetheless, received a few unappreciative looks while wearing her Naquib. The three explored the memorial. They sensed the hallowed nature of the grounds. The names of over three thousand victims were inscribed on bronze parapets, surrounding recessed pools set within the footprint of the Twin Towers. They observed a cascade of water flowing into the pools. They walked amid rows of deciduous trees, surrounding the fountains, colored with red and yellow fall leaves, a symbol of birth and renewal. They viewed with sadness a twisted metal remnant of the Twin Towers, kept as a reminder of what had once been.

In front of this memorial, Doron said a Jewish prayer, Saron in turn recited a Muslim prayer, and Nadina, a Bahai prayer, as several people observed them in quiet homage.

Several hours later they left, deciding on a taxi cab ride, instead of another experience on the New York subway system. The cab driver was Italian with a deep Brooklyn New York accent, greying temples, with an old Brooklyn Dodgers baseball cap he wore backwards. He drove at 40-60 miles per hour through downtown New York City. He tried to run over a group of gay rights activists as they crossed fifth avenue and 32nd street. "They may think they own the country, but I own the streets, and I'm taking the street back!" Then he tried to run over several black teenagers, jaywalking as they crossed 7th avenue and 42nd street while the light was red. When he got to 50th street he bounced lightly off a bicyclist who careened onto the sidewalk. As the cabbie drove past Central Park, he approached a horse and buggy. When he lay on his horn, the horse whinnied and stood up on his back haunches in fear, with the cab swerving under the horse's legs. At 139th street and St. Nicholas Avenue he tried to run over two lovers kissing in the street, apparently oblivious to his cab until it almost hit them.

When they finally made it to Washington Heights, they were all shaken as they disembarked. Doron turned to Nadina and Saron.

"Maybe we should have taken the subway..." They both nodded affirmatively.

Then he remembered their ordeal on the subway. "And then again," he added, "maybe not." As they recollected their subway ordeal, all three started laughing. It was the first hysterical laughter any had felt in years, all due to a crazy Brooklyn New York cabbie.

Before they went to sleep late that night, they turned on the news, only to hear about their exploits on the subway system. "The New York subway system was the scene of several remarkable events today," a reporter stated. "A striking red-haired woman, possibly Indian or Muslim killed a bomb-carrying terrorist who apparently intended to detonate the bomb at the 9/11 memorial. On the same train, a Muslim woman was protected by an Israeli-American from several assailants trying to rob her. The Israeli-American was visiting our city from Israel. Only in New York, on the same evening, on a New York subway, could you have a Muslim protecting the city against a terrorist bombing and a Jew protecting an elderly Muslim woman from attack. Go figure?" The reporter ended her telecast with her head shaking in bemused amazement.

The next day, Doron, Saron and Nadina flew to Evanston, Chicago, for a private ceremony at the Bahai National Center where Nadina was welcomed into the Bahai faith.

CHAPTER 39
NADINA:
"REVERENCE FOR LIFE"

NADINA WAS NOW 16 years old. Eight years had passed since she was brought to Israel from Iran. She had a tutor who gradually taught her to speak Hebrew and English and she picked up both more quickly than expected. She rarely thought of her father. More and more she considered Doron her father. Perhaps because of how little life was revered in Iran, how close to death she had come herself, life became more precious to her. She refused to eat meat and became a vegetarian. One day Doron saw her take a spider from inside the house and gently carry it outside, talking to it, like a long lost friend. A few weeks later Doron was bringing her a towel when he saw Nadina removing something from the toilet bowl.

"Nadina, what are you doing?" he asked surprised at her antics. "The toilet bowl is dirty. Get your hand out of there."

"There's a ladybug in there. I need to save it before I flush the toilet!" Nadina picked the bug off the sidewall of the toilet and showed it to Doron. "See how pretty it is. It wants to live as much as you or me!"

"Nadina, when did you decide this? Don't you know it is OK to kill a bug? Everyone does it. If we didn't they would take over." Doron sat down on the bathroom floor with Nadina who proudly held up her ladybug that was walking along her finger.

"I went on line and Googled "who thinks life is precious" and came across an old man with white hair and a large curly moustache named Albert Schweitzer. He believed in 'reverence for life,' and so do I. He didn't kill things, even mosquitoes, so I don't want to either, even ladybugs, even if they are in my toilet!" Nadina laughed, and that surprised Doron, who had not often seen her laugh. "Just because people have always killed bugs, doesn't make it right." Nadina looked at her ladybug. "Dear miss ladybug, do you want to be alive or dead? Do you care if I kill you, flush you down the toilet?" The ladybug just sat there, then fluttered its wings, rising off Nadina's finger then landing on it again. "I think she is telling me she prefers life over death."

Doron was amused by Nadina's newly found philosophy. If only she could go back to Iran and convince the Iranian people to choose life over death. If she did go back, Doron knew the religious theocracy would simply have her killed, with no more concern for her than with a bug in a toilet bowl.

"So young lady, what are you going to do with your newfound friend?"

"I'm going to take her outside and let her fly to visit her ladybug friends, of course!" she said matter-of-factly as she stood, careful not to disturb the little creature on her finger tip.

She went outside the house and shook her friend off her finger. It flew off, carried by a gentle breeze. "Goodbye, dear ladybug. Have a great life!" Nadina called after her. Then she waved to her friend as she flew off. The ladybug was not an it, but a she, Nadina had decided.

Doron followed her outside. "So are you going to go visit all our neighbors and check their toilet bowls for bugs?" he said with a laugh, as he picked up Nadina and swung her in a circle.

"Just ours," replied Nadina emphatically. "Our neighbors can check their own toilet bowls,"

Doron laid her on the front yard grass. Then he joined Nadina, laughing at the thought of everyone examining their toilet bowls.

CHAPTER 40
HURRICANE 2

DORON AND SARON were inside a small private home on the shores of the Caspian. A mass demonstration and protest march in downtown Baghdad was planned in two days. They had become the symbol, the poster child of the opposition movement to the Iranian theocracy. Together they rehearsed the speeches they were to give the next day. Saron spoke the words she had written. "If an Iranian terrorist and an Israeli army lieutenant could find a path to love in the midst of enmity and hate..." She was sitting at the living room table and paused to glance up at Doron, who was closing a window as a rainstorm began. She was still astounded at their relationship. At night she'd awaken thinking it was all a dream, until she turned to see Doron sleeping beside her and she would nestle into his arms for comfort and realize her dream was the reality she was living. Saron put her speech down and went to help Doron close the windows.

The importance of the couple to the opposition movement was not lost on the Iranian government. They had been kept in hiding and moved from one secret hiding place to another.

Early that evening Doron and Saron called Nadina who was now fifteen.

"Nadina. We wanted to let you know we are looking forward to seeing you in a few days." Saron told her daughter. "Is Rosamund taking good care of you?" Rosamund was an 18-year-old niece of Doron who had become friends with Nadina.

"Yes, she is. We are walking through the Baha'i Gardens. It is where I often go when you leave me." Nadina tried to hide her concern but the sadness in her voice gave her away. Nadina and Rosamund were walking to the prayer sanctuary, where visiting Baha'i prayed but was off limits to others. When Nadina was ten she had attended a lecture on the origins of the Baha'i faith.

She learned how the faith had begun with the vision of an Iranian who was killed for his faith and out of his death had arisen the Baha'i faith. A friendly compassionate minister had let her attend a worship session usually restricted to Baha'i. She then started attending their worship sessions on Sundays. Then one day she asked to speak and had shared her life-of-a-terrorist upbringing of near death as a child suicide bomber and how the only place she felt at peace was in the Baha'i gardens and then quietly asked to become a Baha'i. She was told she was too young, that the Baha'i had agreed not to proselytize in Israel and so she could not be allowed into the faith at this time. But since she was Iranian they would allow her to pray with them.

As Nadina spoke to her mother, she and Rosamund walked to the prayer sanctuary inside the golden-domed Shrine of the Bab and were allowed inside.

"Doron and I are preparing for a rally tomorrow and in a few days we will be home. We're safe. Don't worry about us. We miss you. We will be home soon. You listen to Rosamund."

"Yes, mother. Don't worry about me. I am fine." With that she hung up but in the prayer sanctuary she knelt in prayer. "Dear God. Watch over my mother and Doron. I know how many people have been killed in Iran. Don't let anything happen to them there." She and Rosamund stayed for a few more minutes, praying silently. The phone call, however, was intercepted by Iranian intelligence and the location traced to a house on the shores of the Caspian.

"This is what we have been waiting for," Jamal Rahman murmured to himself. He was trained in security hacking in Russia and was now head of security in Iran. He called his superior, Achmed Sebul, head of the Iranian Guard. "They are at 807 Rashad Street in Stabenz, a small house on the Caspian." There was a click as the phone at the other end was summarily hung up. He had done his thankless job.

Achmed called a Lieutenant Amadinajab. "Raoul, take two hundred troops and surround the house and the neighborhood at 807 Rashad Street. This is where our traitor, Saron, and her Israeli spy are in hiding." In the next several hours two hundred troops as requested were sent to surround the house and nearby streets. Slowly they were distributed, 270 degrees around the house all within a few streets. Ninety degrees abutted the Caspian which was its own security barrier. The waves in the Caspian grew in height as the rain blew into a storm.

"In a few hours all our men will be in place. Do you want us to storm the house?" Lieutenant Amadinajab radioed to his superior. At headquarters the information was shared with the supreme leader of Iran, 70-year-old Theos Rezvan. His weathered wrinkled countenance conveyed a man seasoned in world politics, where deceit was just one more method of diplomacy. His head was bowed in thought. "No, don't storm it now. That will make them martyrs. They will come out on their own in a couple days, probably at night. When the eyes of the world cannot see, we will shoot them and dispose of their bodies on the bottom of the Caspian." He looked up smiling, envisioning victory in his game of chess with the West. They had played this game of nuclear negotiation with U.S. presidents from Bush and Obama to now Gomez. Each thought they could negotiate a nuclear disarmament with Iran. Each deluded themselves rather than face war with Iran. If they started a war, they could not win and they would unite all the Arab factions. If they did nothing but negotiate appeasement, someone other than themselves would one day have to deal with a nuclear Iran as Iran inexorably advanced to a nuclear power. This would occur after their term of office. Each would blame the others and each would deny culpability and all would deny responsibility. Once the genie was out of the bottle, Iran would take control, step by slippery step. The supreme ruler rubbed his hands together, as though awaiting a lavish meal.

The Iranian drive to nuclear parity with the West had been slowed down by recent weather-related events but he envisioned it now about to accelerate once again.

Within their safe house, Doron turned to look at Saron and their surroundings. The last time he had been in a house on the Caspian, he'd been Saron's prisoner—now he was her lover, her shared poster child for the Iranian opposition and her soul mate. On the wall were ancient Iranian swords, museum pieces giving the living room an eerie unsettling feeling. The owner of the home promoted peace but collected weapons of war. Just one more anachronism but no more so than his own presence in this Iranian home.

Saron returned to sit at their living room table, wearing glasses, studiously reading over her speech to be given in a few days, making small changes, not knowing if she would be speaking to a few hundred or a few thousand.

Doron glanced at this woman who a few years ago was minutes from killing him, now joined with him, physically, emotionally and spiritually all in a common cause to bring peace to the Middle East. As he looked at her in the early evening there was a flash of light that swept across a window on the other side of the room lasting only a few seconds.

Doron drew back a window shutter but could see nothing. Then he went out the back door, crouching to hide his presence as he went. A block away, he saw a group of Iranian militia. A rain was falling and he could feel the damp humidity rising off the Caspian. As he searched further, he saw several others, about ten in all.

He might have escaped on his own, but instead went back to the house, not knowing that instead of ten there were several hundred soldiers surrounding their home.

"Saron," Doron told her, "we have company. The Iranian militia have found us." She looked up at Doron, putting down her glasses.

"How many are out there?" she asked standing, peering out the window, at the side of the window shade. She could see nothing.

"Five to ten," he replied. "I'm going to relay Israeli Intelligence to get us out if they can. I am sure the Iranian soldiers have the nearby streets under surveillance."

"We could try to escape during the night," Saron suggested.

"Let's see what Israeli Intelligence can do." Using the functional MRI device implanted on his cerebral cortex, Doron relayed a message to Israeli Intelligence, asking for their help.

A few hours later the rain outside grew in intensity, empowering the waves on the Caspian which rose as though it was the shores of an ancient ocean and not a sea. Outside, drenching in the rain and growing storm, Sergeant Jamal called his headquarters. "We have a storm brewing and it is getting harder to watch the house and any people that may leave. What do you want us to do? The soldiers are starting to hide from the storm and so are not watching the house."

Resvan replied. "If any don't keep watch, shoot them as a warning to the others. They cannot escape. If they do, it will be your head that will be cut off! Is that clear?"

In spite of the cooling rain, Jamal was sweating, knowing Resvan would do exactly as he promised.

"Don't do anything tonight," Resvan commanded. "Too easy for something to go wrong in the chaos. Maybe the storm will pass tonight and we can deal with the traitor and the Israeli tomorrow."

Raoul spent the evening watching the house and keeping his soldiers awake and alert, but the storm did not decrease in intensity. By morning the storm had escalated in strength unlike anything he had ever seen. Thunderheads filled a blackening sky. A shelf cloud formed as the storm spawned a hurricane. He called his supreme leader, but the communication failed. As he waited to get through, the wind ripped shingles and then signs until Raoul was afraid his soldiers would run from the scene. He finally got through to headquarters. "I see the weather is getting worse," said Resvan. "Storm the house, kill them and throw them into the Caspian, but I want pictures of them dead as proof!"

"Alright, I'll take care of it myself." Thirty-three-year-old Raoul wanted the glory of killing the infidels and thereby reaping the adulation of his supreme leader. The only life he knew was based on hating the West, its culture, its lack of Muslim values. His sister was studying medicine wanting to help people, while he had learned a culture that taught killing of anything not fundamentally Muslim in value or thought.

Raoul told Bandar, his second in command, to accompany him into the house. It was easy to break in a back door with the noise of the storm camouflaging their own entry noise. They slowly made their way down a narrow hallway to the living room where they could see one person at the dining room table. It was Doron with his back to them.

Raoul whispered to Bandar. "You go in and stab the Israeli. I will watch out for Saron. If she shows up I will shoot her." Bandar was happy to oblige and get the credit for killing a Jew. The only light in the room was a lamp on the dining room table, the pouring rain pummeling the windows and the wind howling through the shrub evergreens along the Caspian shoreline and through the alleys of the seaside town. As Bandar slowly inched forward, the old floor creaked, giving him away.

Doron turned as Bandar lunged at him. Doron turned sideways and leaned out of the knife's path, grabbing Bandar's arm at the wrist, twisting it, until the knife was released. Then Doron turned and gave Bandar a sharp elbow to the head, sending him spread-eagled to the floor.

As Bandar attempted to rise, Doron punched him in his midsection. As Doron readied another punch, he could hear the click of a revolver and turned to see Raoul now approaching. As he turned to face Raoul, Bandar asked to have the honor of killing the Israeli. As he was handing Bandar his gun, Saron entered the room holding one of the Iranian display swords she had taken off the wall. Using the sword, she sliced Raoul's arm off at the elbow and then plunged the sword into his upper abdomen, slicing through his aorta. With a horrible moan, he fell forward.

As Bandar lunged for the gun and grabbed it, Doron struck him with an uppercut, knocking him out. It was then that Doron heard the wind howling outside, more ominous in intensity. The vortex, now a tornado, ripped off the roof and started swirling the contents of the room. Doron grabbed Saron, holding her as the storm hit. The updraft lifted the entwined couple. As they entered a spiral of debris, Doron could make out several hundred soldiers with guns pointed toward the house. He realized that if they'd left by the front door they would have been immediately riddled with bullets.

Outside, two hundred soldiers were still waiting for them to leave the home through a door, rifles and spotlights trained on both front and back. The entwined couple instead exited skyward unobserved, rotating like two Olympic ice skaters as the door and the rest of the house suddenly exploded outward.

The twisting storm took out most of the soldiers, as it spiraled outward from a vortex centered within the destroyed wood frame house. Doron and Saron were carried 100 feet upwards and a similar distance toward the Caspian, crashing down through a wave on the Caspian, shaken but alive. They might still have drowned save for an old sturgeon fisherman who had not believed the weather report of a passing storm but was now racing for the beach.

As the two rescued passengers huddled in towels, Doron managed to contact Israeli Intelligence. "Tsvi. Thanks for creating the storm again. You saved two lives this time! But why no helicopter? We almost drowned in the Caspian!"

Tsvi listened, but was momentarily speechless.

"Tsvi, are you there?"

"Yes, we are here."

"Why don't you answer me!"

"Because we never got any message from you! We had been waiting, but nothing was received. We did not create the storm! I'm sorry but we did nothing to save you. We need weeks to convert a storm into a tornado. Even if we'd gotten a message, there would not have been time to do anything. I am sorry but we're not the heroes!"

As Tsvi spoke, there were rolls of thunder and lightning over the Caspian as shimmering from water to sky and from cloud to cloud. Doron and Saron stared heavenward, grateful to be alive. Within half an hour, they made it to shore where a car picked them up and took them to yet another private home further inland, far from the storm. Having barely survived the Iranian plans to kill them, their commitment to attend the opposition rally in one month was now an even greater, albeit harrowing, necessity.

CHAPTER 41
ISRAEL WEATHER CONTROL COMPANIES JOIN THE NASDAQ

MEETING TECHNION ISRAEL INSTITUTE OF TECHNOLOGY. HAIFA, ISRAEL.

AT THE MEETING were Tsavi Rosenberg, vice chairman of Israeli Intelligence, Yuri Goldberg, head of Israeli Intelligence and the heads of three Israeli weather control technology companies, Anemoi, Harpyiae and Chaos. In addition, there were several Iranians, the heads of the Iranian resistance movement. Saron and Doron were also in attendance.

Myrani Telmon, head of the Iranian resistance movement spoke. "We are planning a major

resistance rally in a month. Due to recent events, the hurricane and storm that freed Doron and Saron, the chemical cloud that formed in Syria and the Israeli response in saving the lives of many Palestinians, our support in Iran has never been greater. This has also caused the autocracy to try even harder to quash our movement. However, some of the military has even joined our ranks."

"And how have you managed that?" asked Rosenberg, vice chairman of Israeli Intelligence.

Telmon replied, "Some believe that God is supporting us, as they see these natural events saving the lives of Doron and Saron. Based on their religious beliefs, these people want to be on God's side. There are others that feel they are tired of endless war, of the suffering of the Iranian people, the lack of jobs, the lack of food, the lousy economy, inflation causing ever-increasing prices of petrol and basic commodities, including food. But this has only convinced about 10% of the military to join our side. We need to find a way to raise this support, so that when we have our major rally in a month, they are willing to let the rally go on without just shutting us down,"

Rofsan Jami, associate head of the resistance movement, nodded. "We need to find a powerful method to convince many of the military to join our ranks?"

Saron spoke, "I thought that was the purpose of the major planned resistance rally next month?"

Jami nodded. "Yes, it is, but first we need to get enough support on the part of the military, that the hardliners are stopped dead!"

Chaim Rabinowitz, the CEO of Chaos Technology hesitated. "Maybe it is time for the incubator babies to go public."

"What do you mean?" said Goldberg, head of Israeli Intelligence.

Rabinowitz replied, "There are over twenty weather control technology companies that have been quietly doing research and advancing their ability to affect storms. If you include drone-related companies and those working in the A.I., artificial intelligence field, it's closer to fifty. By our actions, saving Doron in the storm several years ago, the movement of the chemical cloud saving many lives, and our own internal research, our future potential may dwarf that of the internet companies that took the NASDAQ by storm, pardon the pun, in the 1980s. Many believe one of our companies used their technology to save Saron and Doron in the recent storm. We don't have to tell them otherwise. Many of those internet start-ups at the time, had no income, yet their stocks went from ten to over one hundred dollars in one day. A thousand percent returns for companies with no income! Some did eventually go bankrupt, but some have returned many thousands of percent over the ensuing fifty years. If we offered investment in our companies to members of the Iranian military we could make many of them millionaires in short order when our companies join the NASDAQ. That might entice them to join the

Iranian resistance movement." He looked up at his audience. They were uniformly startled by his idea.

Telmon said, "It sounds a little crazy, maybe even a little outrageous, maybe even impossible, but that's why the more I think about it, the more I like it. However, we would need to show the military we offer this to, that we are not just offering them worthless paper. How will we convince them that these companies will have skyrocketing stock prices?"

Chaim Rabinowitz, the CEO of Chaos technology spoke up. "It is not public knowledge, but we have been in private conversations with the city of New Orleans, to use our technology to protect the city from future storms such as Katrina. For monster storms of that size, our technology is not currently powerful enough, but in the next ten years maybe it will be. The city of New Orleans has offered us millions of dollars to provide whatever help we can, even now and with increasing payments as our technology is implemented and achieves the ultimate aim of protecting New Orleans from another Katrina. If this information were leaked out prior to a listing on the NASDAQ, our ten dollar initial offering price might rival the movement of the early internet companies. Of course, in addition to the weather control companies, there are the drone companies, the artificial intelligence companies and computer modeling companies that will likely see similar spikes in their stock prices. The stock market as you know is anticipatory. If it recognizes a new disruptive technology of seemingly unlimited potential, it will skyrocket whatever company is suspected of being a long term winner."

A few days later Goldman Sachs was contacted and an agreement made to let them handle the initial IPOs of several Israeli companies that would have a joint listing on the Israeli exchange and on the NASDAQ. Twenty companies qualified for listing in the next six months. Chaos, Climatron and Harpyiae were chosen to start the IPO NASDAQ calendar, with the remainder scheduled as dependent on the market reception of these three, so-called trial balloons.

There was both a healthy mix of skepticism and emotional exuberance when the date of the IPO was announced. There were interviews with the CEOs of all three companies on CNN, FOX Business, MSNBC, Bloomberg, Barrons Roundtable and Mornings With Maria Hines. Mary Hines interviewed Susan Grunfeld, the CEO of Harpyiae. "I am here today with Susan Grunfeld, the CEO of Harpyiae, one of three young Israeli weather technology companies going public in two weeks with joint listings on the Israeli and NASDAQ exchanges."

"Congratulations, Susan. Must be an exciting time for you?"

"Very exciting to say the least."

"What does the name of the company stand for?"

"Harpyiae is the Greek god of the whirlwinds."

"And why did you choose that name?"

"Our technology attempts to control the wind speed inside a storm."

"'Attempts' sounds equivocal. To what extent can you actually do this?"

"That depends on the size of the storm. Just the wind energy generated in a typical mature hurricane can generate energy equivalent to half the total electrical generating capacity on the planet! That doesn't take into account the energy generated through the formation of clouds and rain. During the life cycle of a typical hurricane, not one equivalent to Katrina, a hurricane can expend as much energy as 10,000 nuclear bombs!"

"So how can you expect to affect such a large energetic storm?"

"We don't wait for it to get to its full size. We affect it earlier in its development. We take up to 10,000 measurements per minute of wind speed and direction, temperature, turbulence, wind shear and instabilities in these parameters."

"What do you do with this information?"

"We have proprietary computer programs that analyze this data using artificial intelligence techniques that determine in real time the most effective means of either dismantling the storm, changing its path or preventing its development of say a shelf cloud into a tornado."

"And could you turn a storm into a tornado if you chose to?"

"The same technology could be used for that purpose if we chose to. But that is not the main direction of our research. We prefer to use our technology to control a storm not create one."

"So how do you collect this information? Does someone have to fly into the storm?"

"No. We use drones."

"One drone gets you all this information?"

"No, 10,000 drones. Microdrones capable of withstanding 300 mile per hour winds, all networked together to function like one giant drone, together capable of affecting local wind speed, temperature, pressure and wind shear."

"I believe you have brought a video, showing the capability of your company's technology in affecting a small storm. Let's watch it now." A video portrayed a small storm hitting St. Martin, destroying many homes. Then a second video was played where a storm similar in size developed. Thousands of drones flew into the storm—some flashing, some glowing, interacting in some concerted unknown manner. Before the storm enlarged to a destructive size, it veered from the coast of St. Martin, harmlessly dispelling its power over open ocean."

"And your company's technology accomplished this?"

"This was a joint accomplishment of several Israeli weather control technology companies working together."

"I suspect there could be considerable military uses of such technology. What is your opinion of that?"

"All technology has potential military applications. Weather control technology has been evaluated, and is still being assessed by your own military as well as ours."

"Have they had any discussions with you?"

"We are not at liberty to divulge any ongoing projects or potential clients."

"Has the city of New Orleans been in contact with you? Could you prevent another Katrina?"

"Again, we are not at liberty to discuss any ongoing potential clients. But if you're asking, could we prevent another hurricane of that approximate size, that would be our ultimate goal. We could never stop a Katrina once fully formed. That was never our vision, never an expectation. We want to dispel, divert or otherwise control large storms in their infancy, when they are 'baby' Katrinas, if you will, before they have a chance to grow into a monster storm."

"And how do you determine when a small storm needs to be controlled? When it might otherwise develop into a Katrina?"

"Artificial intelligence proprietary software."

The price targets of these companies was widely debated by all the financial analysts on TV, newspapers and financial institutions. There were those that said, for many of the weather control companies, the price target should be zero since they were not profitable, their technology unproven and the likelihood of success infinitesimally small. Other stock market gurus and talking heads, said the winners providing the most disruptive technology since the birth of the internet could rival the stock charts of Apple and Amazon but only if their technology proved successful. Others likened these technology companies to the biotechnology

sector. Both had many companies that started with no earnings, only a few patents and a visionary dream. The biotechnology sector had produced many thousand percent gainers and some major disappointments as well. New newsletters were created to take advantage of the interest, "The Weather Control Digest" and "Tornado Stocks to Rocket Your Portfolio." Analysts from Merrill Lynch held a conference on their stock choices. All three of the initial weather control technology IPOs were oversubscribed by 100%. A few days before the

IPO of the first three Israeli companies opened on the NASDAQ, there was a rumor that the president of Chaos Technology had met with the mayor of New Orleans and that the president of Harpyiae had met with several governors of states along tornado alley in the Midwest. This was like throwing matchsticks into a pile of firecrackers.

Chaim Rabinowitz, the 28-year-old president of Chaos Technology, rang the bell for the NASDAQ the day his company went public. The stock, with no current earnings, went from an opening price of 10, briefly hitting 200 at 10:00 a.m. before settling at 186 at 4:00 p.m. All the administrative heads in the company were instant millionaires and a few like Rabinowitz were instant billionaires! Time Magazine put his picture, along with Ruven Rosenberg, the Chaos Technology officer on the cover, with the caption, "Ruven Rosenberg: the kid with a stutter becomes a billionaire!" All of a sudden stuttering was in. Maybe that was somehow, in some inexplicable way, a key to his talent, to his technological brilliance! Stutterers were courted, given preference in hiring by technology companies and in other unexpected ways revered.

Harpyiae's 10 dollar stock price, opened at 46, and skyrocketed to a high of 146, before closing at 89, a 790% gain on its first trading day. Anemoi, which had had little publicity in the days preceding its IPO, saw its stock price of 10 dollars only go to 25 till 3:00 p.m., when a rumor circulated, that their president had traveled to St. Martin in the Caribbean a few months earlier.

The stock then went from 25 to 125 in 15 minutes, before closing at 121 at the 4:00 p.m. close of trading!

That evening, every newscast covered the remarkable first day of the Israeli weather control technology IPOs. How many others were there? How could one get shares at the IPO price before they skyrocket?" was this for real or a fad that would fade. Debates were held on the delusion, the mania of crowds. The Dutch tulip mania and bubble occurred in Holland in the 1600s when the value of a single rare tulip sold for six times the average person's salary! Was this similar greed and speculation or was it the next set of FANG stocks! No one knew, but there was a tremendous fear of missing out on the most disruptive technology anyone had witnessed in years, combining science, technology, climate change and artificial intelligence into one explosive growth trajectory!

As the stock holders in the U.S. and Israel celebrated their newfound wealth, there was also a small group of stockholders celebrating in, of all countries, Iran! Three Iranian generals had privately been given stock in the Israeli IPOs and were now all millionaires. They were now new supporters of the Iranian Resistance Movement. One was seen driving a Tesla around the streets of Teheran, another was seen driving a Porsche. Six other generals and military officers, the friends of the original three were now also interested in participating in the stock market bonanza and were more than willing to throw their allegiance behind the resistance movement in return for a chance at real wealth.

Amidst the jubilation among the stockholders of the weather control companies, there were a few stock analysts expressing a warning that the amazing rally was overdone. That many of the companies were trading at PE values in the thousands, that some of the companies had no earnings at all, and might never have any! And of course, there were those picking out the most likely short candidates. Stocks that might fall 50-90% when reality again set in, and of course the risk or inevitability, as the shorts maintained, that some would ultimately go bankrupt!

It was amidst this tug of war between those expounding on a "limitless" future and those warning of a major correction that a storm, named Matilda, rose in the Caribbean heading toward Cuba and southern Florida. A meteorologist named Henrietta James on CNN reviewed the local weather situation in southern Florida and New Orleans. "It is now mid-August, close to a twenty-five year anniversary of the original devastating Katrina. Katrina you may not realize rose unspectacularly on August 23, 2005 as a minor tropical depression, according to NOAA records, over the Bahamas."

On the large meteorologic display screen behind, the development of Katrina was displayed. Using a laser pointer, James showed the varied intensities of Katrina during its development. "Katrina was only a category one storm when it passed by the Keys. Wind shear at the time in the Gulf of Mexico was very low, and the temperature very high that August time period, resulting in a very rapid intensifying cycle, turning Katrina in one week from a Category one to a Category five storm on the Saffir Simpson scale. Had Katrina made landfall as a category five storm, it would have wiped out coastal Louisiana, including New Orleans far beyond the 108 billion dollars in damages it produced when it made landfall as 'simply' a Category three storm! Something to keep in mind! As a Category three it still had sustained winds as high as 120 miles per hour. When Katrina passed over southern Florida on August 25th, it again lost energy and was only a Category one hurricane. During this first landfall it further weakened and was reclassified as a tropical storm, not even a hurricane at all! But once over water again it stalled beneath an upper level anticyclone, rapidly gaining strength as it transformed from a tropical storm to a major Category five hurricane with maximum sustained wind speeds of 175 miles per hour! It was then that the storm turned north toward the Louisiana coast, making landfall on August 29th as a Category three storm now with sustained winds of 120 miles per hour.

"Matilda, now in the Caribbean as a tropical depression does not seem especially dangerous. But recognizing that in five days Katrina went from a tropical depression to a Category five storm, no one is ignoring Matilda. Unfortunately, our weather modeling cannot predict what intensity Matilda will have when it makes landfall and where exactly that landfall will be!"

Not initially reported, when Matilda passed through the Caribbean, skirted by St. Martin and narrowly missed Cuba, there were three Black Hawk helicopters flown by Israeli-trained pilots and owned by Israeli weather control companies. They were thought to be transporting patients from Miami International Airport but they headed directly into the oncoming developing storm. During the night of August 25th, at 11:00 p.m., the three copters released a payload of drones that headed into the heart of Matilda. The copters were owned by Chaos, Harpyaie and Anemoi, all jointly hired by the city of New Orleans. The drones released had a surface coating and electronic components that made them invisible to normal radar or visual detection. As with Katrina, the Matilda storm stalled in the warm waters of the Gulf of Mexico where there was a growing risk it would gain strength and imperil New Orleans. The drones were detectable by Israeli technology. On large meteorological screens at one of their shared private Miami offices, the technology officers of the three Israeli companies monitored the 10,000 drones, computer-directed by artificial intelligence software in real time, as they flew, like one networked interconnected flying bird, given the moniker, a pterodactyl, by one research scientist, because of the large wing span of the networked drones, reminiscent of the prehistoric winged creature. The pterodactyl of drones flew unafraid and unemotionally into the tropical depression known as Matilda. All the emotions were, however, on full display by the Israeli engineers and computer scientists watching the drones, monitoring the slowly-changing physical parameters being affected at the margin and within the eye of the storm.

In the late afternoon, at 3:45 p.m. right before market close, the meteorologic reports from NOAA's Miami office warned that Matilda had the capability of becoming a major storm. With that news, the NASDAQ exchange where the Israeli stocks were listed, took a sizable swoon, closing down 25% and the Israeli stocks down 60% from their recent highs, anticipating the weather control technology would not work, and believing the Israeli technology was not, at least initially, having a major impact on the storm. In addition, the meteorologic reports from NOAA's Miami office warned that Matilda could also spawn tornado activity. For a few hours the situation looked grim as

Matilda became a Category 1 storm and did spawn a tornado from a Matilda-originating shelf cloud. The enhanced Fujitsu scale for tornados became operational on February 1, 2007. It assigns a tornado 'rating' based on estimated wind speed and related damage. The tornado spawned by Matilda had a wind speed of 111 mph giving it an EF rating of 2. High enough to do serious damage and complicating the overall Matilda storm picture.

On Fox Business, Mary Strayhorn displayed the stock market futures alongside meteorological reports on Matilda and the stock prices of several of the Israeli weather control companies. The slightest change in the meteorological reports caused exaggerated changes in the stock prices of the Israeli companies and the NASDAQ market as a whole. Strayhorn asked a popular commentator from the Street.com, Jim Mayfield, for his opinion. "All I can say for sure," he replied, "is that in the morning, depending on how things play out, there will be some people very wealthy, maybe new millionaires or even billionaires and some people, very much poorer or bankrupt. Right now it's a crapshoot. Unless you are either very smart or very lucky, I wouldn't play this game!"

When pressed as to which side to bet on, Mayfield replied. "Figure out what the majority believes and take the bet against the majority. Somehow the market tends to prove the majority wrong. It inevitably tries to screw the majority opinion. That opinion appears to be a moving target, but if I took any position, which I am not, I would take the contrarian position against whatever the majority propose will happen."

In the evening, the Category 1 storm intensified into a Category 2 storm. The network of drones, over the ensuing five hours gradually managed to modify local temperature, wind speed, pressure and wind shear in a concerted fashion, as darkness closed in on southern Miami and New Orleans. An evacuation of New Orleans, coastal Louisiana and the west coast of Florida was ordered but with most residents not adhering to the orders. All bets were off on exactly where and when Matilda was going to make landfall and as what category of storm.

Overnight on Bloomberg and the Wall Street Journal Report there were predictions in every direction imaginable, but with the majority expecting the weather control stocks to burst like every other stock market bubble. When the markets did open at 9:30 a.m., to the surprise of the majority, Matilda had reverted to just a tropical depression. The small tornado that had spun off when Matilda was a Category 1 storm, had been veered back into the gulf. At 3:00 a.m., 50 miles south of Cuba, there were reports of a series of small explosions like fireworks going off, at the base and eye wall of the tornado, captured on a video by NOAA's Miami office and confirmed from a weather station in Cuba. In the morning it became clear on the NASDAQ exchange that Matilda had faded into a tropical depression and that New Orleans had presumably been protected by these Israeli weather control companies. Five were now given the nickname CHAZE for Chaos, Harpiaie, Anemoi, Zephyrus and Eos. The anticipated flooding was mild. Everyone now watched the reaction to stocks of the Israeli technology companies. Not only did they regain the 60% lost the previous day, but they went further into uncharted territory to new all time highs, 40% higher than their previous high values, all opening with gains of 100% from the previous day's close.

The technology officers from three of the CHAZE companies, Chaos, Harpyaie and Anemoi were asked to appear on all the business TV networks. On Fox Business, Maria Hines interviewed the three technology officers.

"Congratulations on your success in veering Matilda away from coastal Florida and in particular New Orleans and the rest of Louisiana. How does it feel to know you have saved lives and at the same time made everyone who owns your stock, including yourselves quite wealthy?"

Louise Snyder, technology office from Anemoi, spoke for the

group. "We are humbled at the opportunity to help save lives; that is our major driving influence."

"But I am sure it doesn't hurt to become multimillionaires or billionaires in the process."

The three technology officers all laughed. Tom Einhorn, the technology officer from Harpyiae, said, "I guess I can afford a house now in Israel but maybe not a large property in Malibu!" They all laughed again, with Maria Hines joining them.

"So how the hell, excuse my French, did you pull it off?"

Stanley Zimmerman, technology officer from Chaos spoke. "As we stated in our last interview, we try to affect a storm before it becomes too large to control. We model weather depressions for the likelihood of developing into a major storm."

"And how is that done?"

Petite twenty-five-year-old Louise spoke. "We use computer modeling techniques and artificial technology to forecast in real time any changes that can intensify a storm, using drone-generated physical parameters within the eye of the storm."

"And that was done in the case of Matilda?"

"Yes," Louise replied.

"And what if you had done nothing. What would have happened to Matilda?"

Einhorn, the technology officer from Harpyiae, said, "I don't want to overstate this, but we believe Matilda had the potential to become a Category five storm, possibly larger than Katrina, which only temporarily was a Category five but made landfall as a Category three."

Maria spoke. "Do you have any idea how many cities on our coast are at risk for catastrophic storms?"

Louise said, "An average storm season in the U.S. produces about twelve named storms, including six hurricanes of which three become Category three storms or above, with top wind speeds of over 111 mph. NOAA predicts an increase in storms due to a combination of global warming and cyclical changes in weather patterns. It is believed that warmer than normal sea surface temperatures off the coast of Africa and in the Caribbean will provide more fuel for tropical cyclone formation and intensification."

"Sounds like your business will only grow in the years ahead. I have heard rumors that a number of U.S. companies have bought stakes in your start-up companies. Companies like Intel, Facebook, Google, Apple and IBM? Is there any truth to these rumors?"

Einhorn said, "All of the companies you mentioned have technology offices in Israel and work with many Israeli companies. We have had preliminary discussions with them that we are not at liberty to discuss, but have been grateful for their support."

"And what do you wish for the future?" Strayhorn asked.

Louise said, "We would like to think our Israeli companies can help save lives in many other countries around the world. This helping to save lives may direct humanity away from tribal animosities lingering from the Middle Ages. And maybe humanity will search for peace instead of dwelling on these age old hatreds. I'd like to see all of humanity joined together. We are all in this brief thing called life, living out short lives. Together we should join hands and reach for the stars and not Armageddon. Our current path could lead to an end to life on earth, to the last human, to even a last butterfly, for the very final time fluttering its translucent gossamer wings in the wind, trying courageously to fly to a flower through the gentlest of late summer breezes. I have my own vision that once upon a time helped create Anemoi, our weather control company. But I also have a longer term vision, not of Armageddon, but of a more hopeful future for humanity, a vision afar into the future. Maybe a thousand years from now, after we terraform a distant planet light years from earth, covered with flowers brought from earth, we will bring hibernating cocoons, lying dormant in their chrysalis, containing the larval stage of future butterflies, that on the distant planet are released into a new gentle wind, allowing this delicate species to join us on our journey to the stars

A young man once wrote, 'The last, the very last, So richly, brightly dazzlingly yellow. Perhaps if the sun's tears would sing against a white stone...'

"Would we really want there to be a last butterfly?"

"Who wrote those beautiful words?" Maria asked.

"Pavel Friedman in 1942 from Terezin Concentration Camp where he was imprisoned and died."

"His words are beautiful and that is quite a vision you have. Quite a hopeful vision, I might add. Let us hope one day humankind takes the path fulfilling your vision. I can see where the creativity came from to envision all your weather control companies. All most remarkable. Thank you all for joining me, and again congratulations on your remarkable accomplishments regarding Matilda."

CHAPTER 42
THE SPIDER WOMAN
WEAVES A WEB

LI JUNG CHANG, the North Korean president, had observed the resistance movement growing in Iran through Korean observers, members of the Korean diplomatic core, stationed in Iran. She was also aware of Israeli weather control technology exploding onto the NASDAQ and dreamed of potential military and civilian implications of such technology. Except she had none of it. Chang was also aware of the growing strength of the opposition party movement in Iran. This led Chang to certain decisions, formulating her own plan, weaving her own inimitable intricate web to take advantage of the Middle East chaos.

Li Jung Chang called Rachman Solidar, finalizing their agreement. North Korean nuclear technology for Iranian oil and U.S. donated dollars. Iranian millions, courtesy of the U.S., were now transferred to North Korea through a Swiss intermediary and additional millions were also transferred to Chang's personal Swiss bank account. Only a worthless smattering of North Korean nuclear technology was however transferred to Iran, with only promises of more to come.

A few weeks later, Chang met with Gamal Raksan, a member of the Saudi Royal Family, Abdul Salam, a member of the Iranian resistance movement and Avrahim Rosenberg, an Israeli secret agent and member of the Israeli Secret Service. The meeting was in North Korea. Monies were exchanged from Saudi Arabia and Jordan again to Chang's personal bank account which appeared to be ballooning. Chang now also had insisted on and obtained an investment in several future Israeli start-up Weather Control Technology IPOs. Chang told the visiting contingent, "With our agreement, I will promise not to provide Iran with any of our nuclear technology for a ten-year period. We can renew our agreement under new financial terms at the ten year anniversary of our agreement." Now Chang had financial agreements with Iran to provide them with nuclear technology and agreements with Saudi Arabia, Jordan, the Iranian resistance and Israel not to do so. Her moniker, the spider woman, appeared well earned.

CHAPTER 43
IRANIAN RESISTANCE RALLY

THERE WERE OVER ten thousand people in attendance at the opposition rally, "Rally for World Peace," as it was named, spread across a 50-acre field in a country suburb of Teheran. Certainly most people were from Iran, but there were young and some not-so-young that had come from all corners of the earth. There was a contingent of black ministers from the southern U.S. There were Arabs from other countries, such as Jordan, Saudi Arabia and Kuwait, a diverse assortment of people young and old from European countries, such as France and Germany. Even a few from China, Japan and Singapore. There was however, only one Israeli, Doron, and he stood onstage with Saron.

Presidential Palace, Teheran, Iran. The Iranian generals were expecting orders from their supreme leader on how to deal with the resistance rally now in progress. They had previously met, planning to disrupt the rally and kill the leaders of the rally should it actually occur. The Russians had warned them not to do this as it would cause a major backlash at the U.N. and hinder Russian attempts at supplying Europe with oil and gas. Solidar had told the generals, "Lying in the name of Iranian interests is not a lie but a duty. It is our policy, as I have told you before. The Americans accepted our lies about our nuclear program and the Russians will accept our lies about our plans for the opposition rally. They have no choice."

The Iranian generals were waiting for a command from the supreme leader before taking any action. Seven of the thirteen were now supporters of the resistance movement brought into the fold by a combination of debate and desire for a new destiny for Iran, religious belief that it was God's will, a divine wind blowing above the desert sands, and for some the desire for almost instant wealth and freedom from poverty. For a few it was the heady taste of freedom from autocratic control. Yet all expected new orders from the supreme leader. When there were none, some of the generals went into the supreme leader's palace home seeking him out. They found him outside in a courtyard adjoining his bedroom. At first they thought he was asleep in a lounge chair, but when he could not be stirred they felt his pulse and there was none. Rachman Solidar, the Iranian supreme leader, was dead. There was no sign of injury, clearly no bullet had killed him, no penetrating knife injury. He was known to be hypertensive and to have heart disease but had refused stenting, believing Allah would protect him. Had it been a fatal heart attack or arrythmia? A forensic autopsy might take weeks. One of the forensic pathologists, noted faint red lipstick on the supreme leader's cheek, but did not put it in his report for fear of having this type of remark associated with the supreme leader and his name, so this information was not included in the autopsy. The general, therefore, had no orders from the supreme leader. Those already supporting the resistance movement made up their own orders, which were to let the rally proceed, saying they did not want to anger the Russians or cause a worldwide backlash or further rioting by their populace. And so the rally proceeded without military intervention.

The vast numbers in the rally would have made it difficult for the Iranian theocracy to intercede in any event with a mass killing that would have been necessary to stop it and then the resultant world condemnation. So the generals acceded to the Russians' warning not to interfere with the massive rally. A large stage had been set up for the speakers and musicians. It was more reminiscent of a scene at

Woodstock than any rally previously held in Iran. The scent of pot did nothing to counter the comparison. The emcee for the evening was a philosophy teacher at Teheran University, Jamal Isvan, a Nobel laureate, that prize probably accounted for his longevity.

Isvan said, "Our first speaker is 20-year-old Ahman Banishan, a political science student from Teheran University." He then gave Banishan a brief introduction and handed him the microphone. Banishan looked out at the crowd spread over many acres, viewing faces as far as his eyes could see. Speakers and TV screens were set up within the audience because of the distance to the stage for those in the crowd that could barely see the stage.

"We are gathered here to express to our government in Teheran and to the world at large, our desire for peace. We believe the final destiny of Iran is to be a sacred home of and for peace. Peace with Israel and peace with our Arab neighbors. The events of the last few years, countless deaths, destruction of towns and cities, here and in Lebanon, Libya and Syria have shown us that more killing in the name of God, in the name of Iran only leads to more deaths and a hopeless future for us and our children."

He left the stage and several musicians came on stage, along with a group of black Christian ministers from South Carolina. Arm in arm, the mixed group of Southern Black ministers and Muslims together began the spiritual black civil rights chant, "We shall overcome some day...." Slowly people in the audience picked up the chant, holding hands with their neighbors, a tribute to the black civil rights movement in the United States, now taken up in a new movement for peace in the Middle East.

Other musicians played songs of peace and worship. A young Iranian boy sang: "Let there be peace on earth, the peace that was meant to be. With God as our father, brothers all are we...."

Jamal Isvan took the stage again and spoke to the audience. "A movement has begun in Iran, begun quietly, slowly, furthered by social media, by the internet, by Facebook and Twitter, by Google and Apple and cellular networks too diverse and now too widespread to disrupt and impede."

Doron and Saron were invited onto the stage to a standing ovation from the crowd. A young girl of about ten was in front of the stage, holding a bouquet of flowers, planning to come up the stage stairs and give them as a gift to Saron. Saron saw the girl and her mother, with the mother, talking to the girl before she went onstage. Her mother seemed very nervous and then Saron turned to a nearby security guard. "Don't let her on the stage, pointing to the girl. I think she's being used as a suicide bomber. Her mother acts like I did when I said goodbye to Nadina and put her on a plane to blow it up."

Security immediately stopped the girl, detected the metal signature of a bomb, cutting one of the leads before it could be detonated, saving the girl's life, everyone onstage, and probably several thousand people at the front of the opposition rally. The mother and child were driven away for questioning. Two other bombs were detected by bomb-sniffing German Shepherds on the grounds of the rally and dismantled. The rally continued as though nothing untoward had happened.

Saron spoke with Doron at her side. "Two days ago, Doron and I were in a small house on the shores of the Caspian, surrounded by Iranian militia ready to kill us. That we have survived to be here is only by the grace of God, a God that wants our message heard by the theocracy in power and by the world at large." Saron stopped to a thunderous standing ovation, spreading out from the front of the audience in a wave to as far as one could see. Saron was dressed in traditional Muslim garb, with a jet black niquab hiding all but her green eyes and her raised reddish black eyebrows as she looked throughout the vast crowd.

Saron continued with words she had thought of inside the small house on the Caspian a few weeks before. "If an Iranian terrorist and an Israeli army lieutenant could find a path to love in the midst of enmity and hate, maybe it is time for two countries and their warring citizens to do the same. It is time to stop giving out candy when an Israeli child is killed. Maybe it is also time to discard the theologic ethics of the 12th century, where hatred and death are honored, for a new ethic, taught to me by my daughter, Nadina, and developed by a gentle elderly man, with a fluffy elegant mustache, Albert Schweitzer, in 1915, while living in Lambarene in Gabon Africa, in a word: 'reverence for life.' Let us teach our children the value of all life, of their lives, of the lives of our neighbors and our neighbors' children." Again the crowd rose to cheer. Saron stopped until the crowd settled and sat down.

Saron then continued. "Imagine a world where our children have a chance to be children, without guns and bombs strapped to their bodies. Where life is cherished and not suicide bombings. Where the character of a man or woman is more important than their religion. Imagine a world where people choose not to kill, choose not to die for extreme religious beliefs. Imagine all the people in the world living in peace. Imagine a new ethos for the world, creating a world at peace."

Jamal Isvan retook the stage. "Thank you, Saron." He gave Saron a heartfelt hug. He then turned to the audience. "As the sun starts to set and we approach dusk, please take a candle from the people now passing them out." These were lit as two pianos were brought out and the music behind the words of Saron were played on the two pianos and on the large screen behind Saron a video of John Lennon was displayed, with a video of Lennon singing the words of his song, "Imagine." The song instantly became a symbolic theme song of the opposition movement. Isvan went on. "The words were composed by John Lennon one morning in early 1971, on a Steinway piano, in a bedroom at his Tittenhurst Park estate in Ascot, Berkshire, England." With the shimmering candlelight as a backdrop, the words and accompanying video of John Lennon singing his song, "Imagine," rang out.

This song was then followed by a video displayed on the large screen of a ten-year-old girl, Jackie Evancho with an angelic voice singing Pie Jesu. Isvan explained the background of the song. "The song is part of Andrew Lloyd Weber's Requiem, written as a response to the story of a Cambodian boy forced to murder his mutilated sister or be executed himself. A second event inspiring his writing was the death of a journalist who had interviewed Weber weeks before being killed in Northern Ireland as a result of the IRA conflicts. The requiem Mass in the Catholic religion honors the deceased."

As Pie Jesu was sung, pictures were portrayed on a giant screen. Isvan turned to his largely Muslim audience. "We were taught in our history classes that there was no Holocaust, no imprisonment of millions of Jews, but if we are to ever create peace with our neighbor, Israel, we should try to understand their history, their true history, not the revisionist history we have been taught. Isolated societies can deny the truth, create their own 'truth.' But today with all manner of social media, truth is like water seeping into a river valley. Water will find a way. And people will ultimately, in the end, prefer truth over lies and deceit. A closed society can imprison those who disagree, can kill those hidden away in prisons, those who seek an open society where open discourse and truth has a chance to flower. Is Darth Vader so compelling that the Dark Side should win over a just truthful society? Do people, when given a chance, truly prefer suicidal death for their children over life? Lies over truth? War over peace? So let us begin by showing some of the history left out of our textbooks. The pictures now being displayed were drawings from Terezin Concentration Camp from 1942-1944. Of 15,000 children interned in the concentration camp at Terezin, only 100 survived. And this is one of the poems penned in Terezin by one of these children, Pavel Friedmann." By the evening's full moon, by the light of hundreds of shimmering candles, Isvan recited to his largely Muslim audience, the words of Pavel Friedmann written in Terezin Concentration Camp many years before.

"THE BUTTERFLY
The last, the very last.
So richly, brightly, dazzlingly yellow
Perhaps if the sun's tears would sing
against a white stone.."

Surrounding the words were yellow butterflies flying around Pavel's words, the ground in the video covered with the dandelions in Pavel's poem. Isvan went on. "Pavel Friedmann died in Auschwitz September 29, 1944 at the age of 23."

Pie Jesu was sung and then a young gifted teenager sang "Angel," as pictures of scenes from bombings in Lebanon and Syria were displayed, as well as individual children lying among the rubble, heads covered with bandages. Isvan continued in a more subdued reverential tone. "This song, *Angel,* written by Sarah McLachlan, was initially intended as a description of drug addiction and the 'angel' drugs taken by these addicts, but we have a different interpretation of the lyrics. The angel described in the words, we interpret to be many angels whose arms now envelop the dead from countless wars and atrocities. These people have been silenced, but through us we give them a voice. We are their voice." The angelic voice of the young teenager continued the song.....

"You're in the arms of the angel(s)

May you find some comfort here..."

There was the fragrant scent of pot and hashish in the air, with all manner of water pipes and rolled cigarettes. There was also something else wafting skyward toward heaven, embodied in the dreams and prayers of the throng below, emanating from the hearts and souls of the people present, blossoming into a new growing hope for peace.

A TV special on the opposition rally played in many diverse countries in the ensuing weeks, with a telecast of the rally and commentary from multiple news media. In Iran it was banned on public television but could still be seen on YouTube. As Bill O'Malley on Fox News stated, "Something remarkable is certainly brewing in the Middle East, centered in Iran of all places, unexpected, unbelievable, perhaps miraculous is the general consensus. And I would have to agree with that consensus. We will follow and share these events with you as this new Arab spring unfolds."

CHAPTER 44
SCHEHERAZADE

ONE EVENING, AFTER a long discussion between Saron, Nadina and Doron, Saron slept in bed alongside her daughter, holding her through the night, thinking and dreaming. The next evening after Nadina fell asleep, Saron went to Doron's bedroom. As she entered, Doron grabbed for his Beretta pistol, which he always kept by his bed. The moon gave enough light for Doron to observe the red sable haired, tattooed woman climb into his bed, as he turned slowly toward her, still lying on his back.

Saron was on her knees lying over him. Saron without saying a word, quietly unbuttoned Doron's shirt. Then she pulled off her blouse exposing full breasts and sleek body. Saron bent down to kiss Doron. He tried to turn away, but she cupped his head in her arms and kissed him gently on the lips. A kiss he did not return. Then she kissed his cheeks and nose and forehead, working her way down his body. When she returned to his mouth, he resisted less and less.

Like Scheherazade the Persian Queen, Saron took her, once again, captive Israeli on a different journey than the night she danced around him with a knife at his ribs. This night was to be an amorous adventure. Saron had been won over by the love Doron held for Nadina. Saron had seen how Doron treated her daughter, how he had saved her life on multiple occasions and now she had personally witnessed his bravery and compassion, on multiple occasions, with her own eyes.

Sometime during the night the Beretta fell to the floor and clothing was shed. Later that evening, Doron's dormant feelings and longings awakened in ways he had neither wanted nor ever again expected. Two bodies joined, rolling together, legs entwined, Iranian and Israeli, unexpected, as inconceivable as anything imaginable on God's earth. Two sworn enemies bridging an endless war, joined now at the hip by their shared love of a young Iranian child, now a teenaged young woman, sleeping soundly in the next room.

"Why now? Why me?" Doron pondered silently.

Together they experienced the only type of death they had not expected, the death the French call "the little death," "la petit mort," as Scheherazade, Queen of the Persians led her Israeli captive on a magic carpet ride, feelings and bodies melding together in their most unexpected union.

Outside, a full moon was setting. The sun would soon be rising as a cooling gentle divine wind blew across ancient desert dunes.

CHAPTER 45
RABBINICAL STUDY AT ROSH HANIKRA

SEVERAL RABBIS LED by Rabbi Shimon Perez met with about 20 of their students in the caves at Rosh HaNikra to discuss the recent events. Events that had heralded what appeared to be a new long-awaited era of peace in the Middle East. They all had their individual theories. Samuel, a ten-year-old, said it most simply, voicing what he believed. "It is because God made a promise years ago to protect Israel and had not forgotten. God was now honoring this age old promise."

Rachel, a twelve-year-old girl, said it was to reward Israel for all the suffering through the ages, through the pogroms of the Middle Ages, through the horrors of the Holocaust. Stanley, a major in the army, said it was not because of God, but because of the weather control technology Israel had created. "It is because of new Israeli technology," Stanley stated, "technology that has caused Iran to be outflanked and outsmarted."

This brought an outcry from many of the participants filling the seats in the auditorium. "What about God?" they questioned. "Can't you see his handiwork in all this?"

"What handiwork?" Stanley questioned.

Mollie, an 11-year-old girl responded, standing in the third row, speaking for many of those present. "How could an Israel soldier unite with an Iranian woman, fight together, join the resistance in Iran without the help of God?" This went on for hours with a secretary transcribing all their thoughts and comments. These were compiled and then restudied and again argued, the way Rashi, the commentator on the Torah, had once analyzed each word of the Torah.

Out of these discussions, came a joint statement read by Rabbi Perez. "Because a child's parents were killed on 9/11, an Israeli/American teenager traveled to Israel. Because he came to help Israel, he became a soldier. Because he became a soldier, he was captured in Iran. Because he was captured in Iran, an Iranian child's life was saved. Because her life was saved, an Iranian mother came to Israel. Because the soldier again saved the life of this child, his life was also spared. Because of the mutual love of this Iranian child, an Israeli soldier and a female Iranian militant joined forces to support and grow the Iranian resistance movement. Because, together, they had saved the life of this single Iranian child, God saved them from the Iranian military. Because of God's actions, the resistance movement grew until the military joined the resistance movement, causing the Iranian theocracy to collapse and go into hiding. Because of this simple act of love in saving an Iranian child, God did not destroy the Middle East, Iranian nuclear ambitions were thwarted, nuclear Armageddon avoided and the world was saved." They then returned to their prayerbooks, completing their evening prayers in Hebrew.

CHAPTER 46
EPILOGUE

A FEW YEARS later, Doron and Saron moved to the small town of Uz on the shores of the Caspian, near the scene where so many storms had occurred. Nadina was now a beautiful young woman of 21, having inherited the sculpted features of her mother. It was in this small rural town, on a cliff overlooking the Caspian that Doron and Saron were wed. The ceremony was surprisingly uneventful, at least that was the opinion of those present. They were, however, oblivious to several uninvited guests. Two Al Qaeda Iranian terrorists had secretly joined the wedding party. If they couldn't prevent or destroy the new Iranian resistance movement, the remaining Iranian extremists would try and kill two of the main proponents of the new freedom peace movement. One was at the back of the wedding party. A second was ten rows away, also near the back of the main wedding seats.

The terrorists, dressed as welcome guests, mixed with the true wedding guests in the reception before the wedding ceremony. Together, silently they prepared for the final demise of the couple despised by the Iranian autocracy.

Instead of a white wedding dress Saron wore an emerald green satin dress. Saron knew of Doron's prior marriage and out of respect for Sarah chose something entirely different, trying not to compete or show any disrespect for his previous marriage. The gently flowing dress was captivating. Saron also wore a green satin band on her forehead, framing her emerald green eyes, and highlighting her wedding dress, which shimmered in a gentle wind.

As the ceremony began, a gentle rain started. Doron and Saron were under a cupola with a black Christian minister, Hosiah Watson.

Rather than have a rabbi or a Moslem priest, they had heard of Hosiah from a YouTube broadcast of a recital he had once done at the Kennedy Center. Once they had heard his booming baritone voice, they both agreed to have him perform the ceremony. He suffered privately with an aggressive malignancy. He left a hospice hospital bed unannounced to the staff, for one last trip.

The wedding guests stood in the rain and out of respect for them, Doron and Saron stepped out from under the protecting cupola to join their guests in the gentle rain. Saron's dress, now clinging to her body, exposing the attractive contours.

Hosiah, in his inimitable silky-smooth baritone, recited verses from the Bible. His face was gaunt, his grey hair and stubble of a beard belied the voice that was still strong, still unaffected by the cancer ravaging his body. Hosiah somehow knew he had been given a final reprieve from death to perform this, his last ceremony.

"Where were you when I founded the earth? What were its pillars built on? Who laid its cornerstone?" Hosiah's voice boomed, reciting words from the Book of Job, as though it was God himself, speaking through his human instrument.

"Where were you when I wrapped the ocean in clouds?

Have you ever commanded morning or appointed the dawn to its place?

Who cuts a path for the thunderstorm and carves a road for the rain?

Who has begotten the dew and given voice to the whirlwind?" Before continuing, Hosiah took a moment, looking up at his rapt audience, taking it all in.

"If you shout commands to the thunderclouds, will they rush off to do your bidding?

Can you send lightning bolts on their way, and they will say to you, 'Here we are?'

Who gathers up the storm clouds?"

Sitting alone behind the invited wedding guests, one of the terrorists aimed a luger at the couple and certainly would have killed one or both, save for the presence of Nadina. Standing behind the closest terrorist, she thrust an 8-inch Russian Zooni knife, a gift from her mother, into his back. Before he fell, she pulled it out and with the skill taught to her by her Iranian mother, threw it at the other terrorist also drawing a handgun. The knife sliced cleanly into his larynx, the front edge extending two inches outside the opposite side. Both fell silently, almost simultaneously, to the ground. The second jerked out the knife and flailed, but could not breathe. At that exact moment, no one else but Nadina knew what had just transpired.

Nadina glanced around for other terrorists in the immediate area, but saw none. Both Israeli and Iranian officers from the outskirts of the perimeter rushed in to secure the area and evacuate the terrorists.

Nadina joined the guests, watching as Saron tossed her bridal bouquet into the crowd of guests. Saron then spun her head, freeing her gently waving red mane, as rain flew off her hair in a crescendo of sparkling droplets.

Saron turned to face her fiance, looking into his eyes as she spoke to him. "Would you have me as your wedded wife? I am not a Jew. I am a Muslim and proud of my faith but not of those who choose to misuse and abuse its tenets. I have been taught to hate the Jew, to hate you. I once wanted to kill you, dreaming and planning it for many months. But God, it seems, had a different plan for me. All has changed, caught up in a mystery, not of my will, unexpected, and certainly not of my choosing. It is as though I have been given new eyes. And now I see you through the lenses of those new eyes."

Saron looked up at Doron, standing beside her, and then continued. "I see the transformation in my daughter through your care and love. I see a man who has suffered great loss and had every right to curse God for his plight, but did not. I see a man who taught me and my child reverence for life, rather than the passion for death instilled in me as a child. You have made me a believer in strength of character over religion, both mine and yours. I witnessed your selfless actions in saving my daughter's life, many times, in many ways. This created the seed that eventually blossomed into love." Saron looked up at Doron with those same piercing eyes, and with a most endearing tone spoke to her betrothed. "Would you still have me, as I am, knowing what I have been, as you find me now, as I believe, now loving you, now to be your wedded wife?"

Doron looked for a moment upon this Iranian woman, looked deeply into her eyes, into her soul, this woman who had once held a knife to his ribs but who, against all expectations, had captured his heart. "Yes," Doron replied simply, "if you will have me, a Jew and an Israeli soldier?"

Saron nodded affirmatively, and then they both smiled. There was a palpable unmistakable physical and emotional attraction between the couple, above and beyond all else.

The couple placed rings on one another's ring finger as Hosiah proclaimed, "What God and only God could truly have brought together, let no man break asunder!" As though on cue, overhead, intracloud lightning flashed in the heavens above as thunder boomed.

Hosiah continued, looking at the couple now facing him. "By the legal authority invested in me, I now pronounce you, Doron and Saron, husband and wife!"

Doron kissed his new bride to the cheers of everyone present. Together they turned to their guests, hand in hand, perhaps the most unlikely union the Middle East had ever seen. Rolls of thunder and intracloud lightning flashing in the skies above. The Kabbalists later said nature's display was not God speaking in anger, but God blessing the union of this most unlikely couple. They noted that if God had been displeased, the lightning would have struck the ground, if not the couple themselves. That was a given.

After the ceremony, several songs were played during a small reception. The most unusual, a recommendation of a distant cousin of Doron's, living in Nashville, Tennessee. "Love Can Build a Bridge," once sung by a grey-bearded American country singer, a rotund cowboy, replete with a cowboy hat and an American swagger, named Sundance Head.

Nadina came up to the couple congratulating them. They noticed a new look emanating from her eyes, a rainbow appearance. "How did you do that?" Doron asked Nadina.

Nadina replied. "I always admired my mom's green eyes, and wanted something unusual instead of my ordinary brown eyes. So I found rainbow colored lenses. What do you think?"

"Very striking. Very beautiful," Doron told her. "But I wouldn't want you to upstage your mom on her wedding day." He laughed.

"No one can upstage my mother," Nadina replied, laughing as well.

Pictures of both Saron, Doron and Nadina made it into many local Iranian and Israeli papers and several national papers in the U.S. as well as on social media.

In the ensuing weeks the song became popular in Iran and the rest of the Middle East. Occasionally it was played with the second stanza rewritten, with the word 'heart' replaced by the word 'country':

"Love can build bridge
Between your country and mine..."

It was stated by many observers that if love could flourish between an Iranian militant and an Israeli soldier, literally anything might now be possible in the Middle East. They added that a country song sung by a southern cowboy named Sundance Head had hit the number one charts in the Middle East, further proof that anything, might now be possible.

In the years that followed, a university was created with two divisions.

In Israel it was called "The Israel Iranian Institute of Technology." In Iran it was named "The Iran Israeli Institute of Technology." For short, it was called the Double I, sometimes written out as the Double Eye. Its symbol were two watchful eyes.

In the years that followed, the new institute, in the fields of applied physics and mathematics came to rival MIT in Cambridge, Massachusetts. Likewise, in the forest of the Albors Mountains on the shores of the Caspian were the eyes of the stealthy but silently observing Iranian tiger, now making a comeback. Likewise, were the piercing green eyes of Saron, still at times peering out from underneath her only occasionally worn niquab. With Doron by her side, she often looked out from their home at the vineyard the couple had created on a hillside in their town of Uz on the shores of the Caspian, yielding wine rivaling the red wines from the south of France. Somehow, the rain always seemed to come when the grapes were at their most thirsty. And above them all, was the single eye of God watching over all earthly things.

In distant North Korea changes had occurred as well. Li Jung Chang had an Asian-themed garden planted on five acres of land, complete with an assortment of Japanese Bonsai, Hong Kong orchids, miniature red maples, Hawaiian orchids surrounding a one acre Koi pond and a stream flowing through it. Chang particularly enjoyed a small specialized garden filled with purple and blue aconitum whose vibrant appearance was only matched by its toxicity. Then there were also poisonous mushrooms, containing scoparius with cardiac toxicity. Adjacent to these were tall multicolored flowering foxglove, containing digitalis. Contrasting the color was bell-shaped white flowering Lily of the Valley with red berries. There was also a ground cover of autumn crocus containing colchicine, a member of the arsenic family, completing the collection of the world's most poisonous flowers. Chang allowed one black widow spider to inhabit the garden. She had no need to keep out other spiders, as the one female black widow tended to eat any intruders, catching all manner of insects in her intricate beautiful web. Chang reserved visits to this private garden for "special" guests and their children. As Li Chang stated, "My secret garden seems to have a calming affect on unruly children." The Li Chang North Korean Gardens, as it came to be called, rivaled anything in the West, as well as the Baha'i Gardens in Haifa, Israel, perhaps because Israeli engineers helped create it.

On the front of the Iranian Israeli University was an oval, walnut sculpted sign, depicting the image of an elderly stooped man, supported by a gnarled wooden staff, a spotted fawn at his side. The elderly man was Albert Schweitzer. A quote from the man curved above the scene, "Reverence For Life." The quote a direct refutation of the terrorist suicidal ideology and their promotion of death over life.

It took several months for the forensic pathology report on the death of Supreme Leader Rachman Solidar to be released. The only thing unusual was a trace of the neurotoxin VX but the quality of the chromatography was not adequate to separate this drug from a contaminant, and so it was ignored and left out of the final report. The final report simply stated Rachman Solidar, the Iranian Supreme Leader, had died of a myocardial infarct, brought on by a fatal arrhythmia.

Over 50 worldwide companies made donations to the Double Eye Institute. They donated computers, internet access, as well as many cell phones. This further opened the closed Iranian society to the fresh air of free human discourse and knowledge. It was through such avenues of written and spoken dialogue that younger generations came to refute the hardliners of the Iranian theocracy and came to further cement the peace so long sought after. A million small planted seeds slowly sprouted and eventually took hold in the desert soil, growing over many years into a mighty sequoia whose branches signified freedom. The words of Doron were often quoted, spoken by Doron at the commencement of the first class of students at the Double Eye in Iran. "Any one person can be killed. But it is much harder, if not impossible to kill an idea whose time has come." Doron also quoted the words of George Bernard Shaw paraphrased by an American statesman and U.S. Senator Robert F. Kennedy, "Some men see things as they are, and ask why. I dream things that never were and ask why not." Doron exhorted the students to follow their dreams. "Dream of a better world," he told them, "and use those dreams to create one." Looking out at his audience, he paused, appearing to look beyond his current audience to future audiences, that might one day read his words. He went on. "Some people would say even my very presence here should be and is impossible. But recognize that a synonym for the impossible is: the future. It is not by accident that within the word impossible is embedded the word possible." Doron looked out at the young students making up his audience and then concluded with one final remark. "You are here to envision the impossible and one day make the impossible, not just possible, but a new reality."

The newlyweds received a congratulatory letter from the president of the United States, Vivian Tyson. Surprisingly, her most prized accomplishment was not becoming the first female president or even the first female black president, nor even her help in bringing peace to the Middle East, but the resurrection of the black family unit, with 75% of black children now raised in homes with a mother and father supporting them.

In Iran the end of the religious autocracy brought a sense of freedom that was described in songs and books and said to be comparable to the American black history of freedom from slavery. Of all members in Iranian society the change was most poignant, most dramatic, most revealing among Iranian women. They could now attend soccer games or any other sport with or without accompaniment by a man. They were no longer required to wear a Hijab or other compulsory headscarf or full body covering. Many chose to wear jeans, skirts and show off a beauty that had long been hidden.

Saron's picture made the cover of Time magazine, with the title

"The new face of Iran." The cover showed off her emerald green eyes, red hair in fancy curls, blood red lipstick and penetrating eyes, without any head cover. The article included an editorial on all the recent unexpected events throughout the Middle East. Inside the magazine was also a picture of Nadina, wearing the unusual contact lenses she had worn at her mother's wedding. The rainbow lenses gave her eyes a most striking appearance. With the newfound freedoms in Iran, her picture with her rainbow contact lenses made it to the cover of several new women's magazines in Iran and Cosmopolitan and Vogue in the U.S. The magazine covers complemented her rainbow contacts with rainbow makeup, giving her a sensual, alluring look that soon became the envy of young girls everywhere. The simple caption under one of the pictures: "The girl with the rainbow eyes," became Nadina's new title. With a social media following of over one million teenage girls and young women supporting her, Nadina started a makeup company, called, as expected, "Rainbow Eyes." On the U.S. shopping networks everything she designed sold out, often in minutes, showing that an Iranian woman, given the freedom to do so, could be every bit as entrepreneurial and successful as American women entrepreneurs. Nadina's makeup line was then followed by a clothing line, "Rainbow Eyes Clothing, Inc," as successful as her makeup line.

Her religious beliefs, centered on the Ba Hai Religion and Albert Schweitzer's dictum "Reverence for Life," led her to start "Rainbow Rescue," which rescued stray dogs and animals throughout Iran. This was her most rewarding creation and only further endeared her to her growing following on social media. In her home, were often 10-12 rescued dogs, whose lives Nadina has saved.

Nadina was asked to write her story by many book publishers, and one day promised to do so, already knowing the title, "The Girl With the Rainbow Eyes: What I believe." And below the title, the words, "An Iranian girl's life, from suicide bomber to entrepreneur." When the book came out a few years later, her editor changed the subtitle slightly, based on her skyrocketing business success: "An Iranian girl's life from suicide bomber to billionaire entrepreneur."

Nadina and Ruven Rosenberg, the technology head of Chaos technology had been secretly dating for a few years. When Ruven told his parents, Sasha and Mordecai, he was dating, they asked about the girl. "Well, he told them, "Nadina is not Jewish." His parents were reform Jews. They were not very religious but strongly respecting of their Jewish heritage.

"That's not good," Sasha told him.

"There's more," Ruven said.

"Yes," his father said, almost afraid to ask.

"Nadina is Iranian," he replied with a slight stutter.

"That's even worse," Sasha replied.

"And anything else?" his father asked solemnly.

"There is a little more," Ruven replied.

"Yes?" his mother asked, again.

"Well, she was once a suicide bomber," Ruven replied, barely getting the words out. Surprisingly, his parents both started laughing.

"Why are you laughing?" he asked them.

"Well, now we know you're joking," they said. "You are quite the jokester," his mother added.

"Well, there is one other thing."

"What's that?" his dad said.

"Nadina is an ex-heroin addict."

Both his parents almost fell off the sofa in laughter, and Ruven started laughing as well, realizing the only reason his parents were laughing, was that they hadn't believed a word he was saying.

It was a year later, one evening while alone in his own home, that Ruven told Nadina the response from his parents when he told them about her. "Well, do you think I am a joke?" she asked him, looking up at him questioninglywith her rainbow eyes."

They had planned to go to dinner that evening and she was dressed for an evening out, her rainbow makeup alluring as usual.

"You're no joke to me." He laughed, reaching for her. "When I look into your eyes, I know there's a rainbow in heaven."

"Why is that?" she asked.

"Because when I look into your rainbow eyes, I'm there, in heaven," he said, kissing her eyes.

"Do you know eye color has to do with Rayleigh scattering and the amount of melanin in the iris?" she asked.

"Don't talk physics. I'd rather you talk dirty to me."

"But physics turns me on!" Nadina responded laughing.

"Well then," Ruven said, "as I said, you can talk physics to me anytime you want!" Grinning, Ruven drew Nadina close to him, as she melted into his arms. They never did make it out to dinner that night.

A few years after her book came out, Nadina and Ruven Rosenberg were married in a private ceremony on the shores of the Caspian. Ruven's stutter never did turn off Nadina. She admired him for overcoming his handicap to become a scientist and the main technology officer of Chaos Technology. As she stated, "If my mother, the ardent Iranian terrorist, can marry an Israeli, so can I."

With the end of the autocratic regime, came the end of the U.S. embargo, freeing up investment into Iran. Companies raced to bring business to Iran. Iranian entrepreneurs joined the world business community and it was discovered that, given the opportunity, Iranians were exceptional engineers, scientists and very willing to become capitalists.

Of all the successes, the most honored was a 23-year-old Iranian girl, Zumi Mosana, who had been genitally mutilated by her parents as a child. Based on her introverted nature, she chose to study mathematics and at the age of 23 won the field medal in mathematics, the first Iranian of either sex to do so. Using her notoriety to help sponsor a bill in the new Iranian legislature, all forms of genital mutilation were outlawed. Other Iranians won prizes in literature, including one Iranian woman winning the Nobel prize in literature for her description of Iran's path from enslaving the minds of its people to promoting freedom of thought, freedom of worship and the rebirth of the religion of Islam from a means of controlling the population and glorifying death and suicide bombings to a means of promoting life, glorifying freedom and individual liberty. The religious autocracy, they said, had hijacked the Islamic religion for their self-serving militant terrorist ideology and now it had been freed, its chains cut and the original intent of the Islamic religion to promote life and individual freedom reclaimed by and for the people of Iran and Muslims in the world at large. An Iranian renaissance developed encompassing, literature, science and business. It ushered in financial rewards that grew the economy out of the depression it had stagnated in for generations, and with it brought a new pride in being Iranian that spread like a tidal wave among the Iranian people.

On the shores of the Caspian, numerous hotels were built by Marriott, Hilton, Four Seasons and several new Iranian-owned luxury brands.

In the late afternoon, a surprising foursome was seen at the Four Seasons golf course on the shores of the Caspian playing a round of golf. There was Vivian Tyson, the current U.S. President, Jamie Watson, recent winner of the U.S. Open and two previous presidents, Shane O'Malley, a Democrat and Evan Rumpsky a Republican. O'Malley and Rumpsky had shown such ardent distaste for one another during their campaigns that two New York papers stated flatly, " O'Malley and Rumpsky would become friends only when hell froze over" and "it would be a cold day in hell when they became friends." A reporter in Idaho, shortly thereafter, pointed out a recent news story in the Idaho Snake River Gazette titled, *Hell Freezes Over.* The story went on to detail that Hells Canyon Crater Lake formed by the Snake River bordering Idaho, eastern Oregon and eastern Washington had indeed frozen over, but the New York papers both chose to not cover this news story, or otherwise chose to bury it. That only incentivized people on

Facebook to reprint the story below a copy of the New York papers' articles and of course to add insult to injury, someone else posted a video on YouTube of the frozen Hells Canyon Lake which garnered a few million visitors in the following week.

Following the lead of Israel, President Tyson announced a new NASA initiative. "Our new initiative is a ten year plan to control weather-related storms in the U.S. following the lead of the Israeli weather control companies. We will be working with them, NASA and NOAA, joining in partnership with many of them. We have aptly named it, 'The Katrina Initiative'."

Along with the technologic creation of this new initiative and the success of the Israeli NASDAQ IPOs, NASA, NOAA and other meteorologic educational centers were deluged with new student applicants. NOAA, particularly, saw a flood of applicants for its jobs and training programs.

In a ceremony at the White House President Tyson awarded Doron ben Avrahim the Presidential Medal of Freedom. Doron was standing alongside Tyson as she spoke. "The Medal of Freedom is our nation's highest civilian honor. This medal is reserved for people who have made 'an especially meritorious contribution to the security or national interests of the United States, world peace, cultural or other significant contributions to our nation.' Doron ben Avrahim fits firmly into the mold of such a person. It has been said that when the crisis occurs, the hero will appear. There was Lincoln helping save the nation at the start of the Civil War. There was Churchill at the time of the German blitzkrieg against England, helping England and the world defeat Hitler. There was Einstein writing a letter to Roosevelt leading to the Manhattan project, the development of a nuclear weapon, and the defeat of Japan in World War 11. Heroes come in unexpected forms and at unexpected times.

"Today we celebrate the heroism of an Israeli American citizen whose trials began at the young age of thirteen, at the 9/11 tragedy with the murder of both his parents. I believe his father wanted his son to be an engineer, which was not Doron's desire, and this caused some discord between father and son. Doron's path then veered from what he and his father both wanted. This led him to follow a path chosen by the death of his parents, with a desire to avenge their deaths and help Israel fight terrorists. Doron became an Israeli army lieutenant, volunteering for the most dangerous missions, causing him to be tortured in captivity with his life at grave risk on multiple occasions. Who could ask for anything more? I am sure both his parents are looking down upon him from heaven immensely proud of a son who has helped Israel and America and the world in this time of ultimate crisis." Tyson turned to Doron. "The world owes you, and people with character like you, people who choose country over self, a debt of gratitude, a debt we cannot repay, but which we symbolize by the Presidential Medal of Freedom, we present to you today." With that Tyson placed the medal around Doron's neck.

Doron looked up heavenward, wondering if his father in heaven might now finally approve of him. He had never become the engineer his father had hoped for, nor had he become the artist Doron himself had set his heart on becoming. Circumstances had ultimately chosen a different path for him, the soldier's path now being honored.

In the small audience, largely filled with the White House press corp were the Israeli ambassador to the U.S., a few other Israeli officials, and two Iranians, who stood out from the rest of the audience--Saron and Nadina.

Tyson shook Doron's hand, then gave him a warm embrace, whispering a Hebrew prayer to him, saying "May God watch over you, protect you and keep you in all our prayers." President Tyson turned to the small audience and concluded with the words, "And may God continue to watch over the United States of America."

Not lost to the excitement were the computer software companies, creating new computer games developed by Activision, Electronic Arts,

Take Two Interactive and Microsoft. Games with the names, Tornado Alley, Katrina, Whirlwind and the most popular Pterodactyl Tornado Drones Inc.

Not to be outdone, Disney developed a new theme park, Tornado Alley, complete with a Pterodactyl Drone Cove. There were flying exhibits where you could take a ride on a Pterodactyl through a hurricane and then through a tornado. There was an exhibit of robotic flying Pterodactyls along with a scientific exhibit of the Pterosaurs of the late Jurassic period. Here it was pointed out that Pterodactyls were properly called Pterosaurs and were not dinosaurs but flying reptiles.

GoDaddy's stock doubled in price as every conceivable web address related to storms, hurricanes and tornadoes was bought and resold multiple times. Pterodactyl Tornado Inc. sold for a cool million to the Israeli company with the same name. They could easily afford it as their stock shot up to a valuation of $25 billion!

Kids asked their parents, "What do Pterodactyl's eat for breakfast?"

"I have no clue." was the usual reply.

"Tornadoes!" the kids responded, while eating their Pterodactyl crunch cereal and chewing their Pterodactyl One a Day vitamins.

IMAX partnered with Disney and came out with an IMAX Tornado movie and a Pterodactyl 3-D movie of Matilda and the tornado spawned from it.

Meanwhile, Doron and Saron enjoyed their lives together on the shores of the Caspian. Together, they had three daughters. The eldest daughter they named Dove, the second, Charity and the third, Tranquility. In all the world there were no women as beautiful as their daughters, save for their mother Saron and Saron's first daughter, Nadina.

One late summer evening, Nadina visited. Her parents were outside standing on a small parapet overlooking their vines now pregnant with grapes to be harvested. As Nadina came inside she noticed a small unadorned little box on a shelf in the corner of the living room. She opened it and started reading the faded yellowed pages, recognizing a story that would have seemed impossible, except that it was her story and the story of an Iranian terrorist and an Israeli army lieutenant. She sat down on the living room couch and continued reading. Nadina looked up as a gentle breeze, then a sudden wind rustled the pages in her now trembling hands. Meanwhile, Saron and Doron came inside to visit with her...

After this, Doron lived for well over a hundred years. He lived to see his grandchildren and his great-grandchildren and died at a very great age, living to see peace finally come to the Middle East, the setting where visionaries had once upon a time recorded for posterity the sacred words when God first spoke to Mankind.

And of course there was always the risk that framed by the reddish hue of the setting sun, with a blood moon rising, white billowy cumulous clouds would once again turn grayish black, the heavens part as a gentle rain turned into a torrent, the wind howl a prescient warning, a thunderous cry reverberate through desert sands, the risk that nature's wrath would once again tear asunder the frail constructs of humanity, undoing mankind's fervent hopes, as the Voice in the Whirlwind, an omniscient Divine Wind, trumpeted God's presence, once again heralding His return.

CHAPTER 47
HUMANITY'S FUTURE DESTINY

1000 YEARS IN THE FUTURE.

IT IS NOW one thousand years in the future. Fermi's paradox has finally been answered. It has now been confirmed: humanity on earth is the only conscious life in the universe. As such, it is alone in the universe! There are no aliens. In this future world, everyone now living on earth will, of course, be dead, but Armageddon has been averted. Earth narrowly skirted Armageddon, to the surprise of many. Everyone living in this generation had died of natural causes and limited wars but not because of Armageddon. Human immortality develops 950 years into our future, but, unfortunately, too late for everyone living today. The multiverse sought after by physicists working at the border of science and philosophy was never found.

A black Latino physicist, Archimedes Hernandez, won the Nobel prize for his "proof" that the multiverse did not and could not exist. Theologians honored him with their own prizes. Physics, widely expected to ring in the death knell for belief in God, had, instead, become its savior. A Time Magazine cover read: "Physics Proves the Existence of God (?)" A question mark was left, like an asterisk, as some scientists, including some physicists, denied the proof was valid. With no aliens to be found and with no multiverse, Deism, which had seemed on the verge of widespread rejection because of physics, instead made a remarkable resurgence through the surprising insights of physics! Isaac Newton's ideas of theism also made a comeback and, with it, his "Philosophiae Naturalis Principia Mathematica," was reprinted and restudied along with his religious views. At some colleges and universities a new course was taught, "The physics of God." This proved widely popular and was offered in the curriculum for degrees in astrophysics, philosophy and religion.

In this far future time, a starship named Noah's Ark has landed on the terraformed planet Osiris, 100 light-years away from earth. The captain of the ship is Enrico Salvatore, an Italian, and a distant relative of Enrico Fermi, his namesake. En route to Osiris, deep in a hibernation state, his thoughts turn inward to his ancient relative, and the question he posed years ago.

Included in the starship's baggage compartment as they voyage to Osiris are hundreds of butterfly larvae lying in their individual butterfly chrysalis. These have been placed in trees that were previously planted on Osiris, which is also now covered with earth grasses and an assortment of flowers as well. Osiris orbits a double dwarf star system and has a single large moon, now rising in the eastern sky. The butterflies are of many different species and their wings are a multicolored rainbow of light shining through translucent wings. The butterflies are just now testing their wings before their maiden flight. The shimmering display of colors is dazzling but perhaps the most dazzling are the yellows, "so richly, brightly, dazzlingly yellow. As though the sun's tears were singing against a white stone;" a lingering collective memory of times gone by... A seeming unexpected ode to a young Pavel Friedmann when he wrote words filled with anguish and tears from a distant past within the depressing depth of Terezin Concentration Camp.

Mankind has indeed made it to the stars and, it would appear, has chosen not to be alone in the void of space and distance. The butterflies fly around the Italian astronaut, as though dancing in gratitude, in appreciation of their new home. The scene then transforms to Doron's painting created as a very young child of a far-off world, of a double star, of an astronaut letting butterflies fly off his hand, exactly the image now visible, the vision Doron had dreamed and painted as a child, has now indeed become reality in this far distant future.

On Osiris, the moon rises further in the eastern sky and the double suns together set low along the western horizon. As darkness descends, all that remains to be felt or heard is a gentle breeze, a gentle wind echoing through the canyons and river valleys of Osiris.

Before leaving Osiris, Enrico Salvatore planted a wooden plaque into the virgin ground of Earth's new sister planet, inscribed with simple ancient words, hopeful and prayerful, first transcribed in the city of Jerusalem by a prophet named Isaiah, son of Amoz, 8 centuries before the Christian era:

> *Nation shall not lift up sword against nation,*
> *neither shall they learn war anymore.*

> *(Isaiah 2:4)*

A DIVINE WIND—REFERENCES

Ahmed, Qanta A, MD. In the Land of Invisible Women, Sourcebooks Inc., 2008

Alter, Robert. Wisdom Books, W. W. Norton & Company, New York, 2010

Asimov, Isaac. I, Robot, Doubleday,1950

Baer, Robert. The Devil We Know, Dealing With the New Iranian Superpower, Crown Publishers New York, 2008

Bassett, Maurice (Editor). Reverence For Life, The Words of Albert Schweitzer, Albert Schweitzer, 1993, 2017

Butterman, Bella, Avner Shalev, (Editors). To Bear Witness - Holocaust Remembrance at Yad Vashem; Avner Shalev, Editor

Belfiore, Michael. The Department of Mad Scientists: How DARPA is Remaking Our World, from the Internet to Artificial Limbs, Harper Collins, 2009

Berenbaum, Michael. The World Must Know. The History of the Holocaust as Told in the United States Holocaust Memorial Museum. Little Brown and Company 1993

Burt, Christopher C. Extreme Weather, W. W. Norton and Company, 2004

Campbell, Joseph. The Hero's Journey: Joseph Campbell On His Life and Work, Chapter one, The Call to Adventure, page 34,2018

Campbell, Joseph. The Hero With a Thousand Faces, 2008, (original edition 1949), New World Library

Challoner, Jack. Eyewitness Hurricane and Tornado, Eyewitness Books, DK Publishing, Inc., 2004

Clancy, Tom. The Sum of All Fears, Berkley, 1991

Clark, Arthur C. The Fountains of Paradise, first copyright 1979, Electronic ed 2012, Rosetta Books LLC, New York

Condon, Richard. The Manchurian Candidate, Wolfpack Publishing, 2020. (Originally published in 1959)

Crichton, Michael. Jurassic Park, Ballantine Book, 1990

Crichton, Michael, Anne-Marie Martin (Screenplay). Director Jan de Bont. Twister, The Movie, 1996

Eban, Abba. Heritage, Civilization and the Jews, Summit Books, New York, 1984

Emanuel, Kerry. Divine Wind, The History and Science of Hurricanes, Oxford University Press, 2005

Frankenheimer, John, director. The Manchurian Candidate, 20th Century Fox, 1962.

Friedman, Pavel. I Never Saw Another Butterfly, Children's Drawings and Poems from Terezin Concentration Camp, 1942-1944, Edited by Hana Volavkovd, Schocken Books, New York, 38-39, 1942, The Butterfly

Gabriel, Brigitte. Because They Hate, St. Martins Griffin, New York, 2005

Gutterman, Bella, Shalev, Avner, Editors. To Bear Witness, Holocaust Remembrance at Yad Vashem, Yad Vashem, Jerusalem, 2008

Hart, M. H., Zuckerman, B. eds, Extraterrestrials: Where are They?, Pergamon, New York, 1982

How it Works Book of Extreme Weather and the Science Behind Earth's Forces of Nature, IP Imagine Publishing Ltd, 2016

Hirschberg, Peter. "Netanyahu: It's 1938 and Iran is Germany, Haaretz, November 14, 2006

https://www.history.com/topics/world- war - ii/trinity-test

Hitchcock, Mary. Iran and Israel, Harvest House Publishers, 2013

Hitchcock, Mary. Wars and Rumors of Wars, Iran and Israel, Harvest House Publishers, 2013

Hoffman, Ross N. Controlling the Global Weather, Bulletin American Meteorological Society, September 25, 2001, "Technological Advances over the next 30-50 years may make it possible to control the weather. If we can, should we? Are "weather wars" inevitable?"

Hoffman, Ross N. Controlling Hurricanes, Can hurricanes and other severe tropical storms be moderated or deflected?; Scientific American, 2004, 69-75

Israel. Insight Guide, Apa Publications (UK) Ltd, 2012

Jacobsen, Annie. The Pentagon's Brain, An Uncensored History of DARPA, Little, Brown and Company, 2015

Kaku, Michio. The Future of Humanity, Our Destiny in the Universe, Doubleday, 2018

Janzen, Gerald J. Job, Interpretation, Westminster John Knox Press, 1985

Kaku, Michio. Physics of the Future, Doubleday, 2011

Kaku, Michio. Physics of the Impossible, Doubleday, 2008

Kardeshev, N.S., Transmission of Information by Extraterrestrial Civilizations,"
(1964), Soviet Astronomy, 8, 217

Krauthammer, Charles. Things That Matter, Crown Forum, 2013 (I wish you could have tarried a little before leaving us. The world right now more than ever could use your wisdom, your insightful analysis, your counsel, your unwavering honesty and your self-deprecating humor in the face of life's hardships)

Kushner, Harold S. The Book of Job, When Bad Things Happen to a Good Person, Schocken Books, New York, 2012

Kushner, Lawrence. Honey From the Rock An Easy Introduction to Jewish Mysticism, Jewish Lights Publishing, 1990

Kushner, Lawrence. The River of Light: Jewish Mystical Awareness, Jewish Lights Publishing, 1990 (especially Quotation at beginning of Chapter 6, adapted in quotation prior to Chapter 1, " A Divine Wind.")

Matt, Daniel C. The Essential Kabbalah, The Heart of Jewish Mysticism, Harper Collins, 1998

Melman, Yossi and Meir Javedanfar. The Nuclear Sphinx of Teheran, Carroll and Graf Publishers, New York, 2007

Muller, Richard A. Physics for Future Presidents, W. W. Norton and Company, 2008

Netanyahu, Benjamin, Speech to American Israel Public Affairs Committee (AIPAC), March 5, 2012

Ossala, Alexandra. Injectable Mesh to Interface with The Brain; Popular Science Your New Brain, Time Inc Books, A Division of Meredith Corporation. 2018, 58-59

The Physics of God, lecture 12, The Great Questions of Philosophy and Physics, Steven Gimbel, www.thegreatcourses.com, The Teaching Company, 2020

Physics Today, 38, 8, 11, (1985); https://doi.org/10.1063/1.2814654

Physics Today, 38, 8, 13, (1985); https://doi.org/10.1063/1.2814655

Puig, Manuel. Kiss of the Spider Woman, Vintage Books, 1978

Reynolds, Ross R., et al. Weather, Dorling Kindersly Limited, 2008

Safdie, Moshe. Yad Vashem: The Architecture of Memory; Joan Ockman, Moshe Safdie, 2005

Snodgrass, Eric R. The Science of Extreme Weather, The Great Courses

Smith, Jerry E. Weather Warfare, The Military's Plan to Draft Mother Nature, Adventures Unlimited Press, 2006

Tornado Season (Video), Saloon Media, 2016

Twain, Mark. Complete Novels, OPU, 2018

Walsh, Michael. Last Stands, Chapter 3, Masada (73/74 AD) and Warsaw (1943), St. Martin's Press, 2020

Webb, Stephen, If the Universe is Teeming with Aliens... Where is Everybody? Springer, 2015

Wells, H.G. The War of the Worlds, (originally published 1897), Read Books Ltd, 2016

yadvashem.org

Zurich, Moshe, Zur, Head Editorial Board, Haifa Tourist Board, Baha'I Shrine and Gardens, Mount Carmel, Haifa, Haifa Municipality, May 2001.

IN REMEMBRANCE OF JAKE AND ZEUS

WRITING CAN BE a lonely private endeavor, but I was rarely alone when I wrote "A Divine Wind," because two of my dogs, Jake and Zeus, followed me wherever I went, just wanting to be with me. Jake and Zeus were always lying near my side as I wrote the words of "Divine Wind," sometimes in the morning and at times late into the night. They never complained, as long as they could be near me. So I never felt alone as I wrote, at least while they were still alive. When I took a break from writing they were ready to play with me, run into our yard, jump into my arms, lick my face, bowl me over in Zeus's case (He was a 140 pound Rottweiler mastiff mixture!).

Because of my novel dedication to them, I thought it appropriate to share their story, at least a small part of it, so readers can better understand why I made this dedication.

Jake's life story: Jake was a white, fluffy curly haired little Bichon, as all such purebred Bichons are. His first owner didn't take very good care of him, resulting in a broken leg at a very young age. He was then given to a relative who had a farm, and summarily abandoned in a barn where he was covered in mud and otherwise ignored. After being there only two weeks the owner called my wife, Cheryl, and asked her to take him and find him a home. She said she couldn't stand him. So Cheryl went to pick Jake up, planning to find him a home--we already had enough dogs. He was five or six at the time. Jake was so filthy Cheryl had the lady (I use the term loosely) bathe him before she brought little Jakey Jake, as my wife decided to call him, home.

When Jake came to our home, he was six months old. I was sitting on our couch in our living room. When Jake saw me, he ran to me, jumped into my lap, and from then on he was my dog.

My wife took some offense to that. She saved his life and Jake took one look at me and from then on, I was his and he was mine! I don't know why he did that. I am nothing special. I have all the frailties of being human. And humanity, I strongly believe, is overrated, vastly overrated. Yours truly more so than most, and deservedly so, I am forced to admit. But for Jake I was the end-all and be-all for him. I could do no wrong. It is only in a bond with a dog that I have felt such selfless unconditional love. And of course, we never even considered finding him a home. He already had one, ours. For the sake of honesty, I should admit that I love dogs, all dogs. I only tolerate people. If I had to choose between a rabid dog and a human, any human, I would take the dog.

Jake had only been with us for about a month when my wife informed me that she felt unsafe in our country location in Southern Ohio, a part, I said, of Appalachia. I have tried to convince Cheryl that where we live is safe. Then she pointed out a black bear on two separate occasions, heard the howl of coyotes at sundown, glimpsed gray foxes stealthily hunting in the late evening, neighbors shooting off guns, trespassing on our property to hunt deer, and a confrontation with an occasional snake, her favorite. Somehow in the presence of all these creatures, my words had not convinced her our property was safe. So one day, she showed me an ad for a Rottweiler mastiff puppy for sale in a nearby town. I took her hint and went and picked up 8-week-old Zeus, the "runt of the litter," the last to be sold. At eight weeks of age, Zeus was about the same size as 6-month-old Jake. They played together like old friends but it didn't take long for Zeus to be too big to safely rough house with Jake. So Zeus played with Harley. Did I forget to mention Harley, our Bernese Mountain dog?

This isn't a letter about Harley, so I'll try to be brief about him. Harley was and is a character and he was big enough as a puppy to play with Zeus. When Harley was eight he developed osteogenic sarcoma in his left front leg which was amputated. Of course, it would be him. He was such a gentle giving soul. He was the only one of our dogs that would let another dog eat out of his dog bowl while he was also eating! It took Harley a month to recover and then for many years he never lost a step. He was supposed to live three months to at most one year after diagnosis, that was four years ago. I have never written a novel before, but have written many radiology professional articles that may have in a small way advanced the field of medicine. But of all the articles I've published, the one I am most proud of is the article I wrote about Harley, about his brave heart, what he went through and how he had overcome an osteogenic sarcoma. Our local paper, published the article and graciously put his color picture on their front page.

My wife Cheryl and I live in the country with a 3 acre pond in front of our house. To mimic the cherry blossom trees in Washington DC, I planted a row of them around the pond. On a clear sunny spring day a few years ago I drove up our long driveway to take the garbage to where it gets picked up—something I do every week. On the way, I stopped to admire the cherry blossoms that were in full bloom. They only last about a week. When I got back to our house, my wife was screaming at the top of her lungs, "Jake's gone! Jake's gone!"

We have a fenced-in yard attached to the house. When we want them to use the "bathroom," we just let them out the back door and call to them in a few minutes and they all run back inside. Cheryl was afraid little Jake had burrowed under the fence or slipped through a hole in it. She also knew Jake would never run from me if I called for him--he would immediately. So I ran around the perimeter of the fence calling for Jake as loud as I could, but there was no response. Then we searched again within the fence. We found him unconscious or dead lying a few feet from the back of the fence. With trembling hands, I picked up Jake's little lifeless body. He had had a haircut just a few days before. We asked for a puppy cut and instead they shaved him, which had upset him. My wife yelled at them for having hurt him. Without all his hair, it was even more apparent just how small and frail Jake was. He felt as light as a feather. I ran with him to a small deck nearby in the fenced-in yard and did CPR on my child. I am a physician trained in CPR, but it is very difficult to do on a dog. The success rate is only 6%, mainly in veterinary hospitals, and close to zero in the field. An hour later there was still no response and I stopped.

I took Jake inside and cradled him in my arms while we decided what we would do. Those four hours were the last time I held my son in my arms. We placed Jake in a plastic container with his favorite toys and wrapped him in a blanket. We buried our son on a grassy knoll overlooking the yard he shared with his brothers and sisters. Cheryl set up a little cross to mark his grave and we laid some flowers on his grave. I am Jewish and found my Hebrew bible and said some Hebrew prayers as we said our last goodbyes. Jake was 11 years old. In all of his pictures he always looked a little apprehensive, maybe even a little fearful. I think he was always afraid of being hurt, of being neglected, of being abused as he had been before we adopted him. Maybe it was a premonition of what was to come. It always made me try to be extremely gentle with him. He never got spanked or scolded. Most meals I would sneak a little of my food to him, to let him know what was mine was his as well. This loving treatment was so special to Jake, as though he was saying, "You mean someone is actually willing to love me?" Jake just wanted to be loved. He was so grateful for this bond we shared, so unexpected for him, he wouldn't let me out of his sight when I was home. Jake, I believe, knew he was loved.

About three months before Jake died, construction had started on a swimming pool in our backyard, not so much for us but for our dogs, to give them another way to exercise and have fun. By this time we had about eight dogs, most of them rescues that would have died without our adoption. A week before Jake died, Cheryl had bought Jake a life jacket to use in the pool. She told me it fit perfectly. The pool was completed just a few days after Jake died. One of the contractors asked me what I thought of it when it was all done. "It's beautiful," I replied. "Just what I wanted, except..."

"Except what?" the workman responded.

"Except I don't need it anymore," I replied, teary eyed as I walked away. My wife apologized for me and explained to the workman what had transpired.

Zeus's life story: Zeus had the dark velvety black coat of the Rottweiler, trimmed in brown, so he had the look of a Rottweiler, but the "runt" grew to the size of a mastiff, "a Rottweiler on steroids," as my wife often remarked. When he was full grown at about two years of age, my wife no longer complained about feeling unsafe when I was gone to a meeting or at work at our local hospital. Many of our dogs have bonded much more closely with my wife. Zeus, however, like Jake, was totally devoted to me when I was home and would follow me everywhere I went. Zeus was the only dog my wife would let me walk off-leash on our property. He wouldn't go further than about ten feet from me. If I was outside with him and someone was on our property--workers, friends or strangers, Zeus would not bark at them, he didn't need to. He was so impressive, so powerful a presence, it would stop people from whatever they were doing. Zeus would just observe them, how they acted toward me. Then he would take a few steps to stand between me and them. People on the property spotting Zeus would wisely stop about ten feet away and let me know why they were there. Zeus was intimidating by his presence, by his stance, by the aura of subdued power, by his Rottweiler deep black and brown coloration and his mastiff size. When he ran with his slow loping stride, it reminded me of a race horse cantering gracefully, a beautiful thing to behold.

As Zeus reached older age, he developed many medical conditions. Diabetes insipidus for which my wife gave him drops in his eyes twice a day, hip problems, spine problems that made it difficult to get up and walk, mitral regurgitation and atrial fibrillation. He took it all in stride. Dogs, they say, live in the moment. They don't dwell on their disabilities. They made our time together more poignant and significant. And like Jake, he would lie near me as I wrote the words of my novel, " A Divine Wind." When he was 10 and a half years old, he developed a limp and we immediately had his leg x-rayed. It was an osteogenic sarcoma, even more aggressive appearing than Harley's. I found some medication that made him feel a little better and because of that he walked more for a day and seemed less in pain. Unfortunately, walking more caused it to fracture. I called a major nearby veterinary hospital but they wouldn't speak to me because I wasn't a vet! I called back and begged them to speak to me and find a way to help Zeus in his emergent need. They still refused, which I found then and still find today, unconscionable. Our local vet told us there was nothing we could do but end his suffering. We put a harness around his chest and abdomen to help lift him so he could get outside and relieve himself. The vet was supposed to come that evening and euthanize him in our home. We called it off. The next night, he had spent the whole night crawling off his dog bed to pee on the floor and not soil his bed.

We took him outside one more time to let him relieve himself. He spent a moment looking around across our pond and the woods, inhaling the late spring air for the last time. I remember, it was surprisingly quiet, solemn like a prayer; no birds were singing, only a gentle breeze was blowing. We then brought our child inside. It was at that moment that the ground Zeus had walked on, the place he had run on, romped with his brothers and sisters and me on, that just a few minutes earlier was red clay dirt, had been transformed, and was now hallowed ground. That evening we let the vet come and euthanize Zeus to end our child's suffering. For one day I thought I had done the right thing by ending his suffering, but then I started missing him and I was filled with a helpless hopeless longing. I felt Zeus would have tried harder for me. As someone wiser than me has said, "If I was half the person my dog is, I would be twice the human."

There is a reason they use mastiffs to hunt lions. Zeus would never have given up on me. I found myself speeding home from work, not understanding why. Until it dawned on me, months later. My brain knew he was gone. My heart still had hope. But hope for what? My heart, I came to realize, felt there was still a one in a million chance that this was all just one big terrible nightmare and when I got home I would wake from the nightmare and Zeus would be there running into my arms, as I ran my fingers through his thick velvety hair around his neck and nuzzled into the warmth of his chest and looked into his beautiful brown eyes. The heart, as they say, has reasons the brain cannot fathom. Zeus was cremated with his urn now resting on our living room fireplace mantel. My heart thought I could get another Rottweiler mastiff and then I realized it would not be Zeus. And then I thought, again thinking with my heart, I could get a thousand Rottweiler mastiffs and then surely I would find him. And then, once again I realized it would still not be Zeus. I thought of the words by Judith Viorst in *Necessary Losses*, "Losses are necessary because we grow by losing, by leaving and letting go." And I beg to differ. Losses are not necessary, at least not for me. I could live without them. One day, maybe a thousand years in the future, after we cure malignancies such as osteogenic sarcoma and heart disease, death will also be cured, but unfortunately I was constrained to live in the present with unbearable losses wrapped in feelings of inadequacy and depression, having let Zeus down. Zeus died only three months after Jake. The body is 70% water, but I think it can also adapt to a person's condition and mental state. In my case, I think my body has at times gone to about 98%

water, as it has never run out of tears when the darkest of nights come, like a thief in the night, the times of extreme loss and anguish.

After Jake died, Cheryl and I had fallen into a clinical state of depression. After several weeks wondering how we might recover, I wondered if we should be medicated. Unfortunately, I felt there weren't enough drugs in the world to help us. The drugs might numb us but not deal with the depression itself. I didn't want to be numbed to where I didn't feel or remember the love I had known with my son, Jake. So what could we do? And then it dawned on me. We could never replace Jake, but maybe we could rescue another dog and by doing so in Jake's memory, we would honor Jake's memory and by helping this new rescue ease the pain we were feeling.

A local rescue in Ashland, Kentucky, "Aarf," was having an adoption day at a nearby "Petsmart," that weekend. I had to work but Cheryl said she would go and try to find us a rescue.

I think she was particularly worried about me and my own severely depressed state.

So Cheryl went to the adoption clinic. She took out a few dogs asking me if one particularly appealed to me. They were all little mixed breeds. One did catch my attention. She had this black coloration around her eyes that was very striking, like a mask. So 'Blossom,' was the one. You know Blossom, like the Kwanzan Flowering Cherry Trees I had loved and admired that incredibly sad day Jake had died. When we picked up Blossom, I noticed another dog in a cage that was wagging its tail at Cheryl. He had thought maybe Cheryl was coming to pick him up. He was a little terrier they had named Spike because of a tuft of hair standing up on his forehead. Unfortunately for Spike we weren't coming for him. When he realized it, he just sat in his cage depressed. Aarf had forgotten to give us some of Blossom's adoption papers so I went to get them a few days later. While I was there, I again had a chance to visit Spike. I asked them to get Spike out and let him wander around the room I was in. He seemed very depressed and not very active.

Not the type of dog most people would want. Little Spike had been rescued by Aarf from a kill shelter only a few days before he was to be euthanized, and before that he had been in another shelter. No wonder he was depressed.

Watching Spike listlessly wander around, clearly depressed, there was no strong reason to adopt him except for one fact. The only things more depressed that day were Cheryl and me. I thought maybe if we helped Spike get out of his depression, doing so would also help us get out of ours. I called Cheryl and asked what she thought, and she said, she had felt sorry for him as well, and what was one more little dog to feed. I think we were then up to about eight. Nonetheless, we brought little Spike home. We changed his name to Winston. We felt he needed a more distinguished name. The terrier appearance looked British to me, so we named him after Winston Churchill. It took about two years for Winston to realize he had a forever new home and to gradually come out of his depression and enjoy his life, and in so doing, with Blossom's help, our depression eased as well.

Blossom by the way was never depressed and somehow, like Jake and Zeus, she bonded inseparably with me. We noticed Blossom had a slight limp when we took her home. We immediately had her legs x-rayed. No tumor. However, the radius of her left leg was not long enough to support her elbow joint. Untreated she would develop severe osteoarthritis in the joint and would probably be euthanized. The surgery in a little dog would be difficult with no guarantees and would cost several thousand dollars. One of the nurses at Med Vet offered to take her if we chose to give her up. Blossom is Miss Personality Plus, is full of herself and can charm anyone. Of course we said no thank you. She had only been with us less than a week, when she was operated on. MedVet kept her for about two weeks. They did a surgical fracture, osteotomy of her radius, placed pins across the fracture and widened the fracture gap a millimeter per day until the radius was the length needed to support the elbow joint. We took Blossom home, where she had to be confined for three months, wearing a cone most of the time. Blossom never got depressed. She would have none of that nonsense. She was too full of herself. When I was depressed, or teary eyed or just plain crying, Blossom would have none of that either. She would lick my tears away and just keep licking until all I could do is start laughing from her uncontrollable adoration.

Cheryl insists it was a little miracle, that we were meant to find her, and she was the cure I needed. Blossom it turns out is part Pomeranian, beagle and hound dog. She also, like Zeus, has no fear. We have two 60-pound German Shepherds. Blossom thinks all the toy bones are hers. She used to wait for the Shepherds to drop their bones before snatching them. Now she just takes them out of their mouths, and the Shepherds let her do it. She only weighs about 23 pounds. At the time of her surgery she was probably less than a year old. Now she is one of our fastest dogs without any limp at all.

During the cold days of winter, whenever it snowed, I would look out at Jake's grave and feel a gnawing emptiness deep inside, that little Jake was out in the cold. Of course, as my wife pointed out, it no longer mattered to Jake. Yet what my mind knew as fact my heart would not accept. So one spring day a friend and I dug up Jake's grave, still in the plastic container holding him and I had Jake cremated. His urn now sits alongside Zeus on our living room mantel. It also allows me to do one more thing for both Jake and Zeus. Whenever I took a nap or slept on our couch, Jake would sleep on top of me and Zeus would sleep on me as well just below Jake. When I die, we will once again be united together, as we had slept together so often in life. Of course it no longer matters to them. They will never know of these plans. But I am not yet dead and I know, and my heart knows without any uncertainty what they, my precious children, would have requested.

May you rest in peace, my precious children, Jake and Zeus. Your lives ended way too young. Your memory will forever be with me, living within the deepest recesses of my heart.

Norman (Norm) Jacobs, MD, MS
Wheelersburg, Ohio
July 8, 2020

THOUGHTS ON WRITING
A DIVINE WIND

WHEN I FIRST considered writing a novel envisioning one country's development of weather control technology, I was initially a skeptic, myself, regarding the weather control science proposed, my own worst critic. Could I make this idea plausible? Could I make it believable? Was it too far-fetched? If I were to successfully draw readers into my novel, I first needed to convince myself that weather control was at least theoretically possible. I began with a search of Scientific American articles and came across an article by Ross N. Hoffman in the 2004 Scientific American. At the time, Hoffman was a principal scientist at Atmospheric and Environmental Research (AER) in Lexington, Mass. He has been a member of several NASA research teams and was a member of the National Research Council Committee on the Status and Future Directions in U.S. Weather Modification Research and Operations. His article in Scientific American is titled, "Controlling Hurricanes. Can hurricanes and severe tropical storms be moderated or deflected?" His excellent article convinced me that weather control was being looked into seriously by members of the scientific community. I was now motivated to search on!

Then I decided to look into the U.S. military interest in the use of weather as a weapon. There were numerous articles on the subject, including an entire book, "Weather Warfare. The Military's Plan to Draft Mother Nature." There have also been congressional hearings and UN policies on the military use of weather modification and control. After reviewing these books, articles and documents, my conversion from skeptic to casual church-goer to a full-fledged true believer progressed! Even a recent sci-fi movie, "Geostorm," has as its theme: "He who controls the weather can control the world." The question in my mind is no longer whether weather control is achievable, but rather what country will first achieve it, in what time frame, how will it be regulated, if at all, and for what multiple purposes will it be applied?

Recent storms, Harvey and Irma have raised questions debated on social media. Has military testing in the ionosphere such as through HAARP (High Frequency Active Auroral Research Program), contributed to these storms? I was now surrounded by other believers, all mutual converts to a weather control religion, ideology and belief!

My novel mixes known science with speculation and makes no attempt to separate fact from fiction. Understand that all science begins with a speculative hypothesis. General relativity was a speculation in the mind of Albert Einstein before his mathematical proof and scientific testing confirmed it as a fact. The laws of thermodynamics, and in particular the laws governing entropy and chaotic systems, imply that stable systems become less stable as entropy increases. Viewing the atmosphere and its underlying weather as such a system implies that weather-related events are likely to become more erratic with a greater degree of wind and temperature variance. This may be furthered by global warming, but would occur even if there were no global warming.

Although these changes ultimately play out over hundreds or thousands of years, they seem to be playing out in our current lifetimes in both frequency and volatility of current storms and other weather-related events. The problems are only compounded by larger populations, living close to large bodies of water, be they large lakes, seas, bays or oceans.

Every day, somewhere around the earth, extreme weather is occurring. This includes about 1800 thunderstorms. Tropical cyclones can release as much energy as 10,000 nuclear bombs, making clear the destructive power of large storms. The average annual damage from such storms exceeds $5 billion dollars. The financial cost, not to mention the human and animal lives lost, the hopeless, helpless suffering incurred in weather-related events, together drive financial, ethical and human interest in using evolving advanced technologies to develop weather modification methods and tools. The most deadly hurricane in U.S. history was the Galveston hurricane of 1900 resulting in 8,000 to 12,000 deaths, far exceeding the death toll of the 1906 San Francisco earthquake. According to a report in Science, the number of Category 4 and 5 hurricanes has almost doubled in the past 35 years. The potential strategic advantage of weather control technology has certainly not been lost on the military as my novel, "A Divine Wind," relates.

Weather is chaotic, appearing to behave erratically yet still subject to specific laws of chaos theory. The hope for ever improving weather prediction was shattered in 1961 by the work of Edward Lorenz, a professor of meteorology at MIT. A chaotic system such as the weather, he showed, is highly subject to initial conditions such as water temperature, ambient air temperature, humidity, large and small scale wind currents and nature and distribution of rain clouds. This has been termed "The butterfly effect," whereby a minuscule perturbation in winds, such as caused by a butterfly flapping its wings in China can, theoretically, effect a storm in the Midwest. Computer simulations have borne this out, confirming that small perturbations in the initial conditions of a storm can potentially veer a storm from an approaching land mass, saving many lives and billions of dollars in repair costs.

A country capable of making repetitive small changes in the initial conditions of a weather system could, likewise, modify a developing storm or tornado. This is the theoretical scientific basis underlying my novel, "A Divine Wind."

ADDITIONAL THOUGHTS
AND REASONS FOR WRITING
A DIVINE WIND

WITH MY TEACHER, my Rabi, we first studied the Torah. Then we reviewed the commentaries on the Torah by Rashi and his followers. We then studied the secrets of the Kabballah, Jewish mystical writings. Then, in turn, we studied Hinduism, Christianity, the Koran, ethical humanism, philosophy, atheism, and Buddhism. We traveled the world looking for answers to impossible unknowable questions.

"What else can I do for you, my young impetuous soul?" my teacher asked one day, as we stood before the Sermon Mount.

"Can you give me a gun to kill our enemies?" I asked bluntly, my eyes pleading for this gift.

"There are not enough bullets to kill all our enemies," my teacher replied, just as bluntly. His frown expressed to me his disapproval.

I thought upon this for many days. Months passed. "Can I then have a bomb?" I again pleaded, "to blow up our enemies. A bomb," I reasoned, "can kill more of our enemies than a gun."

He looked at me as though I had learned nothing from our studies, from our wanderings. My teacher tried one more time to teach me the lesson I refused to learn. He spoke slowly, with measured words, clearly discouraged by the nature of my multiple requests. His furrowed brow and downturned visage, bespoke a deep disappointment, a pervasive sadness permeating within him and reaching, likewise, deeply into me, as he replied.

"There is no bomb powerful enough, even a nuclear bomb, to kill all our current and future enemies." I recognized by his demeanor that he felt it was he who had failed me, as his teacher, as I knew, as his student, I likewise had failed him.

Years passed. My teacher died, never having provided me with the weapon I desired. Forlorn, I mourned for weeks, large flowing tears creating furrows in my cheeks. As I cried, head bowed, I saw that my teacher had left me a small unadorned box. Within that box was faded yellow parchment, an old quill and a bottle of jet-black ink. Dipping the quill in the ink, upon the faded yellow parchment, I transcribed the words I found nestled deeply within the soul of my heart.

Finding Home (Excerpt)
How a New York City Boy Came to Find a Home In Appalachia,
and Life Lessons Learned Along the Way

I realize today that nothing in the world is more distasteful
to a man than to take the path that leads to himself.
Herman Hesse, Demian

CHAPTER 1
BROKEN HEARTS

IT WAS LATE one cold and blustery wintry evening, when I finally mustered up the courage to call my fiance from my home in Portsmouth, Ohio, a part of Appalachia. "Cynthia," I stammered, hesitating a moment before continuing. "I can't go through with our wedding next week." My voice trembled. A knot in my stomach ached as my words broke the heart of the woman I still loved but could not marry.

TWO YEARS EARLIER. GEORGETOWN, WASHINGTON D.C.

I was just starting a fellowship in ultrasound at Georgetown. I can still recall like it was yesterday first walking along the hallway leading into a very specific suite.

I am walking toward the ultrasound suite in Georgetown University Hospital in Washington D.C. In the hallway I hear the high-pitched sound of a doppler probe as a technologist examines the carotid arteries in the neck of a patient. I grew up in New York City, living in Washington Heights for the first 21 years of my life. I am a recent radiology grad from Duke University Medical Center, now the new ultrasound fellow at Georgetown.

Cynthia, the ultrasound technologist, deftly holds the ultrasound probe over Samuel Denbar's neck, turning the knobs on the ultrasound monitor to bring out the doppler signal emanating from his carotid. The higher the pitch, the higher the narrowing of the carotid. "You can see from the doppler wave form, that Sam has a high grade internal carotid stenosis." During the fifteen minutes of scanning, they often share their life history with her.

One day she informed me, "A nice Jewish man named Moishe Hauptmann from Miami proposed to me today. He is 79 and wants to marry me and take me back to Miami!"

I laughed, but was not at all surprised. All the other technologists were attractive blond-haired women. Cynthia was different, first in physical appearance--black hair instead of blond, intense inside and out, strikingly beautiful, part Cherokee Indian, giving her a naturally tanned complexion. Emotionally, Cynthia had an ability to counsel people, to bring out their deepest thoughts, read the deepest wishes of their hearts.

"Something a little strange, that's what you notice, that she's not a woman like the others." (Manual Puig, "The Kiss of the Spider Woman.")

Just like 89-year-old Moishe Hauptmann, I, a Jewish boy raised in New York City, was likewise slowly, deeply drawn to her.

I watched many patients being scanned over the next few days. "Do you mind if I scan after you?" I asked her one day.

"Not at all, as long as you don't slow us down too much," she admonished me, grinning as she spoke, a sparkle in her eyes as she looked me over.

As I scanned, Cynthia leaned over me, from behind, helping me direct the ultrasound probe to more accurately evaluate the carotid. I could feel her body next to mine, smell her perfume, her hand on mine as she helped me direct the ultrasound probe.

During the next six months I scanned many people, learning the art of scanning from the best ultrasound technologists anywhere. We used ultrasound to cannulate non-dilated bile ducts in the liver, an ultrasound procedure difficult even when the bile ducts are dilated.

After six months of ultrasound, I was offered a junior staff position in neuroradiology at Georgetown, an area in which I had previously done a fellowship during my training at Duke. Many of the patients I did carotid arteriograms on, I also did doppler studies on, allowing me to directly compare the results of both studies. I had written several articles on carotid doppler ultrasound during my fellowship and was asked to write a review article on the subject for Medical Clinics of North America. I included Cynthia as a co-author for all her work, teaching and guidance.

At Georgetown I was earning $60,000/year, as a staff neuroradiologist. I was working very hard, doing six or seven arteriograms per day, reading about 30 CT scans a day, and trying to teach a third or fourth year resident to do six or seven myelograms while I was doing all the arteriograms. At the time, there was no fellow in the neuroradiology department. The chief of the service often was absent and there was no research being done in neuroradiology. So, I thought if I am going to work this hard, I might as well get paid better for it. One day at a staff meeting, a call came in for Bob Zeman, the chief of the CT service. Bob announced, "Does anyone want to make a lot of money and live in Ohio?"

My initial response was, "Can I just make a lot of money and not move to Ohio?" Zeman took that as a positive response and handed me the phone.

Several months of negotiating ensued, with an offer of a partnership in the Ohio group in two years earning, at that time, eight times what I was making at Georgetown. No small difference. Nonetheless, I kept raising the stakes. "Would you pay a down payment on a house?" I requested, thinking they would balk and I would stay at Georgetown. When they offered an extra $25,000 as a down payment on a house, I started believing I might have to check this job out. The offer at that point was $200,000 better than my next best offer. What could be so difficult in adjusting to rural Ohio, I wondered, that would compel them to make their offer so lucrative. A few months later, I would begin to understand the reason for their high offer. Reasons that encompassed the world of difference between Georgetown, Washington, D.C. and rural Appalachia. This difference was still uncertain to me, when I booked a solo trip to Portsmouth, Ohio in mid-February.

I can still recall my first drive from Washington D.C. to Portsmouth. It was mid-February. Winter made the area seem particularly bleak. Skeletal oaks and maples stood out on the hilly terrain, hungry, malnourished, unquestioningly bending in the chilly winter wind. Gone were the crowds filling Au Pied de Cochon, a French Bistro in the heart of Georgetown, for a Sunday brunch of lobster, quiche and wine. Gone too was the ambiance of Chez Grand Mere or of the French country inn setting of La Chaumiere, with its blazing central open fireplace so warm and inviting on a wintry night, the firelight reflecting in the eyes of lovers sipping wine from the south of France. Gone also were the crowds of young people filling M Street, spilling out of the shops during the day and the taverns at night. Gone was the vibrancy, the exuberance, the excitement, the sophistication, the very life and lifestyle that Georgetown emanated.

As I drove through New Boston, a bedroom community to Portsmouth, I felt as though I had been beamed to another world, another time. A coke plant was sending fumes skyward, blackening an already bleak sky with an assortment of noxious chemicals. "How many were carcinogenic?" I pondered. As I continued on, I passed row house after row house just a few feet from the main thoroughfare through town, suffocatingly crowded together, weathered shingles covered with soot, colors faded, as though bathed in a persistent lingering twilight, a surreal mirage dusting the land. No people were in sight. Nothing moving in the ghostlike town but the cars, the dust and a few creaking shutters, as the caravan of cars wended its way through the town much like it did across the nearby Ohio River.

As I drove on to Portsmouth, I came to the Osco Foundry plant in the middle of town, a mass of tanks and pipes spewing forth more gray-black smoky fumes.

As I explored the small town, I noticed no new construction, no growth. As opposed to the large construction cranes dotting the D.C. landscape, there were only signs of decay here. Crumbling buildings left to fall under their own weight.

I passed the Columbia Theater, the one and only movie theater in town. The night before, I had been to the National Theater in downtown Washington to see *Cats*. Here in Portsmouth, the Columbia Theater was playing *The Grapes of Wrath*, and I had a gnawing sensation that it was the original showing.

What was a nice Jewish boy, raised in Washington Heights in upper Manhattan doing in a place like this? Was any position worth the adjustments I would have to make?

Little did I realize at the time the changes I would attempt in lifestyle and identity more radical than the adjustment to the community alone; changes that would lead me to leave this woman I loved one week before our marriage. I would leave the town as well, and give up on the remarkable financial opportunity, to try and find myself, who I was and what was meaningful to me. After a year working as a radiologist in California, I would return to Portsmouth Ohio, believing that hidden in this small town, was the key to finding myself, as I searched for a meaning to my own life.

While living in the town, I would start an internet access company from an initial $1400 investment that became an IPO on the NASDAQ worth $5.4 million the first day it traded on the NASDAQ at the height of the Internet craze. Instead of a cause for celebration, I came to regret the entire achievement. Why this was so--the life lessons learned along the way and the ultimate meaning I found in my own life living in that small Appalachian town, is the story at the heart of my non-fiction memoir: *Finding Home.*

The enclosed picture of a "cowboy" on a paint horse was taken many years ago. I am on Dingo, a paint stallion I rode on a memorable ride through Shawnee State Forest, a local state park, during a violent thunderstorm. A fellow doc gave me the nickname, "Indiana Jacobs," the Jewish cowboy from New York City. How that came to be, as well as the ride itself, is described in my memoir.

Life magazine came to our town many years ago to write a story about poverty in America, with Portsmouth the quintessential representative town. In response, I wrote a previously unpublished story, "The Story Life Magazine Forgot to Write," included within my memoir.

Finding Home, at its heart, is the story of how a New York City boy came to find a home in rural southern Ohio, a part of Appalachia, and the life lessons he learned along the way.

Finding Home: Anticipated publication date, Thanksgiving 2021.